Ready, Steady, KILL!

by

Michael Davies

© Michael Davies

January 2011

Ready, Steady, KILL!

For information address:
info@mickiedaltonfoundation.com

First Printing in Australia, 2012

ISBN: 978-0-6484702-5-0

**Published by The Mickie Dalton Foundation
NSW
Australia**

www.mickiedaltonfoundation.com

Other Works by Michael Davies

The Nightmares of God
The Janus Conspiracy
Accounts of a Killing
A Friendly Killing
Dreamkill
Helix Dreams
Helix – The Second Renaissance

For the Young Adults (12-18)

The Many Worlds of Mickie Dalton
The Many Galaxies of Mickie Dalton
The Many Universes of Mickie Dalton
The Strange World of Mark and Anna

For the 8-12 age group

The Julie Malloy Gang and the Smugglers
The Quest for the Locket
The Secret of Yuri Kirilenko
The United Nations and the Extra-Terrestrial
The Secret of Charlotte's Cello
The Star of the Yshan Kings
The Red Fog of Time
The Star of the Yshan Kings
The War of the Yshan Empire
The Star of the New Yshan Empire
The Mysterious Recorder and The Door to Elsewhere
Prisoners of the Picture
A Step Into the Past
What Can't be Seen Can Exist
How I Spent My Evening

For the Little Ones (3-5)

Mary's World

And in non-fiction

The Business School Approach to Writing Your Novel

To Peter Klare

For his constant support and encouragement during bad times, good times, the failures and the successes

Acknowledgements

Sincere thanks go to Robert Walden, Psychologist of Coffs Harbour for his invaluable assistance and advice on the profile of the serial killer and how such a profile could also be seen in some of the top people in society.

Chapter 1 - Third Blood

"You think that's number three, Doc?" David Hunter looked at the horror hanging from the ceiling water pipe, fighting to keep his face expressionless.

The medical examiner stood back from the dead man. "Almost certainly," she said. "The same knife to the stomach, the same knot holding his wrists, same general type of victim, yes, I'm pretty sure you've got a serial killer on your hands, David."

"How long?"

"Initial estimate, maybe twenty to twenty-four hours. I'll tell you more after I've got him on the table. The crazy thing is that he's still got his wallet and his watch."

"So who is he, then?"

The doctor carefully opened the wallet with her surgically-gloved hands, extracted the driver's licence and read from it.

"Allan Smith," she said. "Born 5th April, 1980, address in Surry Hills, very close to here. There's about $120 in here, various membership cards, Visa and Amex credit cards, Medicare card, some petrol receipts, so we can track some of his movements."

Hunter studied the dead man again, swallowing hard to suppress the queasiness that never failed to appear, even after fifteen years on the job and many corpses.

"About thirty," he murmured to himself. "Stripped to the waist, wrists tied with fairly common rope, hanging from the pipes just high enough so that his toes are touching the ground. Stabbed three times in the stomach, enough to kill him but not instantly. Just like the other two."

He turned back to the doctor who was stripping off her paper overalls. "How long for him to die, Angie?"

She shrugged, a look of distaste on her slender, dark face. "Probably ten, twenty minutes. Long enough to know what was happening, anyway. There are traces of sticky goo around his mouth, so I'd say his killer had stuck duct tape or something to stop him screaming. Just like the other two."

Hunter nodded at the police constable standing next to him. "Have a look around, see if you can find anything that might match."

The uniformed officer nodded and gestured to the others. The scene had already been filmed in much detail, the floor examined for footprints or other potential clues, so there was little need for caution as the new inspection started. The pool of blood beneath the body had already been washed away with a hosepipe and the car-keys uncovered by the stream taken away for analysis and identification.

"What sort of car did he drive?" Hunter asked.

"A Commodore, about three years old," replied the doctor as she packed away her equipment. "Your people checked the registration from the name and address and it matches with the driver's licence."

"Have you found it yet?"

"Not yet, but it's not anywhere close."

"So he was driven here, then," said Hunter.

"Can he go now?" asked Doctor Angela Simpson. She had finished packing away what she called her "bag of gubbins" and stood quietly, dressed in a slim-fitting pants suit in dark blue and a white shirt open at the neck. The removal of the hair cover had let her shoulder-length black hair fall free. Hunter turned to her, as always trying to suppress the small thought that she was a hell of an attractive woman and what he might do about it if she were not married to the Chief Superintendent.

"Yes," he said simply and watched as the rope was cut to allow the corpse to be lowered gently onto a stretcher, covered with a sheet and wheeled away by two young men wearing the expressionless faces of having seen too many such ugly sights. He checked that the scraps of rope were placed into plastic evidence bags for later examination by every high-tech gizmo available. He turned back to her as she spoke again.

"I'll call you as soon as I've finished," she said with a half-smile and a direct gaze into his eyes.

She knows I lust for her body, thought Hunter. *Bugger.* "Yes, please, Angie," he said aloud. "How long, do you reckon?"

She looked at her watch. "It's just after two. I

might be ready by tomorrow evening. There's not a lot on, now that I've done the other two."

He nodded, avoided smiling and turned away as he heard the shout of one of the uniformed cops. *No point in encouraging her*, he thought. *Why can women always tell when a bloke's interested in them?* He walked over to the other side of the basement where the cop had called him.

"There, sir," said the young constable pointing at a screwed up scrap of grey duct tape. He had already placed a numbered post and a ruler by the spot and the photographer had taken pictures from several angles, including the distance from the point where the body had hung. Hunter picked up the scrap with his surgically-gloved hands and placed it in another plastic evidence bag. He handed it to the constable who knew what to do with it. It would be checked for prints, DNA, anything that could point to the killer.

"Okay, let's get out of here," said Detective Inspector David Hunter and walked out while the last few officers hung up the "Scene of Crime – Do Not Enter" strips around the scene of the tragedy. Hunter felt crabby. Serial killings were bad for business. They caused panic in the city and more than the usual stress on the police. He was already exhausted from the long hours spent fruitlessly on the first and second murders and this latest one was the seal that said it really was a series. That made it several times worse as the publicity leaked out.

"Fuck it," he said aloud as he pulled away from the kerbside, and wasn't really certain whether his anger was at the killer or at the delectable, mocking and unattainable Doctor Angela Simpson.

* * *

The rest of the day was filled with routine; ensuring the reports were all completed, the details of the appalling discovery made by a maintenance worker all documented in precise format, the pictures printed and hung up in the situation room and the rest of the murder squad briefed.

It was after six before Hunter could make the call he'd decided to make soon after leaving the killing scene.

"G'day, Jack," he said as the phone was picked up in the house set in two hundred acres a few kilometres north of Coffs Harbour on the mid-North Coast.

"Well, if it's not the young and innocent Detective Sergeant Hunter!" said the deep, familiar voice.

"No it's not, you old bastard!" replied Hunter, suppressing his laugh. "It's the mature, seasoned Detective *Inspector* Hunter."

"Which only goes to show that the NSW Police Promotions Board is staffed with fools, drunkards and dimwits. So, David, why are you calling this old man?"

"I need your help, Jack. This one has got to me, badly."

"Come off it, David. Jack Savage, the world's greatest profiler has retired and well you know it."

"I know it, to my regret. And they call you "behavioural investigative advisers" these days! But there's something very ugly here. Three young men dead, all killed with the same M.O."

"Any murder is ugly, kid. Serial killings are the worst, but they usually give you more clues and there are more opportunities for the killer to fuck up and leave a pointer."

"That's the problem, Jack. Not a clue to be had anywhere. Not a fingerprint, not a scrap of clothing, no skin under the victim's fingernails, nothing. Not a single fucking thing."

"It's really got to you, hasn't it? We covered a lot of murders in our time, David and you never seemed to get this upset. Okay, tell me about them."

"Three young men, all between twenty five and thirty, similar height, between one-seventy and one-eighty centimetres, similar slim build. All found in the basement of an old building, all the buildings within five blocks of each other. All hanging from pipes, wrists tied with common rope bought anywhere, same knot, all killed by three stab wounds to the stomach, left to bleed to death, mouths covered with duct tape then torn off after…"

"Was the duct tape found?" Savage sharply interrupted the description.

"Every time, yes," replied Hunter. "And no, no prints, nothing but DNA matching the victim from where it was ripped away, probably post-mortem."

"Ah," said Savage. "Go on."

"All three stripped to the waist, wallets still in their pockets, wrist watches still in place, one of them an Omega worth a couple of thousand, car keys left lying on the ground."

"What sort of cars?"

"One snazzy new BMW 700 series, one scruffy old

Honda Accord, one common-or-garden variety Holden Commodore, three years old. Nothing in common at all.”

“So you’ve identified the victims?”

“Of course. Nothing in common there either, no single socio-economic connection. One’s a junior partner with one of those humungous accounting firms, one’s a plumber, not rich, one’s a teacher at a high school in the inner suburbs. None of them married.”

A small silence echoed down the line from the Mid-North Coast. “Okay, certainly classic serial killing stuff, but based on fairly obvious physical characteristics. No motive other than the thrill, it seems.”

“But professionally done, Jack. This bloke knows how to cover up. And it’s got to be a bloke, I don’t think I’ve ever heard of a woman doing this sort of shit.”

“Probably right, David. And he can’t be leaving any tracks, because he’s not hiding the obvious clues. It’s certainly curious.”

“So will you come down and help us, Jack? I could really use your specific abilities and it would be good to get the old firm together again.”

“Not a chance, David. Like I said, I’ve retired. I’ve got two hundred acres here, fifty head of cattle, sixty Alpacas and three granddaughters, a horrible golf swing to work on and a wife who insists I wash, clean my teeth and brush my hair every day. How the hell could I solve a serial killing as well?”

“Jack...”

"No, David. You're a bloody good detective, the best I've ever worked with. By all means try another profiler, he or she may help, but leave me out of it. I hate coming to Sydney anyway, the air makes me puke."

"Bugger it, Jack. Can I call you with the odd question?"

"You can do that, kid, but don't expect me to be able to answer it. I think I'm sort of cleaning all that shit out of my head and becoming a farmer instead."

"Okay, Jack. Give my love to Jennie and the family."

"I'll do that. And you know you can come up here for a break any time. The granddaughters want to beat you up some more like last time!"

Hunter couldn't help laughing. He adored the three little girls and it seemed mutual. "Okay, Jack, but I doubt I'll get a minute to myself with a serial killer on the loose. Once the press get hold of it, shit will be flying everywhere, most of it aimed at me."

"Goes with the territory, David. We've both had that before."

"I know it, Jack. I'll call a bit later as it develops. Get back to the cows and alpacas, old man."

"I'll do that! See you, kid."

Hunter replaced the phone, disappointment and worry filling his soul. He had given the evening off to all his team. The investigations into the two previous killings had stalled and Hunter was beating his brains out to think of any other avenues to investigate. Slowly, he filed away the details of the latest murder into his desk, the pictures of the last corpse, the scene in the basement, the notes he had taken. Everything else was with Forensics. His team was briefed to meet at eight in the morning and start the whole detailed, grinding investigation again.

Depressed and worried, Hunter locked his desk and went home to his two-bedroom apartment in Bondi, to sit on the deck and look at the surf and muse on the mysteries of life assisted by a single-malt scotch.

At eight, having grilled a small steak and washed it down with a glass of Merlot, he switched the television on for his weekly treat, watching his sister's television program of current affairs. As always, her charismatic presence dominated the program and he was filled with pride at the fact that this beautiful, intelligent woman on his screen was his elder sister.

At ten, he went to bed, the anxiety and depression about the murders on his patch having taken over his mind again.

Chapter 2 – More Blood

The situation room of the Homicide Squad in Parramatta was buzzing as Hunter walked in a few minutes before eight. Two more detectives followed him in, having been smoking cigarettes outside on the pavement as he reached the entrance. The coffee machine was steaming gently and the most recently acquired detective in the group, Detective Sergeant Jamie Peterson poured a large mug labelled "The Boss" and brought it up to Hunter, the traditional duty of the newest member of the murder squad, despite the rank. Hunter waved his thanks and leaned up against the front desk as he sipped. He wasn't feeling all that good. The single glass of scotch had become three as he reviewed the events of the day, especially the disappointment of not getting Jack Savage to come and work with him.

"Okay, children, let's do some work," he began. A few grins around the room were swiftly smothered. Hunter ignored them. His team was thoroughly professional.

"Now, it's obvious we have a serial killer on the loose," he continued. "Let see if we have anything new. Some of you have already examined the evidence we got from the Kelly Street building yesterday. What have we got?"

"I did the ropes, sir," said a slightly-built man in grey slacks and a black blazer with a military insignia on the breast pocket. He looked about forty with thinning brown hair.

"Yes, Bill?"

"All the same make, without a doubt, sir. I checked the ends where they had been cut, but I don't think they had been connected. I couldn't match the ends of any section with the ends of another. Either they came from different batches of rope or more bits had been cut in between each of the sections."

"Conclusions, Bill?"

Detective Sergeant Bill Hamilton took a few seconds before replying. Hunter waited patiently. He knew Hamilton was a thoughtful man who could be depended on for accurate analyses.

"Each section could have come from a different length or rope. Or, other bits had been cut off between each bit used in the murders. Or, and this worries me, the perp could be a bloody clever sod who deliberately used different sections, not connected in any way to throw us off."

"Or it could also mean he's done a couple of others we haven't found yet." The speaker was Detective Senior Constable Rachel Norman, a solidly-built woman with bad acne and a sharp mind.

"Oh shit," said Hunter. "Well done, Rachel, I hadn't thought of that. Okay, when we're done here, I want you to arrange for a building-by- building search of every multi-storey building in that area. Get the Plod onto that, I need your brains with us."

Rachel nodded. The uniformed police – "the Plod" - had already been instructed by Chief Superintendent Charlie Simpson to give all possible help to this investigation.

"Okay, next?" said Hunter.

"The duct tape," said Jerry Bowler, a newly promoted sergeant and still wildly excited by his new title. Like Bill Hamilton, he tended to a dapper style of dress, wearing a black blazer with a military badge of some sort. "Sorry sir, nothing. No fingerprints, no scraps of any material, nothing but some skin and saliva which I assume must come from the victim. DNA will take a few days to confirm, but like the other two, we found nothing at all on the tape. This bastard is clever."

"Damn right," muttered Hunter. "Anything else?"

"Blood type," said Barrie Roche, a senior sergeant of vast experience. "I ran those to the hospital to identify yesterday's victim and because it looked like a serial killing, I asked them to run full tests on all three. But nothing obvious came out of that."

He opened his note pad and looked intently at a single page. "Victim number one, Paul Aiken, had blood type A, no signs of anything unusual at all. Number two, Jens Carsens was B positive, traces of marijuana and coke, recent use of a commonly-prescribed blood pressure medication and that was it.

Yesterday's victim, Allan Smith, also Type A had some antibiotics in the blood, otherwise perfectly healthy."

"Well done, Barrie. When we're through, get out and find their doctors, get everything you can. If they give you that patient confidentiality crap, remind them what's going on here and they could help save several lives. You've checked the first two people, I know. Let's review the details. Rachel, give us a summary."

"Sure," said Rachel Norman. She opened her notebook. "Paul Aiken is the wealthy one, a partner at an accounting firm in the city. His is the BMW and the Omega watch. Not married. All these blokes were quite heterosexual, it seems, certainly nobody knew of anything different. He was quite well liked according to his colleagues, but the senior partner there said he wasn't seen as going much further. Competent but not brilliant, he said."

"The second?" Hunter knew the details, but the exercise was a good review.

"Jens Carsens was the plumber, worked for a big operation in the Western Suburbs but liked to socialise in the Eastern Suburbs, especially the Cross and out by the beach near Bondi. Single, like I said, apparently straight sexually, smoked a bit of dope, occasionally snorted some coke, his was the elderly Honda. Earned decent pay but had no savings, rented his flat in Baulkham Hills. His mates say he was good at his job, but not driven all that hard."

"Good, now how about last night's victim? Did you check him out too?"

"I did, boss. Allan Smith, teacher at a high school, taught history and geography and was a pretty good football player, so he handled coaching duties for that. His was the Commodore, has a flat in Surry Hills, had been dating a music teacher from another high school for just a few weeks. They weren't out together last night because her mother was visiting from Brisbane."

"Okay, good work all of you, but we have absolutely bugger-all in reality. It looks like we're dealing with a real clever bastard. It could even be a cop himself, judging by the way he knows how to disguise his tracks. But it could simple mean it's somebody who has watched every episode of *"Prime Suspect," "Silent Witness"* and *"Waking the Dead"* on television and studied them carefully."

He nodded as a wave of chuckles ran round the room. "I'm serious, people. Those programs are bloody good, mostly accurate and make our lives rather difficult because they give bastards like this one some good pointers. So for now, those of you with tasks already, get on with them. Jerry, Rachel, go and interview friends and relatives of all three dead 'uns. I know you've already done that with the first two, but there may be something forgotten, something new and now there's a third one to broaden the enquiry. List everybody they knew and then run a cross-check, see if there are any friends, relatives, business connections, anything at all in common. The rest of you, an office by office interview of everybody in the buildings around there, find out if they saw or heard anything, if they were there after regular hours, all that good stuff, you know the drill. We've already done it after the first two murders, now we do it again. All right, you lazy buggers, why are you still sitting there?"

Hunter finished his coffee, took the mug back to the coffee pot and refilled it. He carried it back to the series of whiteboards at the front of the room and began reviewing the data, laying out each fact on the board, connecting with lines where he could see any reason at all and stepping back at intervals to look at the picture from further away. It was a technique he had used for years and almost always revealed unexplored lanes, stand-out factors that needed explaining and connections that had been missed at first.

After an hour, he had seen nothing. His coffee had grown cold, barely touched and his state of mind had sunk into frustrated anger.

"Fuck it," he said and went out to his car. He didn't think the doctor would have any information for him, but he thought he'd take a chance. He had nothing else to do and he felt like talking to her, anyway.

He got as far as opening his car door when his phone rang. He dragged it out of his jacket pocket and opened it.

"Hunter."

"Sir, it's Constable Helen Friar. We're checking buildings like you ordered. You'd better come here. We've found another one."

"Oh Jesus! Another one like the rest?"

"No sir, quite different. It's the basement of the building at 28, Holroyd Street, Alexandria."

"Give me twenty minutes. Call Doctor Simpson."

He slapped the phone shut, climbed into the car and switched on the siren. Something was horribly wrong, probably even worse than another in the series of killings of young men.

* * *

The woman lay on her back, arms outstretched. She was dressed in a black leather mini-skirt, white blouse and her light brown hair had a red ribbon tied around a pony-tail. She would have been beautiful but for the massive, bloody mess where her right eye had been and the blood pouring all over the concrete from the wreck of her skull where the bullet had exited.

A single policewoman stood by the entrance to the underground parking lot. Three others stood outside, all looking ill as Hunter had slammed to a halt near the entrance a few moments earlier. He climbed out and addressed the young woman constable.

"You're Friar?" he asked.

"Yes sir."

"Who discovered this?"

"We did. Nobody else had arrived by car, though a few people had entered the building by the front door."

"Doctor Simpson here yet?"

"No sir. But she's on her way."

Hunter said nothing and walked into the cool, dark building. He stood examining the appalling scene, not walking any nearer than two metres from the body. He looked around the concrete emptiness but saw nothing that made his policeman's senses wake up.

"Not like the others, David," said Angela Simpson's voice behind him. He turned to see her put down her bag of gubbins, open it and extract a paper suit. She had another one by the bag and she handed it to him. The snap of the cellophane covers and rustle of the suits as they unfolded seemed loud in the silence.

The doctor was ready first and she advanced on the body. She took out a clinical thermometer and pressed the opening into the ear, held it there for a few seconds before taking it out and studying the tiny numbers on one side.

"Estimating death about eight hours ago, so sometime maybe between eleven pm and one this morning. Female, aged late twenties to early thirties, expensive clothing, good quality make-up, diamond earrings also quite valuable, though possibly cubic zirconium. I'll know later. Death almost certainly by small-calibre pistol, possibly .22, fired at close range into the right eye. Massive exit wound means the bullet may be around."

Meanwhile, Hunter was moving cautiously around, examining the floor.

"No signs of blood anywhere else, so I'd say she was shot where she was found," he said. "No obvious footprints anywhere." He whistled to the policewoman. "Friar, get those lazy bums in here and start a detailed hunt for a bullet. Stay away from the immediate scene. The bullet could just be a lump of metal if it's hit a wall or pillar."

She nodded and walked out to contact the other officers who walked in and started combing the area. More people at the entrance indicated the photographer had come.

Angela looked up. "It's been dead dry for three days. There won't be any tyre tracks or footprints that you could see. Let the photographer do his thing."

Hunter waved the young man in. "Nothing else you can tell me, Angie?"

"Not a damn thing. No handbag, no identification, no other jewellery, I'll have her taken away as soon as the ambulance gets here."

"What about yesterday's body?"

"Should finish about five. I'll call you."

Hunter walked out. The day had started badly and had become worse before nine o'clock.

Chapter 3 – Getting Stranger

The meeting room was busy again. The scene was much like the previous day, detectives in a variety of casual clothing, one or two more formally in suits, both male and female. Hunter accepted his mug of coffee. "All right, you noisy bastards," he called out. "Let's have some hush in here!"

After a few seconds hush had descended. Hunter took a sip and looked at his crew. He was proud of them. They were hardworking, clever, experienced and quite often funny enough to generate a belly laugh around the room.

"Good morning, boys and girls," said Hunter, leaning up against the desk next to the whiteboard. "We have serious problems and the flying excreta is starting to get close to the rotating blades of the ventilation device. As you know, we discovered another murder yesterday, in the same general area of the other three. This is four killings too many and the fact that they are all in the same area and three of them at least seem to be by the same perp, the brass upstairs is starting to squeal. What do we know about yesterday's death?"

Rachel Norman waved her hand. Instead of her usual autumnal-coloured pants suit, she was dressed in simple blue jeans and a brown sweater.

"No identity yet, boss, but the examiner confirmed death by a single bullet. We're sifting through the most recent missing persons reports. Fingerprints have not produced any identification either."

Hunter nodded. "Let me know if the missing persons reports come up with anything." He took a sip of the coffee. "Okay, any thunks about all this?"

Bill Hamilton vaguely waved his hand. "The latest woman is not part of the series," he said firmly. There was a series of grunts of agreement round the room.

"Why so, Bill?" Hunter knew very well why so, but he believed in ideas being articulated, just in case they led to something.

"Different MO entirely," said Bill. "Wrong victim type, wrong weapon, her handbag taken to cover her ID. The others had all got their wallets, apart from being blokes all killed in the same way. That one's challenging us. This latest one smells of sex motive through and through."

The same murmur of agreement ran round the room.

Hunter nodded. "Right," he said. "The bullet?"

"The Plod found it," said Jerry Bowler, looking as neat as always in grey flannels, black blazer and black lace-up shoes. He wore no badge on the blazer but wore some sort of military striped tie. Hunter couldn't immediately recall what Jerry's military career had been.

"But bugger-all there, Chief," Bowler continued. "It looked like it had ricocheted off two pillars and hit the wall, just a lump of lead, no distinguishing marks at all. Definitely a .22 calibre, though."

"So an illegal handgun, then? Okay, Jerry, look through the files, see who uses a .22 handgun among the crooked bastard fraternity, there may be a pointer."

Bowler nodded.

"Okay, moving back to the serial murders. Anyone come up with useful stuff from the victims' doctors? Barrie, that was yours, I think?"

Barrie Roche shook his head, the ceiling lights reflecting on his bald head. "Nothing, boss," he said. "I went to his school first to give them the bad news and find out about him. They were badly shocked, thought he was a pretty good teacher and he was a well-regarded footie coach as well. He's been dating a music teacher at another school for a few weeks, so I was able to find her. She's badly shattered. She didn't know all that much about his private life but there didn't seem too much to know either. She said the antibiotics were for a sinus infection he'd had for a week or so and when I checked with his doctor, he confirmed that. Apart from the sinus' he was generally a healthy bloke. Boss, he was so normal it's almost abnormal."

"All three are like that," agreed Hunter. "This is bloody frustrating. There's nothing in any of those men's lives to point to why they were murdered."

"No connection between any of them, either," said Bill Hamilton. "I spent half the night listing everything I could think of, writing them up on flip-chart sheets and hanging them all round the room at home. I just can't see anything to connect them."

"Except their killer," added Jamie Peterson, the newest addition to the group. He was dressed in casual fashion, flannels, a sweater and looked like a minor male model, aged thirty, dark and a standard, vaguely handsome face.

"As you say, their killer," agreed Hunter. "Okay, everybody, I have no shame in admitting it, I'm stumped. I can't see which way to go. Nobody had any luck in the house-to-house and office-to-office hunt?"

A series of shaking heads ran round the room like a small whirlwind in a forest clearing.

"Nothing," said Rachel Norman. "It's not a residential block, so there was nobody there at night, it's all offices. Same with the first two, nobody around at night to see anything."

"Shit a brick!" muttered Hunter.

"I don't suppose we could get Jack Savage back, could we?" asked Bill Hamilton.

"Who's Jack Savage?" asked Jamie Peterson.

"Before your time," replied Hamilton. "Best damn profiler we've ever had with us. That bloke, I swear he could get the smell of the killer just from the notes and photos."

"Funnily enough, Bill, I called him yesterday," said Hunter. "I practically begged him to come down. He said he's got his hands full with cows and alpaca and grandkids and stuff. Not a chance."

"Bugger," said Hamilton.

"Sideways! As Jack used to say," said Hunter with a grin. "Alright people, keep grinding away. Something has to turn up soon. I'm going to see the lovely Doctor Simpson."

Catcalls and whistles greeted his announcement and Hunter laughed. "Calm down, you evil-minded bastards! I'm going to get the post mortem results on our last male victim. You keep looking for some pointer as to the dead woman. Keep your mobiles on in case I need to call you or the other way round."

The room broke up as his crew went to their separate tasks.

* * *

Angela Simpson looks quite droolworthy, Hunter said to himself. He was certain that she tailored her laboratory coats to fit extra snugly round her body and somehow maintained a perfectly made-up face throughout the day.

"Do I pass?" she asked as they stood in the corridor outside her office.

Hunter realised he'd been staring at her. "Er.. yeah, well, you scrub up quite well for an old sheila," he said and felt proud of himself for not stammering and stuttering as he could easily have done.

"Well, that's a relief!" She opened her office door and walked in, taking her seat by the coffee table next to the window and waving him to the seat opposite, leaving her desk unoccupied. He knew she preferred to conduct meetings informally like this and he was happier too, being able to look at her legs more easily.

"What have you got?" he asked.

She picked up the manila folder off the table and extracted a single sheet. "Not a whole hell of a lot," she replied. "Young man, exactly what he appeared, very fit and healthy, couldn't find a single thing wrong except for a mild sinus infection. Death caused by three stabs to the stomach with a sharp knife, single edge, probably a common kitchen carving knife but carefully sharpened at the point as well as the edge, or maybe a box-cutter. The stabs were not especially scientific, one got the kidneys, the other two just tore internal organs and all the blows were deep. The victim bled to death relatively slowly."

"That's it?"

"No," she said. "There was a puncture in the right thigh, a needle of some sort, common enough, obtainable by somebody with diabetes, or able to inject themselves with a course of allergy desensitisation mixture."

"Any idea what he'd been hit with?"

"The contents of the hypodermic, you mean? No, but you chose the right word. He'd been knocked out by a blunt object to the back of the head."

"Interesting," murmured Hudson. "So, let's see. He'd been persuaded into the passenger seat of a car, the killer had jabbed him in the right thigh with a potion to put him out..."

"Or just make him dozy," interrupted Angela.

Hunter nodded. "Yes. Probably that, so he could still walk somehow. The killer makes him stumble along to the killing site, ties the man's wrists and hauls him upright before tying off the knot."

"Then why the knock-out blow to the head?" asked the doctor.

"Good point. Did the tox report reveal any appropriate drug?"

"Not a thing," she said. "Whatever it was, it faded fast."

"So maybe that plan didn't work and the killer had to wallop him over the head with what...? A tyre iron, perhaps?

She shook her head. "Blunter than that. The indent was broader than from a tyre iron. More like a cosh."

"So our man came prepared for that requirement. Interesting. But what intrigues me now is that with the victim unconscious, our killer had to haul him upright and tied the rope around the ceiling pipe. He has to be a strong, probably quite large bloke."

"Right. The victim was not a small man by any means, quite muscular, weighed ninety kilos."

"What about the other two?" asked Hunter. "Were they coshed, too?"

"I didn't think so at first," Angie replied. "But when I found that mark, I checked into the two previous cases. No needle marks, but both did have bruises to their heads. Not deep enough to be sure they were coshed, but hit by something, that's for sure."

"Well, shit, eh?" said Hunter. "I think I've got some sort of pointer at last, which is a hell of a lot more than I had before."

"Still not a lot, David."

"It's a start. Bless you, Angela, I think I'd better get back to the team and tell them."

He got to his feet, taking the opportunity to look at her legs under the short skirt as she slid the sheet away in the folder.

"One more thing," she said, glancing up at him and seeing the object of his gaze. She grinned. "I *do* have nice legs, don't I?"

"The entire police department approves. Was that the one more thing? 'Cos we all know that already."

She laughed. Hunter liked the sound of her laughter. "Not that, no! But I found one small mark on the body that I couldn't explain. There was a cross cut into the left shoulder. Not big, just a couple of centimetres. It was done post mortem, because there was no blood on it. There's a photo of it in the folder." She handed it to him and Hunter took it, finding the photo and studying it. The cross was not neatly cut, the arms were not equal in size.

"Not exactly Michelangelo," he said.

"No," she agreed.

"I'd better be going," he said.

"You had."

"See you then."

"See you." She looked at him without expression as he walked out of the office. Something was tugging at his memory.

He didn't get back to his office.

Chapter 4 – Death in North Sydney

"David, it's Rod Hathaway."

The voice rang clearly from the mobile phone loudspeaker. Hunter laughed. He knew Rod Hathaway well and the two men had been promoted to Detective Inspector at the same time.

"Rod, you drunken old bum, what's happening?"

"Too much, mate, too much. I've been reading the reports of the triple killings in Surry Hills. Looks like you've got a serial killer running loose."

"We have, Rod, no doubt. Do you have something to tell me about it?"

"I might. I think we've got another one here in North Sydney. Can you get over here?"

"Quick as I can," said Hunter and put the siren on. He was sure the situation merited the drama. As he accelerated through the traffic, he hit the communications switch to the office.

"This is Hunter. Let all my team know I'm heading to North Sydney. Looks like we've got another serial killer. I'll report back when I can."

"Yes, sir," said the controller. "And a message from DS Roche. He has an ID for the female victim."

"Okay, he knows what to do. Tell him to take Rachel along."

He flipped the switch and concentrated on his driving, sneakily admitting to himself that he enjoyed the process, seeing cars scramble to get out of his way and the curious stares from pedestrians and other drivers.

"Two dead women," said Detective Inspector Rod Hathaway in the conference room at the North Sydney police station. "We'd advised the Homicide Squad when we found the first, but they asked us to handle it for a time until you could take it."

Hunter studied the appalling coloured pictures on the table. "Who are they?"

"Victim one is Vivienne Rawlings, aged 47, divorcee," said Rod Hathaway. He was a relatively short man for a police officer, stocky build with black hair that he kept cut almost military-length. He sat at the head of the table to Hunter's right, while to his left sat two more young detectives, one male, one female. Hathaway had introduced them as Wayne and Jill, both senior constables. "Medium height, good figure," continued Hathaway. "A pharmacist working in the local branch of Brown and Kent, a small but national chain. She attends writing classes on weekday evenings, she's published three short stories in local magazine, plays tennis at club level and rides horses at weekends sometimes. She has two daughters twenty and twenty-three, both working in England.

Lives in a two-bedroom apartment in Chatswood. She's on good terms with her ex-husband who lives in Canberra and works for the Auditor General's department."

The picture showed a trim female form lying face down on a concrete floor. Her legs were straight out, her hands tied behind her back with a simple plastic tether, the sort used to tie plastic garbage bags. Her head was a bloody mess where a bullet had entered the back and destroyed her face on exit. A pool of blood surrounded the head and soaked into the top of the white sweater she was wearing.

"She didn't fall like that," said Hunter. "Was she arranged that way after she was shot or was she shot like that?"

"The doctor thinks after," replied Detective Jill. "Some very small smudges around the top of the sweater suggest she was moved just a little after death."

"When did this happen?" asked Hunter.

"Sometime between midnight and two, four nights ago." replied Wayne.

"Much trouble identifying her?" asked Hunter.

Hathaway shook his head. "Still had her handbag with her, purse, documents everything."

Hunter sat upright. "Just like the other three," he said. "But the victims, the MO, nothing like those events."

"No, agreed Hathaway. "But the second one is just like this one."

Hunter opened the second folder and extracted the pictures. For a moment, he thought he'd opened the wrong folder and taken the first one again. He studied the pictures, feeling his mind whirl in dismay.

The picture showed a similar shape of woman, dressed neatly in what looked like quality clothing. She lay on her face, legs neatly out straight, hands tethered behind her back by a plastic strip, blood surrounding her head, the bullet wound revealed in her hair only by the blood seeping round it.

"Second victim," said Hathaway. "Adrienne Carter, aged fifty-two, widowed after a road smash in Macksville on the Pacific Highway three years ago, one son aged twenty-seven, he's a Captain in the army serving in Afghanistan. We've called the Defence Department, they're going to bring the poor bugger home. Both parents in three years, eh? Anyway, Adrienne has much the same physical appearance as Vivienne, has a house in Lane Cove, works from home as a contractor, a financial accountant, she got most of her business working for the big accounting firms during the tax overload period, she's quite well off from her husband's estate and insurance. She subscribes to the Sydney Symphony Orchestra, goes to every concert in the season. Occasionally, she goes sailing with friends out of Wilsons Bay, some wealthy bloke with a thirty-foot Catamaran."

"And the interviews revealed nobody with any questions over them?"

Hathaway shook his head. "Vivienne's husband was in Canberra that night, some formal do. Vouched for not just by his current lady-friend who has been in residence for over a year, but also the Auditor General who spoke to him at drinks."

"Work colleagues?"

"All accounted for," said Hathaway.

"Writing class?"

Detective Jill grinned. "I had to admit, I thought about artistic jealousy," she said. "Vivienne had three stories published in literary magazines in the last year and none of the others in the class had managed any at all. But they seemed genuinely pleased for her and the class teacher said she knew of no unpleasantness between her and anybody else."

"The snotty, rich boat-owner?"

"He was half way to Coffs Harbour," said Wayne. "Having a shit-awful time of it, he said. I checked the Met Office and he was right. Horrible weather between here and there and the race coordinators confirmed he arrived in Coffs in the middle of the fleet just after dawn. No way he could have been in Sydney overnight."

"So no obvious motive or opportunity for anyone?" Hunter said.

"Not obvious, no," agreed Hathaway.

"Vivienne's contacts?"

"So far, just as barren," said Wayne. "But this was last night, our guys are still checking everybody, but nothing has come up so far."

"Classic thrill kill, then," said Hunter.

"And with two of them, almost identical profiles, classic serial killer," agreed Hathaway. "And just like the other three, this bastard is challenging us. No effort to remove the IDs, but not a smell of a clue anywhere. He's covered his tracks totally."

"And definitely a he," said Hunter. "This is a male killer, through and through."

All three detectives nodded.

"But then there's the earlobes," said Wayne.

"Earlobes?" Hunter looked at him.

"Yes, sir. We didn't see this until the post mortem because of all the blood and mess from the gunshot, but both women had their left earlobes cut off, very cleanly by something exceptionally sharp like a scalpel."

"Were the lobes taken away?"

"No, they were just a few centimetres away, still with the ear-rings in them, in both cases."

"And expensive ear-rings," added Jill. "Vivienne's were diamond studs and Adrienne had opal pendants, also quite expensive. But nothing was removed."

"We're still in house-to-house search mode," said Hathaway. "We're talking to everybody she knew or had contact with, socially or professionally."

Hunter stood up. "This is a right bitch, Rod," he said. "Your Super kicking up a stink, I suppose?"

"Not yet," said Rod with a grin. "We've only had two. When we catch you up, that's when the shit will fly."

"God, I hope we don't get there," said Hunter with a grimace. "This is sick enough as it is."

He made for the door. "Rod, I know that my Homicide Squad should be handling this, but we're loaded. Your team knows what it's doing, so stick with it, will you?"

Hathaway nodded. "I think it's going to get worse, David."

Hunter grimaced. "I think you're right. Somebody's playing with us."

* * *

"That's a bloody ugly sight, Will." The elderly man in a stylish dark grey suit stood erect, almost as if on a parade square. Despite the raw cold of a northern English winter, he didn't wear a coat. He looked calmly at the scene before him.

"Not one I want to see again, sir." The younger man was less formally dressed in blue jeans and white sweater. His face was also calm, but the pale cheeks revealed some distress.

In front of them, the police surgeon from the Greater Manchester police area was bent over the body of a boy aged about fourteen. He wore the school blazer of the local grammar school, grey flannel slacks and a white shirt, now soaked with blood from the hideous slash across his throat. His hands were tied behind his back with simple thin rope and the body lay face up, draped across the bicycle racks of the shed behind the school building.

The two men turned as a policewoman escorted a middle-aged man to them.

"This is Mr John Hanley, sir," said the young constable, her face averted from the sight of the dead boy. "He's the headmaster."

The man's face showed massive shock. He stared at the dead boy with rigidity in all his body. "Oh my God," he croaked. "It's Barton Shelby."

"Mr Hanley, I'm Detective Chief Inspector Greg Robarts, this is Detective Sergeant William Carter.

This is a horrible thing to have happened, but we need to ask you some questions. Can we come and see you in your office in about fifteen minutes?"

The man nodded without speaking, still staring at the boy's body. Robarts nodded at the police constable and she gently took the man's arm and led him away.

"What do you think, doc?" The two detectives turned back to the scene of the murder.

"Death by cutting of the carotid," replied the doctor, standing up and removing his rubber gloves. "Very quick, very nasty, between midnight and three, I think. Hands were tied behind the back, no signs of struggle, so possibly the boy was unconscious or drugged while it was going on. I'll know more when I get him on the slab. His wallet was in his pants pocket, it's Barton Shelby, an address very near here in Whalley Range. But there's an odd thing. His nostrils were sliced."

The senior detective bent over the broad, African face of the boy. Two clean slices opened the boy's nostrils.

"Before or after death?" Robarts had an expression of distaste as he asked.

"After," replied the doctor. "You can see, there's almost no blood on those cuts, probably a scalpel or a box-cutter was used."

"So what the hell was that nose slicing for, then?"

The doctor shrugged. "Beats me, Greg. Can the blokes take him?"

Robarts nodded. "Call me when you have the report," he said and looked at his sergeant. "Let's go and talk to the headmaster, Will."

An hour later, back at their station, the two detectives met in the conference room with six other officers of the murder squad.

"Another one just like this," said the sergeant, handing out computer print-out copies for distribution. "You know about him already, of course. Anver Iwegbu, a fifteen-year old Nigerian boy, killed in exactly the same way, ten days ago. He was a student at Manchester Grammar, found dead in the bike sheds at his school. Both boys were killed the same way, both were wearing school uniforms."

"Racist killings?" asked a young man from the back of the room.

"That's the first natural conclusion, Paul," said Robarts. "But the fact that the profiles of the victims are almost identical, and this signature theme, the sliced noses, that gives me the creeps. There's something else going on here. Ladies and gentlemen, keep an eagle eye open. We need to let every grammar school in the region know about this and have their black kids take extra precautions, suggest parents take them to school and collect them and if that's not possible, have the kids try and travel in groups. Will, put out a request for information around the country, just in case there's anything else happening."

He looked round the room. "We've got a serial killer on our hands. You know what to do, let's get started."

The meeting broke up.

Chapter 5 – Blowing it Open

"Her name is Martina Hall," said Rachel Norman. She sat across from David Hunter's desk and consulted her notebook while Hunter sipped at another in his endless mugs of black coffee.

"She was twenty-six, single, never been married, a payroll officer with the Department of Corrective Services in the City. She was supposed to be going out for drinks with some of the girls last night. She lives in a studio pad in Botany, one of the girls who works with her also has the place next to her. She didn't show up at the pub, and when her neighbour, a girl called Pat Wallace got home, she found a note pinned to her door saying Martina wasn't going to make it. When Martina wasn't at work next day, she eventually called us, about ten."

"You went and talked to her?"

"I did," said Rachel.

"Do you have any idea of where she might have been, Pat?" asked Rachel Norman. She sat at a table in the coffee bar of the ground floor of the office building, the dark, small girl on her right, both of them cradling mugs of coffee. Pat Wallace's make-up was badly smudged from her tears of the crying fit that had hit her when Rachel had told her of her friend's murder.

"I really don't," said Pat, smothering a gulp.

"A boyfriend, perhaps?"

"Really not," said Pat. "She'd dumped her last bloke a few weeks ago, said he was a right bastard and she was off men for a time."

"Do you know his name?"

"Oh yes! Terry Walters! God, I had too much of that turd, what with her bleating about him all the time."

"Bleating? He treated her badly?"

"Yeah, but I think she liked that. Martina did victim like nobody else I knew! I don't think she was happy unless she had some bloke to bitch about how badly he behaved."

"Did you meet him?"

"Just once. Good looking enough, I suppose, but right up himself. He treated me like shit, asking me to get him a beer when we were all in his place in Newtown, as if I was the bloody waitress!"

Rachel carefully noted down the name. "Where in Newtown?"

"Halliday Street, can't remember the number."

"And she was right off men?"

"Well, I think so. Hard to tell with her. She attracts men like moths to a flame, she really is pretty, great pair of legs and she likes to show them off. I'd actually suggested she get on the internet and try one of those dating sites. She laughed, said not a chance, but I wouldn't be surprised, I don't think she'll stay off men for long."

She suddenly looked stricken as if realising she was talking about a victim of murder, no longer her pretty friend in the next apartment.

"Anybody else in her circle?"

"Just the girls," Pat replied. "We occasionally met up with some of the blokes from the office for drinks on a Friday evening, but I don't think there was anybody particularly interesting for her."

"Okay, thanks, Pat. I'm really sorry to have brought you such horrible news."

"I just hope you get the bastard," said the girl, rising to her feet and clacked off across the concrete back into the building.

Thoughtfully, Rachel paid the bill and took a cab back to the police station.

"You've arranged to get her computer?" asked Hunter, sure of the answer.

Rachel looked pained.

"Tell me again now, boss, I make a hole in the egg and then suck it, right? It's already on my desk."

Hunter laughed out loudly. "Okay, lady, get on with it. If you need help prying names of clients out of the dating service, threaten them with a visit from me."

"Listen boss, if I can't scare the shit out of a bunch of computer nerds, I'll give up this policing lark and take up bull-fighting or something just as easy."

"Go for your life, Rachel."

With a wide grin, she left Hunter's office.

Unable to do much but think, Hunter took the task home. His mind whirled and spun for a time until his powerful discipline took over and he began working through the events of recent weeks. He had a serial killer on his hands, that was for sure, a clever one, too, utterly without motive, the hardest sort of murders to solve. And yet the killer had made no effort to clean up the clues as to the identity of the victims, quite the reverse, he was challenging the police. There was nothing at all to point to him.

And what about the dead woman? Not a series, Hunter was certain of that, it had all the common signs of a sexual killing, out of jealousy, abandonment, unattainability, the regular background to a killing, usually of a woman by a man.

Now he had Rod Hathaway's pair of killings in North Sydney. They seemed horribly like his triple murder and yet there were significant differences. Different victim type, different MO, different weapon. But they were alike, much too alike to be coincidence. Hunter knew damn well that Rod would find another one or even more middle-aged women, dead on a concrete floor, hands tied behind them with a plastic tether and shot in the back of the head with a .22 pistol. But Martina Hall in Alexandria had been killed with a .22 pistol. Could they be related? The two murders had nothing in common beyond the weapon and the sex of the victim. But could they be connected? Would there be another thirty-year old male, stripped to the waist, hanging by his wrists from a pipe with three stab wounds in his stomach? How long?

Not feeling like cooking, Hunter took a box of Camembert from his fridge and found the bread rolls in the bread box. A blast of twenty seconds in the microwave and the Camembert was pleasantly soft. He took the plates to his coffee table, switched on the evening news on his television, poured a glass of a gentle Merlot and tried to concentrate on the events of the day.

Only two minutes into the news, the blonde newsreader ruined his evening.

"Police say they have no leads to the string of hideous murders that have occurred in Sydney recently. We have now learned that at least four killings have occurred in the inner city around Surry Hills, three men and the latest, a young woman discovered overnight in a basement car park of a building in Alexandria, just a short distance from Surry Hills."

"What the fuck?" exclaimed Hunter, wine and cheese forgotten. "Who the hell said 'Police say?' It's *my* bloody case, nobody asked me anything about it."

It got worse. To his dismay, the face of the Assistant Commissioner appeared on the screen.

"I have to confirm that what looks like a triple killing has occurred on three separate nights in the inner city suburbs," the Commissioner said. "Three young men were brutally killed by knife wounds. There was also a fourth killing in the same region, a young woman who was shot with a small-calibre weapon. There is not believed to be any connection between that one and the three others. We urge anyone who may know about these murders or who thinks they may have seen anything unusual during the night to come forward or contact us in any way."

Hunter sat in shock. Who had authorised this information to be released? Without tasting it, he took a mouthful of the wine. The Police Commissioner had been replaced by the State's Opposition Justice Minister. Hunter tuned out, only vaguely hearing the platitudes spew out about ministerial ineptitude, poor police morale, funding shortages, etc. But the next face on the screen was not expected at all.

Alan Kinsella was the owner of a national right-wing newspaper and chain of magazines around Australia and the world. Beyond the occasional picture in the newspapers, Hunter had never seen the man. He studied the thin, bony face on the screen. Something seemed wrong with his posture until a sudden change of camera angle revealed that Kinsella was in a wheel chair. Hunter knew a little about the man, it was hard not to, given his profile. He was a multi-billionaire, the sole inheritor of the estates of both parents, his father a US industrial magnate, his mother an Australian high-profile Senior Counsel. Hunter dug into his memory. Born with useless legs, he recalled, but a brilliant business mind.

Kinsella was speaking in a surprisingly attractive baritone voice, obviously highly educated. "This is a disgraceful state of affairs," he said. "The police should be absolutely ashamed of themselves, they're like kids in an adult world. Everyone involved in this debacle, from the Commissioner downward, the detective force, the patrol police, they are all guilty of absolute dereliction of duty.”

“What the hell’s got up his nose?” said Hunter aloud, grateful at least that the murders in North Sydney had not been mentioned and that his own name had been left out for now.

“Shit!” he said and pulled the phone out of the plug. The last thing he wanted was to be deluged by the press this evening at home. He kept the mobile switched on and plugged into the charger. Only his team and his sister had that number

What the hell was going on?

Then he remembered what had been niggling at him since the delectable Doctor Simpson had mentioned it.

* * *

“Christ, Dwayne, that’s just sick.”

The flashing lights of the Toronto Police cruiser flickered across the scene in the cemetery. Three other officers had cleared the onlookers back down the pathway, leaving the two officers who had first arrived on the scene with little to do but wait for the medical examiner and the homicide squad to arrive.

The body of the overweight, middle-aged man lay against the memorial wall that held plaques of those who had been cremated and had their ashes spread elsewhere. Blood had splattered across many of these, thrown out by the bullet that had gone through the man’s head from the back, exiting at the right eye and leaving little of the face.

"What the hell is the point of taking off the guy's shoes and socks and then shooting him through the ankle? You're right, Garry, it's sick."

"You reckon he did that before he shot him in the head, Dwayne, or after?"

"Damned if I know. We'll have to leave that to the examiner. I wish the bastard would hurry up, I hear a Timmy's coffee calling me."

The scene rapidly became crowded over the next few moments as two unmarked sedans arrived and disgorged two detectives in plain clothes from one and a middle-aged woman in jeans and sweater from the other. She took a bag from the passenger seat and walked to the body and studied it while putting on her paper coverall suit. Finally she bent over the ugly sight and began a detailed examination.

One of the detectives came up to the patrol officers.

"You got the call, Dwayne? Who was it?"

"That couple sitting on the bench there, Sergeant."

"Okay. You two guys heading to Tim Hortons, eh?"

"Time for our break, Sergeant."

"Yeah, I know, but bring a couple for us first, will you? I think the doc wants a single cream, no sugar, Harry and I will have double-doubles."

The patrol cops nodded and went to their cruiser, hiding their grumbles until they had driven out of the cemetery.

The detectives split up, one went to the couple on the bench, the other to the medical examiner.

"What do you reckon, Harriet?"

She didn't look up from her inspection of the exit wound. "Well, this bullet didn't give him a migraine. Jim. Probably a .22, soft nose, fired at close range, execution style."

"What about the shot in the ankle?"

"That's just sick! It was done post-mortem. God knows why, unless it's some sort of signal to somebody."

"A gangland killing?"

"Probably. Anyway, time of death estimated between midnight and three and it was done here, but the body was still moved a little after death. See, some blood smudges here and here, they wouldn't have come from the shot itself. I'd say he was kneeling on the steps into this little structure, shot and then pulled into this position. I think that's when the ankle shot was fired."

The detective bent down over the body and examined the rest of the corpse. "Can I move him, Harriet?"

"Just one sec, Jim. Have you guys taken all the pictures you need?"

"Yes, doc," said the photographer who had appeared a few minutes earlier.

"Okay, Jim, go ahead."

Detective Sergeant James Clancy didn't take long making a startling discovery.

"Well shit!" he said. "His wallet is here!" Carefully, he eased the black leather wallet from the corpse's hip pocket and opened it, pulling out the driver's licence. "Claudio Cappano, he's fifty eight, address on Chaplin Avenue, an apartment, I think that's just north of

Eglinton. No pictures of family, one of a dog. A few business cards saying he's a production manager with a company in Markham. We'd better get animal welfare round to his place quick, just in case he lives alone. Could be Mafia, I suppose."

"Stereotyping, Detective Clancy?" said the medical examiner, standing up. "Okay, you can move him, I'll send you my report as soon as I've cut him up."

"Nothing from the people who found him," said the other detective, approaching the group. "They were just taking an early morning walk, saw the body and the blood and called us on their cell phone right away. I've got a statement."

Clancy sighed. "Okay, better get started with a door to door. Maybe somebody in one of those apartments up there heard something. And call a few guys in to look for the bullet. Harriet says he was probably kneeling at the top of these steps, so it could be in that area ahead, if his head was down. But I don't hold out much chance of it. It's probably gone deep in the ground."

His colleague nodded and pulled out his phone. "Where are those coffees?" he asked then punched the numbers.

Chapter 6 – The Bloodstain Spreads

"Angie, that cross cut into the shoulder of that last victim."

"The young man? Yes, what about it?"

"Wasn't there a similar cross on the other two blokes?"

"Hang on a sec, David, I'll check."

Impatiently, he waited as he heard the sound of a desk drawer being opened, a folder being dropped onto the desk surface and the rustle of paper.

"Yes, David, there was, on both of them."

"Identical?"

"Not quite. The first one was very shallow and far more uneven. One arm of the cross looked like the knife had slipped, it was twice as big as the other three. The second cross was more even, still a bit ragged though."

"What about the woman?"

"Nothing on her. I'll email you the pictures of the crosses."

"Thanks, Angie, do that. It looks like he was getting better at it as he went."

"Let's pray he doesn't get expert."

"Amen to that, Doctor Angela!"

He hung up the phone. A few minutes later he had the pictures on his screen. Angie was right, the three crosses had improved in quality with each killing.

David Hunter developed a sick feeling in his stomach.

* * *

"Jack, it's a serial killing, all right. Each of the blokes has a cross cut into his shoulder. I've just emailed you the pictures."

"Yeah, I'm looking at them, now. That first one is a bit ragged, isn't it?"

"And then he gets better."

"Tell you what, young David, I'd say the first one is the result of panic. He hasn't done anything like this before, he has no idea how human flesh cuts and he's still shaking and trembling from killing the poor bastard. Probably took that long to get control of his nerves again and the victim had died before the cross was cut."

"Jack, I really need you down here. Bill Hamilton said the same."

"Bill Hamilton? You've got a good copper there, David."

"I know it Jack, but I need you. The team has gone flat, we've got nothing to work on, no direction, nothing."

"David, I told you, I really can't. I've got a new life here, I don't think I could even know where to start now."

"Like riding a bike, Jack, or undoing a woman's bra. Once you know how…"

Savage's deep laugh echoed down the line from the mid-north coast. "It's been a while since I did either, David."

"Tell me about it, Jack."

"What about those two in North Sydney?"

"Totally different MO, Jack. Different victim type, murder weapon, nothing except the fact that their handbags were left there, no trouble identifying them. And the killer had sliced off their earlobes."

"Did he now? A signature of some sort. The bastard's marking his trophies."

"But two different killers, you think?"

"Definitely not the same bloke, David, unless he's a seriously clever bastard and he's deliberately adopted a different MO. Leaving the handbags, like your blokes had their wallets and car keys left behind, that smells a bit odd. Could be a copycat element there."

"And the young woman who was shot in Alexandria? Not connected? It's close to those others in Surry Hills."

"I doubt it, David. Mind you, there's a sort of link. She was killed with a .22 pistol, like the women in North Sydney."

"Yeah, I thought of that, but there's absolutely nothing else the same."

"What about a signature? Anything there?"

"No, so we all agree it's not connected to the others."

"Well I hope to God you don't get another one like that, or you may have three sets of serial killings to work on."

"Doesn't that even get your copper's nose sniffing a bit, Jack?"

"Just a bit, David, just a bit. But the cow shit all over my paddocks is far smellier and requires my presence rather more."

"Okay, Jack, I know when I'm beaten. I'll keep you informed."

"Good luck, David. Somehow, I doubt you'll have time to come to Coffs Harbour for a while."

"I dunno, Jack. The way some political heavies and that Alan Kinsella bloke are screaming, I might be joining you on the retired list pretty soon."

"That's just for show, David. They know how capable you are. Hang in there."

"See you, Jack."

Hunter put down the phone. Almost immediately, it rang again.

"David, it's Rod Hathaway. We've got a third."

* * *

"Her name is Kerry Holland," said Jill, the young detective on Hathaway's team. "She was fifty-three, single, twice-married before, first time at University to Lennie Graham, an architect, no children, divorced after two years."

The two inspectors and two constables sat in the conference room at the North Sydney police station. A small hum came from the laptop computer on Hathaway's desk and a similar soft sound from the projector that displayed the ugly pictures on the screen.

The woman lay in the same pose as the two previous victims, stretched out, face down, legs together, blood soaking into the expensive white sweater, hands bound behind her back by industrial-size plastic binders.

"The rest of her profile is similar to the other two," continued Jill. "She married again three years later, to Phil Andrews who ran a small engineering company, quite profitable and wealthy, but they divorced after ten years, no children. The first husband lives in the USA, we haven't been able to find him yet, second one still lives in Newcastle where they lived when married, he's had no contact with her since an unpleasant divorce seventeen years ago. She's about 175cm, similar build to the first two victims. She was an office administrator to a company in North Sydney, she has a small house in St Leonards. Worked as a volunteer in her local library some evenings and was studying English Literature at evening classes at the University."

"Definitely the third in the series," said Hathaway. "Shit, David, it's becoming a disease."

"Bloody oath!" said Hunter.

"Her left earlobe had been cut off, too," added Wayne. "She wasn't wearing any earrings, though."

"The doc says the implement was probably a box-cutter," said Jill. "Very sharp, but not as pure a cutting edge as a surgical scalpel."

"And that fact had not been reported in any media, had it?" asked Hunter.

Hathaway shook his head. "Not a copycat killing. And it makes it just that much harder to track, anyone can buy those things at a hardware store."

Hunter rubbed his eyes in weariness. "Any known current relationships?"

"Nothing serious," said Hathaway. "She'd been out a few times with her lecturer at the University, but they seemed more friends than lovers. I don't list him as a suspect. She had lunch on a fairly regular basis with her boss at work, but he's married and his wife knew Kerry quite well. Again, no reason to suspect anyone there."

"This is a real bitch, Rod."

"Tell me about it," the other man said. "And the row is growing. Have you heard what that little runt, Alan Kinsella is saying?"

"I heard him spouting some raving fury a couple of nights ago. He's really got something up his arse."

"He was back the news on last night," said Hathaway. "He seems to be taking aim at the police force, the government, everybody, quite ropeable, he was."

"I suppose it sells newspapers," said Hunter, trying not to get annoyed. "But is it having an effect?"

Hathaway nodded. "At least I've got more boots on the ground now. My Super transferred some more uniforms to help in the questioning."

Hunter stood up. "I need to get back to my place," he said. "Let's keep each other up to date as anything develops."

Hathaway stood up and the two shook hands. "Pray for a break like a farmer prays for rain," he said with a half-smile.

Hunter nodded at the two junior detectives and made his way out of the building.

As he drove over the Bridge, his mobile phone rang. He pushed the button for "hands free" conversation.

"D.I. Hunter."

"D.I. Hunter, this is D.I. Graham Feeney in Brunswick, Victoria."

"G'day to you, D.I. Feeney, how can I help you?"

"David, those serial killings in Sydney, I've just been reading up on them in the system. This hasn't made the news yet, but we've got our own problems, also."

"Oh Christ! What's happening?"

"Three old homeless men, stabbed and left in parks. There hasn't been a lot of fuss, because of who they are, but when I read the details in your files, I realised they're similar."

"How so, Graham?"

"All stabbed in the heart, and then the killer sliced one ear off and left it on the body. All the hallmarks of a serial killer."

"Just like ours. And you've got no clues at all?"

"Not a bloody thing. No motive, no beneficiary, no signs of anything at all."

"There are some sick puppies around, Graham. Will you keep the files up to date so we can follow the story? We'll do the same, of course."

"For sure. There's something ugly going on."
"We'll talk further, Graham. It's got me spooked."
"Thanks, David."

Hunter disconnected the call and continued the drive back. His mind was in a whirl

What the hell was going on?

Chapter 7 – The International Killing

Hunter was starting to feel overwhelmed. Three murders in Sydney, three now in North Sydney. Reports from Perth and Melbourne, serial killings without a doubt, but different MOs between each series. What the hell was going on? This was a plague such as Australia had never seen before.

Only Australia? The thought hit him like a punch in the gut. Could it be elsewhere also? He turned to his computer monitor. His hobby of reading the newspapers from around the world by the internet might yet prove useful.

It was. In less than forty-eight hours, the situation got far worse.

The atmosphere in the situation room was subdued. Somehow the crew had sensed the blackness in Hunter's soul as he walked to the front of the room and the general banter and chatter and faded. The coffee urn still steamed, people still poured their mugs and somebody brought Hunter his own, but things were quiet, depressed.

David took his customary stand, leaning against the desk by the whiteboard and sipped his coffee, gathering himself.

"Okay, people, listen carefully. Whatever we thought was bad before, it's got many times worse. Something hideous is going on. I've been reading a sample of newspapers around the world, just the English language ones. Now all this could just be coincidence, but I don't think so. Here's the situation so far, and I stress the "so far" because I think there's more to come."

He looked down at the sheaf of papers he'd brought in with him.

"Manchester, England," he said. "Two schoolboys, aged fourteen and fifteen have been killed in the last month. They were both black, wearing school uniforms from different schools and they were killed the same way. Their hands were tied behind their backs and their throats were cut."

A stir of horror ran through the room. Hardened as these officers all were into the terrible things that people did to people, nobody ever became callused against the murder of children.

"Jesus Christ," somebody whispered.

"The first assumption by the local police was that this was another racist bastard rampage, not necessarily by one person but possibly a gang, given the common MO. But there was another factor that has only become critical since I sent the query to them and the details of our events here. Both boys had their noses slit, the left nostril from the top of the lip to most of the way to the top. It was done post-mortem, apparently and by the same weapon. It now looks like it was one perp and he left his sign."

Hunter looked round the room. Every face was turned to him, watching intently, clearly expecting more horror. He gave it to them.

"Toronto, Canada. In a cemetery in an area north of the City of Toronto, between Yonge Street and Bathhurst, north of Bloor Street, the body of a man was discovered in the last few days. I sent an official query to Toronto and got the details, some of which were not reported. The victim was in his forties and the description given is that he was quite short and semi-bald, a prosperous business type, not married, and initially the Toronto cops suspected a Mafia killing as he'd been shot, execution style, by a .22 pistol in the back of the head. But there's something about the case that made me call the Toronto guys because it reminded me of our things. His wallet was still there. And there was another odd thing that I got which had not been made public. An additional shot had been fired, into the left ankle, post-mortem."

He put the papers on the desk and stood upright, taking up his mug and sipping it. "Any comments?" he asked.

Bill Hamilton raised his hand. He was in his usual garb of flannels and black blazer with a military badge on the pocket.

"Yes, Bill?"

"I can see the peculiarities, boss," Hamilton said. "The Manchester murders sound like the start of a serial killing spree by a single individual. That slit noses stuff does sound sick, a bit like our guys in the inner city."

"That's what gets me worried," Hunter said.

"That Toronto murder could have me worried, even with just one," continued Hamilton. "The shot in the ankle, that makes no sense at all, nor does leaving the wallet with the body."

"But we've got the same shit here," broke in Jamie Patterson, the newest addition to the group. "Our three here in our patch, all with a cross cut into their shoulders, those women in North Sydney with their ear lobes cut off, they're the same."

"And Brunswick, Victoria," chimed in Jamie Petersen. "Three old homeless blokes, stabbed, one ear cut off."

"What, some sort of signature?" Rachel Norman looked astounded.

Hunter looked hard at her. "Exactly that, I think," he said.

A wave of interest ran through the room.

The door opening broke the wave and a young uniformed constable walked in, carrying a sheet of paper. He looked alarmed and self-conscious in the gaze of so many people as he walked up to Hunter.

"This just came from DS Simpson, sir," he said. "Apparently it's just been on tv and he thought you should see it." He waited in obvious tension until Hunter had taken the sheet and nodded dismissal with a friendly smile then he walked rapidly out of the room.

Hunter scanned the sheet. "Oh shit!" he said and looked around the room. "We've got something in the

USA. This says that there have been four shootings in the Virginia region over the last week, near Washington DC. All political figures, but not Federal, three men, one women have been shot by rifle while attending outdoor events. No reports yet of whether the same rifle was used or what the connections are."

"Were they all the same political party?" asked Jerry Bowler, the newly-promoted Sergeant. "Those Yanks are so politically divided, it could just be a nutter."

"Nothing stated," replied Hunter.

Rachel Norman raised her hand. "That doesn't fit," she said with a dubious look on her face.

"Explain," said Hunter.

"A long-range weapon? All the others were close-up and personal. And what's the signature? You can't leave a signature with a rifle."

"Good thinking," said Hunter. "This may be a wild card and not part of the pattern. I'll get the Super to make some inquiries."

Chapter 8 – First Break

"Boss, this could be something!" Bill Hamilton flung open Hunter's door, some rare excitement reflected in his usually calm face.

Hunter looked with interest at the Sergeant. "What's up, Bill?"

"You need to come down to the interview room. There's an old geezer just come in, says he may have seen something in the Smith murder."

"Well, shit, eh?" said Hunter and got to his feet. "When was this?"

"Just a few minutes ago," replied Hamilton as the two men strode rapidly along the corridor and down the steps to the ground floor. "He came in, said he wanted to talk to somebody. Rachel and I took him, thinking he could be a nutter, you know how they come out of the woodwork, wanting to admit to every murder that happens."

"Bloody oath," said Hunter. "But he sounds sane?"

"Judge for yourself." Hamilton stopped by the interview room door and opened it, following Hunter into the spacious room. Rachel Norman was sitting with her back to the door, across from a tall, slender man who looked in his sixties, Hunter estimated. He was dressed in a well-styled, dark grey suit, a white shirt with cufflinks gleaming at his wrists and an immaculately-tied double Windsor knot in his dark red tie.

"Boss, this is William Chester," said Hamilton. "Mr Chester, this is Detective Inspector David Hunter, in charge of the case."

"Mr Chester, thank you for coming in," said Hunter as they shook hands. "I understand you may have some information on that murder in Kelly Street."

"Possibly, only possibly, Inspector," replied the man. His voice was a pleasant tenor, well-spoken, reflecting a good education. He appeared relaxed and confident, a man who knew how to deal with others.

Hunter sat down opposite Chester who followed suit. Hamilton remained standing by the wall, observing.

"The night of the murder, I was working very late in my office," Chester began.

"Which is where?" asked Hunter.

"On the third floor of Kelly Street, number fifteen, almost opposite the entrance to the car park where the body was found."

"What time was that, sir?" Rachel asked.

"Just after one a.m."

"That's unusual, isn't it?" asked Hunter.

"Not common, no. But I run my own business and sometimes extra effort is required. And I was flying out to Singapore later that day and there was some paperwork that just had to be ready for a client."

"I understand," said Hunter.

"About 1:15, I finished what I was doing, turned off the lights and used a small flashlight to leave the office and take the elevator down to the ground floor. I'd called for a cab to come and get me."

"You didn't use your car?" Rachel asked.

"I don't have one," Chester said with a smile. "I developed some eye problems last year, I had to surrender my licence. Anyway, I have an apartment on Pitt Street in the city, I really don't need a car."

"And so what happened?" asked Hunter.

"I came out of the building, about fifty, sixty metres from the car park entrance across the road. There was a car parked on the road. I didn't really give it a lot of attention, but a man got in and drove off. It was a Jaguar, that I know, but I can't tell you what model. The driver didn't put on his lights, but I saw just a part of the rear licence plate. It began with the letter "Y" and it was one of those plates that has two letters then a dash and some numbers. I couldn't see any more than that. Then my taxi arrived and I went home to get some sleep before my flight."

"And why have you left it till now to come and tell us?" asked Hunter, feeling some irritation.

Chester turned a cold eye on him. "Do you recall that I told you I was to fly out to Singapore that morning? Well, I did and I returned home at six thirty this morning after a nine-hour flight. I went from the airport to my office and that's when my staff told me about the murder. I came straight here. Inspector, I'm

72, I've had a rough week in Singapore and Kuala Lumpur, I flew home overnight and I would like to be in bed, not here."

Hunter felt ashamed of himself. "Mr Chester, I do sincerely apologise, that was bloody rude of me. Could I ask you to stay long enough for your statement to be typed up and sign it then I'll have a police car run you home? Your account may just give us a vital breakthrough, but we're all a bit ragged here with this outbreak of murders."

"I understand," Chester said and finally smiled. Sometime later, he was driven home, after looking as if he needed help to stay awake to sign his name to the document.

Rachel, Bill and Hunter stood in the interview room and looked at each other.

"Well, bugger me sideways," said Hunter. "We may have a break."

Hamilton laughed loudly. "I haven't heard that expression since Jack Savage was here!" he said. "That was his favourite."

"Okay, just have somebody check that distance between the office door and the car park entrance, make sure it's feasible for the old bloke to have seen the rego plate at night, particularly with eyesight problems, like he told us," said Hunter.

"It's about right," said Rachel, "but I'll measure it."

"And I'll get a list of every Jag in the state with a licence plate beginning with a letter "Y" in that form," added Hamilton. "Tally ho, loose the hounds!"

Hunter knew how his sergeant felt. The hunt was on at last.

* * *

The pathologist stood up from the table where the body rested, a sheet from the hips down.

"Got the bullet," he said. "Looks like a nine millimetre, fired from a few feet away, no burn mark on the clothing, but straight into the heart." He held it up in the pincers he had used to ease it from the body of the man in his forties and showed it to the spectators in the observation gallery.

"Hey, this is interesting," he said and moved the bullet nearer his eyes. "There's something here, wait a moment..." He rinsed the bullet under a tap by the metal slab and looked at it again then up at the gallery.

"Sergeant, you need to see this. There's a symbol engraved on the bullet. It's a new moon, or something like that."

"A crescent moon?" said Detective Sergeant Phil Coulson, his attention level rising sharply.

"Could be," said the pathologist. "What, you mean the symbol for Islam?"

"That's exactly what I mean," said the detective. "Just like the one three days ago in Wilmette. We've got a goddammed Jihadist crazy here."

"What about those shootings in Virginia the last couple of weeks?" asked the pathologist. "Do you know anything about those? I wonder if they could be related?"

"I'll soon find out," replied the detective and pulled out his phone.

Chapter 9 – A Death in the Family

"Two in two weeks, Phil, this is bad shit."

"Tell me about it Captain. Wilmette's supposed to be a rich, peaceful area, not the freekin' South Side."

The two men leaned on the rail and looked down into the pathology lab where the medical examiner was bent over the body of a middle-aged man lying on the slab.

"The victim is a man of forty-three and this is known because his wallet and identification were found with the body," the pathologist said clearly for the sake of the recording and the observers. "His clothes have been removed after examination and no burn marks were found. Death initially appears to have come from a bullet straight into the heart and there are no other signs of violence on the body. There is no exit wound so I shall now attempt to extract the bullet."

There was silence all through the gallery as the doctor went about the business of slicing the immediate area of the wound and pushing a pair of forceps into the gap being made.

"Ah!" he said after a short period and stood up, the bullet firmly held in the forceps. He stared hard at the bullet then washed it under the tap nearby. "Phil, you're gonna love this. Another Crescent Moon engraved on the bullet."

Detective Sergeant Phil Coulsen stood up straight. "Goddammed freekin' Islamic fundamentalists!" he swore. "I'm going to arrest every single freekin' one of them in Illinois."

"Let's get back to the office, Phil," said the Captain. "We may have a problem here."

* * *

"It's got me totally freaked out, Deb."

David Hunter swallowed the entire contents of the tiny pottery cup of hot sake and poured another from the little flagon.

Deborah Hunter watched him thoughtfully before expertly taking more ginger from her wooden platter with her chopsticks and adding it to the dish of soy sauce. "I can tell," she said. "Little brother, you don't normally drink that stuff in gulps. Are you drinking more than normal at home, too?"

Hunter moved a slice of salmon sashimi to soak in the soy dish. "I am, Deb. I've never been like this and I'm worried sick. Four murders in the inner west in a few weeks, three in North Sydney, more in Melbourne and Perth and now I think it's happening all over the world as well. And I don't have a single bloody clue."

"What about that lead you got from that old business bloke, Chester? Any luck tracking down Jaguars?"

"Well, it was exciting when we got it, I admit. But we found every Jaguar, in fact every luxury car with a registration beginning with "Y" and came up blank. We did find a handful, but every one of the owners has produced an alibi and not one of them is remotely like any serial killer in our experience. We tried other variations like "T" and "K" because the old boy's eyesight was suspect, like he told us himself, but still came up blank. Sound alibis in all cases. We're taking some serious shit about this, Deb."

"Yes, I know. Our reporters are following up all over the US and Europe. I'm fighting some nasty battles in the studios because the bosses want to make this a massive anti-government campaign and I keep telling them that will only inflate the hysteria."

"Your boss is doing that enough, already," Hunter said with some anger. "What with his news channels, current affairs programs and magazines, I'm getting massive shit thrown at me, so is my whole department."

"Allan Kinsella is a prize prick," she replied. "I can't stand the bastard and his far-right preaching. But it helps to sell papers and magazine and get viewers to his channels and that's all he cares about."

"Yes, I've noticed that your program doesn't join in the blood-thrills that some of the others on the Kinsella networks are indulging in."

"And that's causing me troubles," she said and took a sip of her own sake cup. "I think it will get me fired soon."

"Would you care, big sister? God knows the other channels would love to have you! You're considered a national treasure! You'd probably be glad to get out of there."

"I've no doubt. But if I can hang on a bit, perhaps I can keep some of the more rabid screaming toned down a bit. Any further developments in the matter?"

"Off the record, Deb?"

"Of course. Sounds like you have something."

"I did some studies of newspapers around the world, those I could read, that is. I found an odd report in "The Guardian" from the UK about a couple of schoolboy killings in Manchester. Two boys, similar age, both black, both found murdered. I called the Manchester cops and it took a while, but they finally said the MO was the same in both."

"Was there a sign on them?"

"Their noses had been slit."

"That's horrible," she said with a grimace. "Racist killings?"

"Either that or somehow related to our killings here."

"And the local cops have nothing to go on?"

He shook his head and poured another drink. "Just like all the others. No attempt to take away wallets. The British press is having a field day crucifying them."

"Any others?" She finished the last slice of tuna sashimi and put her chopsticks down.

"Toronto, Canada. Just one, but the bloke had been shot execution-style, his wallet with all his cards and identification left on the body and then the weird thing, he'd been shot again in his left ankle."

"Good grief, David. But only one murder, not a series?"

"Right, but it looks like all of them are being left with some sort of signature, and the common factor of their wallets or handbags being left with the bodies, that says something weird is going on."

"Any more?"

"Another one in the States. Two local counsellors from village governments around Chicago have been shot, but not like that series of shootings in Virginia. The second one I discovered only yesterday! I've started looking through a variety of papers on the web and when I saw this one, I called the local cops. These were shot by handgun, close up, same gun. There was no obvious signature, but when the local cops got the bullets in the post mortems, they both had the Islamic sign of the crescent moon engraved on them."

"Oh lord," Deborah said with a sigh. "Calculated to inflame anti-Muslim hatreds even more, eh?"

"Probably," Hunter said. "And I know the definition of a serial killing is three murders, but my gut tells me there's a serial killer at work, whether Muslim or pretend. He or she may just have got started. Same in Toronto. Somehow, I just know that one is the first of many."

"And there's no connection with that other series of shootings in Virginia?"

"That's the odd thing," Hunter said. "A group claiming to be an al Q'aeda force in the US had claimed responsibility for the first series. But they haven't claimed responsibility for this second one."

"And the right-wing press are stirring things up in their usual fashion, I suppose?"

"You got that right. Fox News is screaming for the arrest of every Muslim in America and Kinsella's network is even louder."

"David, maybe you should consider retiring. It's making you ill."

"Deb, I can't quit in the middle of this. But I tell you, when it's over, I'll give serious consideration to joining Jack Savage and buying some acreage up the coast and spend my days walking in cowshit instead of the human variety."

She laughed. "A great idea, little bro! Now, let's end in traditional fashion and have some green tea ice-cream."

"Damn good idea," he said and waved at the waitress.

Two days later, David Hunter stood on a tiny strip of sand next to New South Head Road in Rose Bay in Sydney's Eastern Suburbs. He stood motionless as Angela Simpson knelt in shallow water under the boat slip of the yacht club and studied the body of the young woman lying huddled on the metal rails. Despite the near nudity of the dead woman, the long, beautiful legs under a short skirt and one bare breast revealed by a torn blouse, the sight was totally sexless.

Finally Angela stood up. She wore plastic boots over the paper suit, but the sea water had washed up over her knees.

"I think she drowned," said Angela. "But there's a nasty bruise above her right ear that could have killed her first. I'll need to get her on the slab, but my first impression is that there's water in the lungs, so she was probably unconscious and thrown into the water some way out in the harbour. Given the water temperature, I estimate death some time between midnight and four this morning."

"Nothing to identify her?'

The doctor shook her head. "No handbag, but a bracelet with the initials "PF" engraved on it." She passed it to Hunter with her gloved hands and he held out a plastic evidence bag for her to drop it into before he sealed it shut. Then he turned and climbed up the stepladder up to the stone wall and over to the pavement. A small crowd was watching and the heavy traffic crawling into town was slowed even more by the spectacle of the police cars and ambulance.

Angela followed him up the steps and began peeling off her protective suit, looking with irritation at the wet patches on her trouser legs. "That's probably buggered," she muttered and slipped on the shoes that were on the grass strip.

"Call me when you have a result," Hunter said.

"Could it be connected to that last killing?" the doctor asked. "It's a different MO, but a similar victim."

"Damned if I know," Hunter said. "I need to get my team out there to see if we can identify a boat on the water at that time. That's going to be damn near impossible."

She took his arm and pulled him away from prying eyes and ears. "David, this is killing you," she murmured softly. "But it will break, you know that.

Somewhere, somebody will slip something that opens up the door. But look, when you come to my office today, I'll give you something to help. I can tell you're not sleeping."

"I'll see you later," he said, saying nothing about the offer of medicinal help.

The atmosphere in the situation room was quite different from that in recent times. People were smiling, some laughing, the sense of celebration high.

Hunter leaned up in his customary position against the desk at the front of the room and his tension-filled face and eyes, shadowed from lack of sleep had relaxed a little.

"I wish all cases were this easy," said Bill Hamilton. He held his coffee mug as if it were a champagne glass and raised it to the room. "Forty eight hours!" he said. "A murder case wrapped up in forty eight hours!"

"Bloody fine work, all of you," said Hunter. "Bill, run us through how it went, so all of us can hear the details."

"It was charmed, boss," said Hamilton. "We got a Missing Person report almost immediately. Patricia Franklin's mother called us by noon that same day the girl was found. Normally, we'd ask her to wait a day, 'cos Patricia was over twenty-one and could just have run off for a dirty few days with her boyfriend, but with this latest body, we took all the details. The mother came in and identified the body and told us her daughter had been dating some bastard called

Raymond Hall from Vaucluse. She obviously didn't like him.

"We checked him out, he has a cruiser he keeps at the Elizabeth Bay Club. Damned if the club didn't confirm he'd been out that night, got in at four in the morning. We found Patricia's handbag on the boat, the silly bugger hadn't even thrown it overboard, and he cracked there and then. They'd had a row on the boat, something about sexual stuff that she wouldn't do for him. He bashed her on the head, threw her overboard and motored home, the lousy bastard. Confession signed and sealed by yesterday evening."

A burst of applause ran round the room and several high-fives were thrown between officers. Hunter held his hands up and the noise subsided.

"Okay, bloody well done," he said. "Is there any chance of a connection with the murder of Martina Hall?"

"None at all, boss," Rachel Norman answered. "We checked that, of course, but the bloke had been in Darwin all that week. None of Martina's mates had ever heard of him or seen him."

"Pity," said Hunter then looked round as the door to the situation room opened. Standing there was his boss, Superintendent Charlie Simpson, Angela's husband. His face looked sombre.

"David," he said and beckoned.

"Okay guys," Hunter said to his team. "Well done again, but we have lots to be getting on with. Get back to what you were doing."

He walked out of the room as Simpson moved from the door. "What's up, Charlie?" he asked. Out of other people's earshot, they were informal with each other.

"Better get to my office, David," the Super replied. Hunter felt anxious as he followed his superior. Something in his face boded no good.

To his astonishment, waiting in the Super's office was Rod Hathaway from the North Sydney station.

"Rod! What brings you over here?"

"David, I've got rotten news," said Hathaway. Hunter felt a cold chill run through him.

"We got a fourth in our series last night," said Hathaway. "David, I'm terribly sorry. It's your sister, Deborah."

David Hunter sat in his office. Since identifying his sister's body on the slab in the morgue in Glebe the previous day, he had felt numbed, unable to function. Refusing his Superintendent's offer to take time away, he had come into the station, knowing that sitting at home would be worse, the scotch bottle would prove irresistible and he would become a dysfunctional wreck.

But he couldn't focus his mind. Blinding rage threatened to overcome him any time he thought of Deborah's white face as the attendant peeled back the sheet, the appalling mess of one side of it where the bullet had made its exit, the utter stillness of the once vibrant, beautiful woman he had adored all his life. He had made a point of watching her programs since she first went before the television cameras as a newsreader a decade ago and the pride he felt in her growing national reputation as a journalist with a sharp mind behind that classical face had sustained him through some bad times in his life.

Her death was certainly the fourth in the series. All the details were the same, a bullet in the back of the head, hands tethered behind her back with a plastic strip, her body laid out straight on the concrete floor of a warehouse building.

Was this directly aimed at him? he thought. Had the killer specifically sought out his sister as a challenge to him?

"Jesus Christ, I'll have that bastard's balls on a stick when we get him," he muttered aloud.

Finally, the years of training and his powerful self-discipline took over. He ignored the pull of the scotch bottle in his apartment and took out the files of the murders in the inner city. There was little to see that he hadn't already scanned repeatedly. Three young men murdered in an ugly fashion, hung up by their wrists in a building basement, stabbed in the stomach and left to die, aware of what was happening to them, nothing taken from the killing scene, not a single clue as to the identity of the murderer.

A small gleam in the darkness had been given to him by the observation of an elderly businessman who had been working late near the scene of the last killing, but nothing had resulted from it. A few cars had been identified as possibly the vehicle seen at the site of the murder, but none had revealed any suspicious owners, all had alibis, none had motivation or any knowledge or connection to the victims. The ugly fog of confusion was thick over the crimes and the Australian media were screaming for somebody's blood, particularly that of the police.

He bent his head over the files and resumed work.

Chapter 10 – The Great Game

Detective Chief Inspector Greg Robarts looked around the squad room.

"As you know, we've had another one. Again at Chorlton Grammar, this time a fifteen year old Kenyan kid called Ashvin Harji, found like the others, throat cut, nostril sliced post mortem."

A small sigh ran round the room where a dozen or so police officers sat or stood.

"And I have something to tell you, and this you absolutely must keep to yourselves."

The room went completely silent in response to the obvious disturbance in Robarts' face. Normally, the Chief Inspector was a calm, controlled individual, but now he showed distress.

"A few days after the first two deaths, I got a call from a D.I. David Hunter of the Homicide Squad in Sydney, Australia. He told me there had been a few serial killings discovered, in Sydney and Melbourne and then later in Perth. In both series, there had been some sort of signature on the bodies. The first one, in Sydney's inner western suburbs, a set of three murders of men in their thirties, all by stab wound, all had a cross cut post-mortem in their left shoulders."

If the room was quiet before, the utter stillness now was like death.

"The second series over the Bridge in North Sydney was of three women, all in their late thirties, early forties, all shot in the back of the head, all had their left earlobes sliced off. Since we talked, there has been a fourth and I cannot begin to describe how this must affect us all, but I've been told that the last one was David Hunter's sister."

"Oh my god!" whispered a woman at the back of the room.

"There were three killings of old homeless men in Melbourne," continued Robarts. "No progress has been made on any of them, and like us, the police forces in those areas are taking a whipping in the media."

He looked round the room, meeting the eye of each of his team in turn.

"Horrible as this is, people, the worst thing is that we've got absolutely nothing to go on. Whoever is doing this is taking great pains to hide all evidence. We all know too well just what hysterical crap we're taking in the media. We're being crucified and I know just how painful all this is for all of you. We haven't had anything like this since Jack the Ripper. So all I can tell you is redouble the efforts. Let's get back to the house to house interviews, somewhere, somebody has got to have seen or heard something. Let's go and find it."

Robarts stood silently while the group dispersed. He poured himself a mug of coffee and went to his office to sit quietly and try to make some sense of the horror.

* * *

"I'd say we've got us a serial killer on our patch."

Detective Sergeant James Clancy stared down at the ugly sight. The body of the overweight, middle-aged man lay face-down in the grass. A few yards away, three police officers kept the gaping crowd away, standing on the boardwalk along Toronto's Beaches district.

"I'd agree with that," said Doctor Harriet Nielsen as she finished donning her paper suit and bent down over the body. "First fact, small calibre bullet in the back of the head, same execution style as the other two, shoes and socks removed and a shot into the left ankle, post mortem. So either a serial killer or a copycat."

Clancy nodded at the photographer. "As many as you need," he said. "Harriet, can you see a wallet anywhere?"

"Hang on," she said and carefully examined the hip pocket of the man, finding nothing. "Okay, can we turn him over?" she asked and Clancy stopped to help her, holding the shoulders of the corpse.

"Oh shit!" he said as the man's face came into view. Little of it was left above the mouth, the rest reduced to a bloody mess by the exit of the bullet.

"And yes, there's a wallet," said the doctor, less moved by the horror done to the man. She opened the wallet and examined the driver's licence. "Mark Halliday, aged fifty, address in this area again, somewhere on Bathurst. Again, no family pictures of any kind, just a few gas purchase invoices, club membership of some sort."

She handed the wallet over to the detective who stood up. "So exactly the same victim profile and MO as the last two, eh?"

"Damn right," said the doctor. "And again, I'd say he was shot while kneeling and facing the beach, so the bullet won't be found then pushed forward onto his face, judging by the little smears of blood here."

"Not Italian," said the detective. "Nor was the first, so that makes it less likely to be a Mafia or any other gang war. This is just thrill-kill stuff."

"I think so," replied the doctor. "Okay, Jim, can you get him out of here?"

Clancy nodded at the two men standing by the ambulance and they advanced on the body.

Something was bugging James Clancy, something needed doing and he wanted to get back to his station and think about it. But as he entered his office, he was handed a message by the desk officer.

"We got a call from a cop in Australia," said the desk officer. "Wants to talk to somebody about those shootings we had. Says could you call him first thing in the morning, it will be evening his time."

Puzzled, Clancy took the message and went to his office to think.

* * *

"According to the stuff I've been reading, Captain, three in a row makes it a serial killer on the loose."

Detective Sergeant Phil Coulsen stood with his Precinct Captain on the observation deck overlooking the mortuary. The pathologist had just held up the bullet he had extracted from the heart of the man on the slab. Both cops looked weary.

"That's what the book says, Phil, and that's what we've got." Captain Jim Ball rubbed his eyes. "Damn, but we're taking a beating! Three victims, all white, forties, similar height and weight, all shot in the heart with a nine millimetre with a crescent moon engraved in the bullet."

"It sure seems like a jihadist thing, Captain."

"Well, Fox News certainly is screaming that, so are some of the other channels and papers. Is there any sign of a link to those Virginia shootings? Some Islamic group claimed those."

Coulsen shook his head. "I think they're different. Those were long range, no common factors at all other than the claims by that bunch of sickoes. Our killings here have all the signs of a genuine serial killer. And there's nothing to link the victims, beyond the same physical characteristics. God knows, we've looked hard enough."

"Something here might interest you," said Carter. "After the second one hit the news, I got a call from a cop in Australia."

"Australia? Why would a cop in Australia call you?"

"He's what they call a Detective Inspector, that's about the same as a Lieutenant. He says they've had a rash of serial killings around the country. And here's the odd thing. Each of them has some sort of signature on the corpses."

"Nothing to do with us, Captain. Ours are all Islamic lunatics, no doubt about it."

"Probably, but keep it in mind, Phil."

"Will do, Captain."

"Good. Now wish me luck. I've got to face a media conference in town and those bastards are going to flay me alive."

"I don't envy you, Captain."

"Nor do I. But that Aussie seems well-informed. You might want to have a chat with him."

* * *

Hunter was about ready to hit somebody. The small gleam of daylight given him when William Chester had indicated that a Jaguar had been around the killing scene had not resulted in any dawn over the horrific waves of blood that were running around the world. Every Jaguar with a possible registration had been identified and the owners checked out. Every luxury car remotely like a Jaguar had been checked, every registration with "Y", "X" or "T" or anything similar had been identified and the owners interviewed. Nobody had seemed the remotest bit suspicious.

The screams of abuse directed at the police, at him personally, and the other police areas where serial killings had occurred were beginning to leave their mark in sleepless nights, bad indigestion and irrational outbursts of rage. He struggled desperately to control the latter when around his staff, but sometimes he failed. But he was blessed with professionals, all suffering the same stresses but who understood that his rage was never directed at them personally.

When his sister had been murdered, he nearly lost all control and came close to resigning from the force, doing as he had considered for some years and following Jack Savage to a rural life away from the cities. But he had controlled the impulse and resumed work. Inside his mind he consoled himself with what he would do to the North Sydney killer when he was found.

He put away the files of the killings, bending down below the desk to place the folders in the bottom draw. It was already after seven in the evening and he was beginning to think about heading home. He heard the door open to his office and sat up, staring at the tall, distinguished-looking man in his seventies, white hair falling over his collar and bright eyes looking down at him with friendly warmth.

"Well, bugger me sideways," said Hunter.

"That's my phrase," said Jack Savage. "Anyway, I thought you needed a hand."

"I'm so sorry about Deb," said Savage. "You know how much I liked and admired her."

"You can help us find the bastard that did it and all the others. I'm bloody glad you're here, Jack."

The two men sat in David's office, sipping their glasses of scotch that David kept there against all rules.

"I was getting damned close to coming down, anyway. Deb's murder just brought it on immediately. This is a completely weird and sick story, David."

"You don't know all of it, old man," said Hunter. He slid the folder containing the reports from other countries across the desk. "Read those."

He sat back and waited while his old friend and colleague quickly read through the reports of the series of killings around the world. Savage's face reflected nothing until he put away the last sheet and looked up at Hunter.

"Jesus Harold Christ," he said softly.

"Exactly. It's a bloody plague, Jack."

"Almost like copycats, David. But I've never encountered copycat killings on this scale and spread around the world."

"All we can do for now is let the locals work on them and we try and sort out our own shit, but it's getting to me, mate, I tell you."

The phone rang and Hunter held up his hand to stop Savage saying any more and picked up the handset.

"Sir, it's Sergeant Andrew Walcott. I'm on patrol on the Pacific Highway near the Freeway entrance at Wahroonga."

"Yes, Sergeant?" *Why the hell had a patrol car asked to be put directly through to him?*

"We just pulled over a Jaguar XK because of a broken rear light and we logged the registration number, first two letters, Yankee Bravo."

"Something suspicious, Sergeant?"

"His name is Robert Worthing," said the voice in

his phone. "Works for a company in Gosford, aged thirty-eight, married, two children."

Hudson switched to a file on his computer and scanned the results. "Yes, we interviewed him weeks ago after we identified every Jag with a "Y" rego. Nothing suspicious and his wife gave him an alibi for the night of the murder." *Definitely not the profile of a serial killer*, thought Hunter.

"But here's the thing, Sir," said the Patrol Officer. "While I was checking his documents, Jenny, my partner was looking in the car. She found a cosh, just sitting on the passenger seat."

Holy Shit! Hunter sat up from his slumped pose at his desk. "A cosh?"

Across from him, Savage's eyes opened, sensing something critical had just happened.

"Yes, sir, a cosh. One Grade A, bog-standard, bang-'em-on-the-head cosh. She's bagged it."

"Sergeant, you and Jenny have made my day. Bring the bastard in."

"We thought you might say that, sir. He's already cuffed and in the back seat. Jenny's drooling at the prospect of driving the Jaguar."

Hunter laughed and hung up. Then he stood and punched the air. "Hooyah! Hooyah!" he shouted. "Jack, this may be it. Come and sit in on the interview when they get here. I'm going to call Charlie Simpson and get you put back on the team."

Hunter and Jack Savage stood outside the one-way glass of the interview room.

"David, there's not a chance in hell that bloke in

there is a serial killer." Savage closed the folder containing the documents filling out Robert Worthing's life details. "There's not a damn thing to suggest it!"

They continued looking at the man sitting silently at the table. He was not particularly impressive. Though of reasonable height, about 180 centimetres and moderately bulky, he was hardly athletic and his waistline displayed an unhealthy mass. He was dressed in a dark blue suit with a yellow shirt, no tie and while neat enough, seemed to be one of those men who had no sense of style and always looked a little untidy. His hair was neat, but thinning.

"Married, two very ordinary kids, this bloke is the absolute definition of boringly normal," continued Jack Savage. "He's on a good income....." He checked the dossier again, "... $115,000 a year, drives a rather expensive car, his wife's a teacher at High School, so not exactly underpaid, his kids go to pretty good private schools."

"What about the cosh, Jack? Why's he carrying a cosh?"

Savage shrugged. "Maybe like he said, he keeps it for protection. But I think if the situation occurred where he might need it, he'd drop it in panic. This is no killer, David, once-off or serial."

Hunter stared at the ground and slapped his thigh in irritation. "Bugger it, Jack! I know you too well to ignore that! You've always been spot on the mark. What the hell is wrong here? I mean, I *know* it seems wrong. Hell, we looked over his details when his car showed up in the search for Jags with the "Y" rego and he seemed an impossible candidate then."

"Well, let me go and talk to him, kid. You stay out here."

"Right-o, Jack. See what you can come up with."

"You're not offering him a lawyer?"

"He hasn't asked for one, he hasn't been charged yet and anyway, this is a pre-interview."

"A pre-interview, kid? That's not really legal. You intending to beat the crap out of the bastard, David?"

"Go and talk to him, Jack."

* * *

Savage smiled at Robert Worthing as he took a seat opposite him. "G'day, Robert, how would you be?" he said.

"And you are?" Worthing looked calm and composed.

"My name's Jack Savage. I'm a behavioural psychologist."

"And why is a shrink interviewing me?"

Savage gave a friendly laugh. "It's all a con job, really. They think it helps, I tell them it helps, it keeps me gainfully employed."

Worthing didn't return the smile. "So what, you're going to ask me about my childhood, my parents, was I abused as a kid, all that sort of stuff?"

"That was the idea. Would I get anything useful if I did?"

"Not a damn thing. I had a normal upbringing, a happy childhood, I love my parents, they never beat me, they're still married. Anything else?"

"Your marriage is okay?"

Worthing shrugged. "We've been married sixteen years, so things sometimes feel a bit stale. But yes, I think we're okay. We've got two great kids, I earn decent bucks, my wife earns decent bucks. I'd say we're doing pretty well."

"You said your childhood was good, Robert. You were happy?"

"I was. This is all very trite, isn't it?"

Savage laughed again. "I have to go through the motions to get my fee, Robert. So play along with me, will you? What siblings do you have?"

Worthing shrugged. "One sister. We always got on well and I never tried to rape her. Will that do?"

"How were you with the girls at school, then? Many girlfriends?"

Worthing grinned. "Yes, actually! I did pretty well."

"So you didn't spend your evenings in your room jerking off, then?"

"No more than the average teenager."

Savage smiled in appreciation. "Certainly sounds good to me, Robert. Are you an alcoholic?"

Worthing laughed in surprise. "Only if a few beers over the barbeque on a Sunday makes me an alcoholic. I'd say not."

"No, I'd agree with you." Savage leaned over the table in a conspiratorial manner. "Have you ever killed anyone, Robert?"

For the first time, Worthing looked startled. "Killed anyone? Jesus H. Christ, Savage, what sort of question is that? No, I have never killed anyone, why the hell do you ask?"

"Well, one thing that interests me is that you haven't actually asked me why you're here, why we arrested you."

"Well, I'm pretty certain it's not for a broken rear light. I'm assuming it's because of the cosh."

"Ah yes, the cosh, I'd forgotten that," said Savage. "So just why do you carry a cosh like that in the car with you?"

Worthing shrugged. "It's illegal, I know, but my job takes me into some industrial areas, driving a rich man's car. I'll admit it, I get frightened, especially in the dark."

"Ever have to use it?"

"Never."

Savage sat back. He looked hard at Worthing for a moment or two and Worthing stared back, no emotion on display.

Savage stood up. "I'll talk to my colleagues about that cosh," he said and walked out, leaving Worthing sitting quietly in his chair.

Outside in the corridor, he walked up to Hunter.

"David, he's a cool customer, the cosh is ugly, but there's no sign at all of a man who has killed several people. His background is so normal it's almost abnormal. He's a bit tense, but so would anyone be when they're in police custody and there's a definite charge pending because of the cosh. There's one odd thing though. He seemed to go out of his way to point out how he's not the classic serial killer profile. But nobody has raised the question of murder yet, so that's a touch smelly. And he's right, he's not your serial killer type, but why has he obviously read up on the subject?"

Hunter slapped his thigh in irritation. "I know he's not fitting the classic profile, but there's something about that bastard that's all wrong."

"Well, let's review, shall we?" Savage folded his arms. "We all know the classic background. More than eighty-five percent of serial killers are white males, the greatest majority under thirty and often quite intelligent."

"IQ usually between 105 and 120," said Hunter, struggling to stay calm. "Dysfunctional families, miserable childhoods, big day-dreamers, heavy-duty wankers, yes Jack, I've read the materials."

"But they're usually loners, not good dealing with society, not married. This bloke here may fit the physical profile, but that's because most men in Australia are white, middle-class, but he doesn't fit anything else. His sex life was quite good as a teenager, he's married, two kids, all terribly normal and not a serial killer's profile. And yet he does know what that profile is."

Before Hunter could reply, a uniformed cop came up and handed him an envelope. Hunter opened it, took out the single sheet and read the typewritten words aloud.

"The cosh had been cleaned carefully, but some remaining materials were analysed. There were minute traces of blood and skin but it's too early to identify if they were human or not. DNA testing will take probably twelve hours or more."

Hunter looked directly into Savage's eyes. "My turn, I think, Jack."

"David, be careful. You hurt him in any way and your career's over."

"You know, Jack, I don't bloody care. That bastard is a killer and if I can't get him to admit it, I shouldn't be a cop. And anyway with all this killing going on, maybe I'll follow you, buy some acreage and grow some cows and alpaca and things. The world is becoming too sick for my taste."

He turned and walked angrily into the interview room. Savage watched sadly. "Be bloody careful, David old friend," he murmured.

Hunter walked up to the interview table, every atom of him reflecting his rage. He leaned over Worthing. "That cosh has got human hair, skin and blood on it," he shouted. "Who did you kill, Worthing?"

Finally, Worthing looked frightened and he leaned away from Hunter. "I told your mate, I've never killed anyone."

"You lying bastard!" roared Hunter. "You killed three young men, you hung them up by their wrists and you stabbed them and left them to die."

"What the fuck are you talking about?"

Hunter's rage finally took over him. He slammed one fist into the left side of Worthing's face and the man fell back against his chair and onto the floor. Hunter stamped round the table, hauled him by his jacket lapels so that Worthing was just standing and he hammered him again, this time in the stomach. Worthing doubled over with a grunt of pain as Hunter lifted his knee into his face, turned and thumped Worthing hard in the mouth.

The man collapsed into the corner, blood streaming from his nose and mouth, gagging from the pain in his stomach. Hunter moved back to him, reached down and grabbed the lapels again, but Worthing cried out in fear, "No! Please, no, please stop!"

But Hunter was almost out of control. He pulled Worthing up to his knees and hit him again, an open-handed slap that pushed him back into the corner, blood all over his suit and shirt, spitting a broken tooth onto the floor.

"God almighty!" croaked Worthing. "Stop it! Yeah, okay, I killed those blokes. For fuck's sake, it's just a game! That's all it is, it's just a fucking *game*, for God's sake."

Hunter stood upright, shock running through his body.

Outside the one-way glass, Jack Savage stared at the bloody, ugly scene of mayhem.

"Well, bugger me sideways!" he said softly. "Now it all makes sense."

The police doctor had come and gone. Not Angela Simpson but a stand-by doctor who occasionally helped with cuts and bruises, provided flu medicines, did the blood tests for drivers brought in with possible drunken driving charges hanging over their heads and performed some minor stitching and bandaging for officers who had seem some violence on patrol. He gave Hunter an angry look at the condition of Robert

Worthing but said nothing as he wiped the blood from Worthing's face, checked him for damage and looked at the missing tooth. He fed the bruised man some pain killers and walked out with just a suggestion that Worthing should see a dentist.

Savage had come in with the doctor and he nodded and Hunter ignored him completely. He continued to stare at Worthing.

"Tell us about this game."

"They said I'd never be found," Worthing muttered, his head in his hands.

"Who said?"

Worthing didn't reply.

Savage leaned over the table and moved Worthing's hands from his face. "Tell us about the game," he said.

"Worthing, here's the situation," said Hunter. "That cosh ties you to the murder of Allan Smith and almost conclusively to the other two men in Surry Hills. Your life is over, you won't see daylight again till you're in your eighties, if ever. Tell us about this so-called game and we'll be able to make things a bit easier."

"They'll kill me."

"Believe me, *I'LL* kill you if you don't. Whoever *"They"* are, they killed my sister. I've stopped caring about legalities. So once more, tell me about this fucking *GAME!*"

The last word was a bellow and Worthing sat back in shock, fear shining from his eyes.

"You get ten thousand for each one," he muttered after a short pause.

"Ten thousand dollars for each murder?" Hunter said. "Who pays you?"

"I don't know."

"Then how do you get paid? Bank transfer? Cheque? Cash? What?"

"Cash. She gives me a package of $100 bills once the killing hits the papers."

"She? Who is SHE?"

"I don't know."

Hunter slammed his hand on the table top. "Listen you bastard!" he shouted. "I've just about had it up to here with you! You want me to start hitting you again?" He stood up and leaned over the table again, lifting his fist high. Worthing sobbed and tried to move away but Savage grabbed his collar and hauled him back.

"You know what?" said Savage. "I want to see him hit you again, so you'd better play along rather better than this."

All the life seemed to go out of Worthing. His shoulders slumped, his gaze became fixed on the table top. Savage watched this then grinned at Hunter and nodded. The two men had worked together for long enough for Hunter to understand the message. Worthing had given up all resistance.

"You get invited in," the damaged man mumbled.

"How?"

"I was just sitting in the pub one evening. A young bloke walked up to me and handed me an envelope and walked away again immediately. I opened it. There was just a single sheet. It said, "You can make serious money and have a lot of excitement if you want to play the game.”

“That was it? Nothing about how to respond or what to do next?”

“That was it.”

“So what happened next?”

“A week later, the same thing, but another young bloke, gave me an envelope again. This time it just said, “$10,000 a time. Place an advert in *“The Sydney Newsman”* saying, ‘I want to play the game. Sign it Jake. Do not use a credit card to pay for the advert.’ That was it.”

“What’s *“The Sydney Newsman?”*

“Just one of those local rags for the inner suburbs.”

“Did you have any idea of what all that was about?”

Worthing shook his head.

“But you placed the advert. Why?”

“I was curious. And the money was worth thinking about.” Worthing was speaking in a low monotone, as if about to fall asleep, displaying no interest in the conversation.

“And then what happened?”

“About a month later, I was walking the dog in the park and a woman came up to me.”

“You’re Jake, aren’t you?”

Worthing stopped. He’d almost forgotten that weird note in the pub and he had to think for a few seconds. The woman looked in her early forties, neatly dressed in a blue skirt and a white sweater, fairly attractive features but without any vitality in her face.

"Er... yes. Who are you?"

"Nobody you need know. You want to play the game?"

"What's it all about?"

"Can't you guess? For that sort of money, what do you think it is?"

"It sounds nuts, but I think I'm supposed to kill somebody."

"A very interesting conclusion, Robert. Whatever it is you do, it's for ten grand a time."

"Ten grand! What for? Why?"

"Robert, you don't need to know any of that. Just be happy for the amazing opportunity you're getting."

"You know who I am?"

"You don't think we'd make an offer like this to just anyone, do you? We spent some time checking you out before that young man approached you in the pub. We know everything about you."

"Jesus Christ!"

"So do you want to play?"

"Yes."

"Okay, here's the deal. Every time you do one, you have a leave a personal mark that proves it's yours. And every one of them has to be similar, same sort of target, same way of doing it. Once we hear that it's done, somebody will give you ten grand in cash in a package. Now, here's the biggie. Do five and you get an extra fifty grand bonus. Do you understand so far?"

Worthing nodded.

"And one more thing. This is big time. You tell anyone about this, you won't see the next day come up, do you understand?"

Worthing felt a chilly sensation in his gut, but he nodded again.

The woman bent down and patted the dog's head and walked away.

* * *

"And that was it?" asked Hunter.

Worthing nodded. "And she said somebody would give me a detailed set of instructions about keeping clear. And then she walked away."

"Did you think to ask why this was all going on?"

"Yeah. She said that was not important, just be happy I was getting the chance to make money."

"And did somebody give you anything?"

"Another bloke in the pub. A week later, he came and sat next to me. He told me to get a set of rubber gloves and paper overshoes like people wear in hospitals. He gave me a tin with a small vial of a drug and a half-dozen small syringes, said it would keep people quiet and easy to deal with. He said never take anything away from the scene, not even money from a wallet. After that, just make sure there's nobody around, do it at night, never move a body 'cos that leaves traces. And don't use a credit card to pay for the personal ads."

"What about the cosh?" asked Hunter.

Worthing shook his head. "I got that myself, just in case."

"I still don't get it," said Hunter. "Why you? Why

does some bloke pick you out of a crowd and offer you a chance to make huge sums of money for killing people? It's a hell of a risk, isn't it? Why didn't you just go to the cops? Almost everybody else would."

Worthing seemed to shrink inside himself and shook his head.

Savage reached over and took Worthing's wrist in a sympathetic gesture.

"You a gambling man, Robert?"

Worthing gave out a short gasp of shock, but said nothing else.

"Big sums, eh?" said Savage. "What is it, horses, casinos? How much?"

Worthing swallowed, his face rigidly staring at the table. "Casinos."

"Ah!" said Savage, speaking softly, as if he were a counsellor helping an addict. "It can run away with you, can't it? How much are you in for, Robert? Ten grand? Twenty?"

"About thirty-two," mumbled Worthing.

"Ooh, nasty," said Savage. "Does your wife know?"

Worthing shook his head. Tears were running down his cheeks.

"And you don't have it, do you?" Savage continued speaking in a soft, friendly, sympathetic voice.

Worthing shook his head again. His eyes were swollen and red.

"And your wife, she'll bloody kill you when she finds out, won't she?"

Worthing hid his face in his hands and a small sob escaped him.

"That's going to bugger up the private schools for

the kids, the Jag goes and gets replaced by a scruffy old Holden or something, the kids will hate you, the neighbours will be laughing at you, all sorts of shit is coming at you, isn't it?"

Worthing buried his face in his arms, flat out on the table.

Savage grinned up at Hunter standing at his left. Hunter recognised the technique, having witnessed it many times before. Savage was gently and surgically dismantling Worthing, removing all barriers and preparing him for Hunter to dive on the victim like a bird of prey.

Hunter moved to the chair next to Savage and sat down across from the man now weeping openly.

"Okay, Robert, let's start with that first murder, Paul Aiken. Why don't you take us through that, from go to whoa?"

The two men settled back in their chairs and waited for Worthing to gain control of himself. After a few minutes, he sat up, his face blotchy from the tears and tried to speak, but his voice was croaky and inaudible. Savage got to his feet, went out and came back a few moments later with a mug of coffee and a sachet of sugar. Worthing slowly prepared his coffee and took a few sips, staring into some dreadful, nightmare distance.

"It was Friday night," he said. "You know, the usual after work thing, everybody was gathering in pubs, clubs, whatever...."

Chapter 11 – A Killing at the Cross

The bar in Kings Cross was rocking as Robert Worthing approached it along the pavement. Crowds had spilled out and filled the spaces approaching the El Alamein Fountain and the noise was growing steadily.

Worthing pushed and shoved his way into the bar, his nerves on edge and his heart pounding. This was the night he would become the image of himself he'd yearned for, the man of power, of influence, of control. He'd arrived some hours before so that he could leave his car parked relatively close and spent the time waiting for the post-work revelries to begin.

He managed to reach the bar and somehow order a beer before moving away to start studying the Friday-night groups of executives, secretaries, lawyers and similar prosperous, tension-breaking, mostly young residents of Sydney. He had the profile of his target in his mind, having picked it after many days of thinking and planning.

As ten o'clock came and went, he began to cut his list of targets down from the dozen or so that he had identified. Three had already left in the company of young women and three others he decided against as being rather larger than he thought he could handle. Finally he moved, bought another beer and eased his way into the vicinity of the young man that might be his first conquest.

Deliberately he stumbled a little against the man's side, not enough to cause anger but enough to provide the excuse.

"Oh, jeez, sorry mate!" he said and grinned. "This place is a bloody zoo, isn't it?"

"No worries," replied the target. "It adds to the fun!"

"Yeah, well, they told me that was the case," Worthing replied. "Reckon they were right."

"Your first time here?"

"Yeah, down from Brisbane on business," replied Worthing. "Got to hang on for next week, so I thought I'd check out the Cross."

"It's usually worthwhile," the man said with a grin. "Seems a bit light on women this evening, though."

"Yeah, I was thinking that," agreed Worthing. This was happening all too easily. "But I was killing time till I go to a mate's club in Taylor Square. I tell you what, that place is always a gold mine. Feel like coming along? It'll be worth it. Ken's a top banker, worth millions and he makes sure his place is stocked with prime talent."

"Now that sounds more like it! You sure it's okay?"

"Hell, yes! Ken and I are old mates. Hey, I got lucky and got a parking spot just near, why not take my car?"

Getting an enthusiastic nod, he led the way out and just half a block down the road and unlocked the Jaguar, aware of the impressed whistle from the target who seemed to lose any reservations about the plan in the face of such obvious wealth.

Pulling into the traffic, Worthing drove slowly in the perennial crawl of Sydney. Carefully, he eased the small package out of the little slot to the right of the steering wheel and found the small syringe he'd prepared earlier. The man in the other seat was well occupied watching the numerous young women walking along and saw nothing suspicious. Worthing drove along towards the Hospital and as he accelerated past the building, suddenly slapped the needle into the man's thigh.

"What...?" said the man and clasped his hand to the point of entry. "Hey!" he yelled and tried to open the car door, but Worthing had pressed the lock and by the time the target had worked out what to do, the drug had hit him. He subsided into his seat, head rolling around and mumbling, just as Worthing's supplier had told him would happen. The man would be able to stand up and shamble along with guidance, but he'd have no aggressive abilities.

Worthing drove at a careful pace to the drive-in garage he'd located in several trips around the area over recent weeks. He drove to the entrance, but parked on the road. No point in taking any chance of an oil drip or some other indicator to the car's identity being left on the relatively clean concrete floor.

He unlocked the doors and reached behind him for his bag, first taking out a pair of paper over-shoes such as used in operating theatres. He turned sideways in his seat, slipped on the shoes then climbed out and walked round to the passenger side, pulling on a pair of thin leather gloves.

He opened the door and grabbed his target by the collar. "C'mon," he said and pulled him out of the seat. The man looked like he was sleepwalking, head slumped as if utterly exhausted and he obediently followed Worthing to the point he'd selected under the pipes.

Worthing took a boxcutter from his pocket, opened out the scalpel-like blade and carefully sliced the man's shirt open and hauled it off his shoulders. Leaving the barely conscious man for a moment, he walked to the wall where he had previously left a small pair of stepladders, only a metre high. He carried the ladder back to the victim, opened it up and then took the rope he had stored in his bag.

At that point, the man stirred, his eyes opened and he seemed to be seeing more clearly. Hurriedly, Worthing took his cosh from his trouser pocket and tapped the man firmly on the side of his head. The light died from the man's eyes again.

He tied the man's wrists, climbed up the small stepladders and passed the rope over the pipe. It took little effort to haul the man's wrists as high as possible with the man even obliging by standing on his toes. Worthing tied the rope round the pipes and knotted it, climbed down and went to his bag again. This time he took out the duct tape, stripped off a few centimetres and stuck it firmly over the man's mouth.

Now his heart started thumping wildly. This was it, the culmination of years of dreaming of doing this wonderful, thrilling thing again. He took a deep breath and plunged the cutter into the man's stomach. The man convulsed, tried to scream and couldn't, emitting instead some muffled sounds like a fish being taken off a hook. Worthing repeated the stab twice more, staring into the man's face like other men watched a sex scene in a movie.

God, he'd nearly forgotten! He climbed back on the stepladder and reached over the man to his left shoulder. He hadn't realised how difficult it would be to slice into the shoulder when it was stretched high as it was. He made a mental note to do this part before tying the victim to the pipe. But he managed to cut the cross in the shoulder, though rather clumsily before climbing down.

For a few moments, he watched with a deep sense of gratification as the man gasped and groaned and blood poured out down his legs to the concrete. He moved close to the body and ripped off the duct tape, deliberately dropping it in one corner. Might as well give the cops something to get excited about, there'd be no traces on the tape.

As the last twitches faded, he folded away the stepladder and carried it to the car, placed it in the trunk, returned for his bag and the man's shirt and put them on the passenger seat. He returned for one final look around, went back to the car, sat in his seat while he removed the paper overshoes then closed the door, started the car and moved off quietly.

He was breathing hard, but he felt wonderful, satisfied and thrilled.

The first one had been completed.

* * *

"You got a real kick out of it, did you?" asked Hunter.

Worthing nodded.

"So what did you do then?"

"I had to put another advert in the personals of that little paper, saying, 'One down, Jake.'"

"And you did?"

Worthing nodded. There was no expression on his face, he looked numb, almost bored.

"How?" asked Hunter.

"They've got a couple of offices, one in Newtown. I went there and did it, paid by cash."

"And when did you get the money?"

"Just a week later. That young bloke did the same as before, he just appeared at the pub one evening and handed over an envelope. I asked him why it took so long and he just said they needed time to check out all the facts."

"And there was ten grand in the envelope?" asked Savage

"In hundreds."

"And what did you do with it?"

"Took it round to the casino the next day and just handed it over as part payment."

"Very commendable," said Hunter, no sarcasm evident in his tone. "And they accepted that?"

"I told them the rest would be coming soon."

"And did it?"

"Yes. I'm clear."

"Interesting," said Hunter and exchanged looks with Savage.

"You just stay sitting here," Hunter said and indicated to Savage for them to walk out of the room. They stopped by the one-way glass.

"Well, bugger me sideways," said Savage, breathing hard as if he had walked a stiff uphill path. "I've heard some sick shit in my life, but that may beat everything."

"What do you think he meant by them needing time to check out the facts?" Hunter asked.

Savage stared through the glass at the man sitting motionless as if in a trance at the table in the interview room.

"Probably making sure that little bastard had indeed killed the man."

"Yeah, but how, exactly? They hadn't seen it. They had nothing to tell them except for that advert. How did they know who had done that thing?"

Savage rubbed his eyes in anger and confusion. "I'm too old for this crap," he said. Then he slammed his hand on the window. The man at the table looked up, startled but could see nothing.

"The Casino," Savage said. "They must be in it up to their necks. When they got the money, that told them Worthing had made a killing. In fact, I bet they initiated the contact, knowing he was deep in hock and desperate."

"We certainly need to talk to them, but that may be giving the game away, Jack. But there has to be another signal to prove the claim."

"The cross on the shoulder," Savage said in disgust. "Somebody had to check that the corpse had the cross cut into the shoulder as Worthing's declared trade mark."

"That's what I think, Jack. And you know what that means."

"Yes, it bloody means they've got somebody inside who can see the corpses, or at least the pathologist's reports. And that's just one of the shit problems we've got, young David."

"Tell me, Jack."

"I bet you're there already, kid, but this is what I see. First problem is what to do with that little bastard in that room. If you shove him in the clink and start prosecutions, you'll let the people behind this know we're onto them and they'll shut up shop right away."

"But we can't just hold him out of sight, Jack. His wife and family will start screaming very soon."

"Right. There's only one thing you can do. Somehow, you're going to have to let him loose on a very long leash, at least for a time."

Hunter looked thoughtful. "The bastard hasn't actually been charged with anything yet. The record of his arrest will show the cosh, but nothing else."

"What about the patrol car crew?"

"I'll tell them we couldn't pin anything on him and let him go with a caution." Hunter stared through the window at the crumpled man sitting face down at the table.

"David, you'll have to keep this so quiet you could hear a mouse squeak in Perth. Will you brief Charlie Simpson?"

"Completely. I've got an idea and it's going to need Charlie's full cooperation. Because the mole we've got in the police department is not the last problem, is it, Jack?"

Savage nodded. "If this is a game, who the fuck are the players?"

"Right. Okay, let's go back in and talk to that piece of shit."

Worthing barely looked up as Savage and Hunter entered the room and took seats across from him.

"This is your lucky day, Robert," said Hunter.

This time, Worthing sat up and looked blearily at him but said nothing.

"We're going to let you go."

"You what?" Worthing's shock was obvious. "Let me go?"

"Amazing, isn't it?" said Hunter with a cold smile. "You can go out of here, get back in your lovely Jaguar and drive back to Gosford to your loving wife and family. As far as we're concerned, we brought you in here for questioning, but couldn't find anything suspicious. We'll take the cosh away from you and you've had an official warning about it, but that's it."

"I don't understand. I said I'd killed those guys."

"Yes, you did. And it's going to come back on you eventually. But this is going to help us, so things will be a lot easier for you later. Right now, you do nothing, live normally, don't kill anybody. But here's the thing. If those people contact you and ask what happened here, you tell them only half the truth. You were arrested because of the cosh and interrogated but you told us nothing. And you'll say that frightened you so much, you're retiring from the game. They'll have to believe you, because there's no way you could be released if we had grounds for suspecting you, is there?"

Worthing shook his head, the first gleam of wakefulness reaching his eyes. "You mean I can go?"

"You can, Robert. But think of this. If whoever is controlling this "game" thinks you've spilled the facts to us, they'll kill you. They won't hesitate, you'll be dead in seconds. So I hope you're a bloody fine actor."

The shock reflected in Worthing's face and he swallowed nervously. "So what do I tell them if they ask?"

"You tell them that you're scared shitless, being arrested broke your nerve and you're not going to kill anybody else. They should understand that."

The fear didn't leave Worthing's face. "And what are you going to do?" he asked, his voice cracking with tension.

"Nothing you need to know about," said Hunter. "Now, fuck off, you worthless piece of shit before I beat the crap out of you some more."

Not looking steady, Worthing got to his feet and walked out of the room.

Savage and Hunter looked at each other.

"I think I know what you're planning, kid," said Savage. "Christ, you're taking a risk."

"Can't see any other way," Hunter replied. "Just let me get that recording out and away from here then I'll you how I'm going to do it."

Chapter 12 – Passing the Baton

The situation room was almost silent, so much so that the bubbling of the coffee urn could be heard. A chair scraped on the floor as somebody moved and a couple of the officers coughed.

Chief Superintendent Charlie Simpson stood by the desk where Hunter normally stood for these sessions. The desk slid a little as Simpson's heavy frame leaned against it. His normally florid face was paler than anyone could remember seeing it.

"I'm terribly sorry to have to report this," Simpson said. "But yesterday, Detective Inspector David Hunter resigned from the force and left with immediate effect, taking sick leave."

A chorus of groans of dismay ran round the room.

"As you know, David was badly hit by the murder of his sister three weeks ago and he was not helped by the massive tirade of abuse he and all of us have taken from the media in recent weeks. It just all got too much for him and he said he could not do the job anymore."

"Did he say where he was going?" Rachel Norman looked like she was almost in tears as she asked the question.

Simpson nodded at Jack Savage sitting at the side of the room. "You all know Jack Savage, by reputation if not directly," he said. "We're fortunate that Jack has volunteered to help us and as David's old friend and colleague, I think he knows more about his plans. Jack, can you take that?"

Savage stood up. "David's a wreck," he said. "He's flying out of Sydney this afternoon, heading for the UK to get as far away as possible, he said. I don't think he has any specific plans, except maybe to sit in a few British pubs, travel around a bit and try and get his head straight."

Simpson resumed control. "So we're going to make a few changes to try and make some headway. First up, I'm following David's recommendations with a couple of promotions."

There was a stir of interest and full attention was directed at Simpson.

"Detective Senior Sergeant Bill Hamilton, as of now, you assume the rank of Acting Detective Inspector," the Chief Superintendent said and smiled. "Congratulations, Bill, well deserved!"

Applause ran round the room and some approving shouts. Hamilton grinned widely.

"Detective Senior Constable Rachel Norman, this was coming soon anyway, you've passed the exams, but you are now Detective Sergeant as of today. Congratulations, Rachel, again thoroughly deserved."

He waited while the applause and cheerful comments ran round the room.

"And now, some organisational stuff," continued Simpson. "These serial killings, they require special attention, so this is what we're doing. I'm setting up a small task force to be a hundred percent dedicated to the problem. That force will be headed up by Acting Detective Inspector Bill Hamilton here, assisted by Detective Senior Sergeant Barrie Roche and Detective Sergeant Rachel Norman. Others from this group will be called in to assist as required and the task force will request help as needed from Uniformed Division. Jack Savage will also work with this group. To give them room, we've taken a small suite of offices in a building in Taylor Square and that will be ready for them by tomorrow morning. Here are the details."

He turned to the white board, picked up a black marker pen and carefully wrote three numbers on the board and an address. "You should already have those officers' mobile numbers, so use those and just use these numbers I've just given you to leave messages. I'll ask you not to go to those offices unless requested by one of the task force or by me."

He began to walk to the door as the meeting broke up then called to Jack Savage. "Jack, a quick word," he said and continued out of the room.

Savage caught up with him as they reached the Superintendent's office and walked in. Savage shut the door and took the seat opposite the officer.

"Christ, Jack!" said Simpson. "We're taking a bloody risk here!"

"Don't I know it, Charlie," replied Savage. "But there's no other way we could do it."

"I know. Hell, I couldn't even brief the Commissioner, there's no way of knowing who's involved. My whole career is on the line here."

"We'll solve this shit, Charlie, I know it. That'll put you on the path to Deputy Commissioner."

Simpson grimaced. "Or on the unemployment list and my wife will be looking for another job, too. You blokes had better perform to save all our necks."

Savage nodded. "This took guts, Charlie, we'll give it everything."

"I know it, Jack. Look after David for me."

Savage got to his feet, waved and walked out.

* * *

Acting Detective Inspector Bill Hamilton looked round his small group. They sat in relaxed fashion in various seats around the small conference room, Barrie Roche and Jack Savage cradling mugs of coffee, Rachel Norman held a bottle of water. Hamilton was in his usual mode of dress, a black blazer with the insignia of the Royal Artillery on the breast pocket, grey flannels and well-polished black shoes. His thinning hair allowed the ceiling lights to reflect off his cranium.

"We've got a hell of a job on, boys and girls," Hamilton said. "Filling David's shoes is a major task and we're under the spotlight. Now, you all know about the killings around the country. They seem to be a set of serial killings, but each set by a different killer. And of course, we have the tragedy of the latest event in North Sydney being David's sister. For that reason, we will liaise closely with D.I. Rod Hathaway who has been attached to the Murder Squad on a temporary and unofficial basis, but nobody else. I cannot stress enough, you must not, under any circumstances discuss our work here with anybody else from North Sydney and nobody else from our group except Charlie Simpson."

He lifted a sheet of paper from the conference table.

"Let me fill you in on the scene around the world. You've already heard about some of the serial killings in the UK, the States and in Canada. In the two weeks since David flew out, we've had another one in the USA, two in Canada and one in Wales." He put the paper down.

"This is all a bit weird, Bill," said Rachel Norman. "It sure as hell isn't Standard Operating Procedure, being here, not talking to others, all this secrecy."

"You want weird, Rachel?" Hamilton grinned widely. "I'll give you weird. But I warn you, once I've told you this, you are on your absolute best behaviour. This must not, I repeat NOT, under any circumstances go outside this group. You mustn't tell your wives, kids, girlfriends, boyfriends, mothers, *anyone* what you are about to learn. If you do, not only will you be gone from this group, but gone from the force and under arrest for interfering with a police inquiry. Got me?" The grin had gone and Hamilton stared each of them in the eye in turn.

Rachel and Barrie shifted uncomfortably in their seats.

"And I will have to kill you," added Jack Savage from the foot of the table. There was no sign of humour in his face.

"A few days before David left us," continued Bill, "we arrested a man called Robert Worthing. He had been interviewed as part of the exercise after we had William Chester's report of seeing a Jag parked outside the scene of the third killing in Surry Hills, but he seemed in the clear. He was arrested because after a routine check on a busted light, a patrol car officer found a cosh in his car. And when we interviewed him at the station, he broke down and confessed to the killings in Surry Hills."

"What?" Rachel let out an explosive gasp of shock. Barrie Roche's jaw dropped and he was wide-eyed.

"Then where is he?" demanded Roche. "Where are the arrest reports, where's he being kept? How come we didn't hear about this?"

Every eye was fixed firmly on Bill Hamilton.

"We let him go," he said.

"You did WHAT?" Barrie Roche was on his feet. "Bill, what the hell is this? What sort of insanity is it that releases a confessed serial killer?"

"Sit down, Barrie, please." Jack Savage spoke softly, but he had a power of command that was impossible to ignore. Roche obeyed, but the tension in the room was palpable.

"Now let me fill you in on everything else," continued Hamilton. "I suggest that before we go on, you go and have a wee-wee, or a smoke outside, refill your coffee cups or whatever for five minutes, because the next half hour is going to blow your fucking minds, I kid you not."

The two detectives walked out, almost in a daze, leaving Hamilton and Jack Savage at opposite ends of the table.

"So how do you think it's going, Jack?"

"About as expected. Once you've played that tape, their lives will never be the same, Bill."

Hamilton swallowed, the first signs of any nerves he had shown since the group had taken over the offices in Taylor Square two weeks ago. "If one of those two is the mole, then we're fucked immediately," he said.

Savage nodded. "Or if you are! But David's worked with each of you for years," he said. "So have I. If either of us is wrong about any of you, we deserve what we get. But that's why we're here and only Charlie Simpson knows what we're doing. Angela does, too, because we need her. And we both trust them too, but there's always the risk. That's why nobody, not the Assistant Commissioner, the Commissioner, the Police Minister nor the Premier, none of them knows what's going on."

The door opened and Rachel walked in with a cup of coffee. As she sat down, Barrie Roche followed and took his seat. Both looked with obvious expectation at Hamilton. He touched a button on the table and leaned back as the sounds of the recorded interview of Robert Worthing began from the room speakers.

* * *

"Holy SHIT!" said Roche.

"Exactly," said Hamilton. "And it's going on all over the world."

"And we have no idea at all who's behind it, who's playing this game?" asked Rachel. Her face was white, but otherwise she seemed calm.

"None," said Savage.

"So what are we doing here?" asked Rachel. "We know who killed those three near here, there won't be a fourth…"

"Not in that series, anyway," broke in Savage.

Rachel stared at him. "Christ, I suppose there could be others, yes. And we'll investigate those?"

"We surely will," replied Savage. "That does remain our real job."

"Boss, it's not clear from that tape why Worthing was approached in the first place."

Hamilton nodded his appreciation of her point.

"You raise a fascinating issue, Rachel. Just yesterday, we got the word that Worthing had actually killed a kid at school when he was fourteen. It was clear then that it was a premeditated stabbing, but of course the wealthy family had a hell of a barrister and got it accepted by the Juvenile Court as an accident. The whole thing was kept secret, he was moved to another school and the records locked away. But Charlie was able to get to them."

"Christ, but that means somebody else was able to get to them as well," said Rachel, her eyes wide. "God almighty, Bill, who the hell are we dealing with here?"

"That's the problem," said Hamilton. "And that's why we have to keep this in such a tiny circle."

"So just how are we going to find out who and what's behind this? Shit, why did David have to run away at this stage?" Rachel looked quite angry.

Hamilton sat up straight. "On which point," he said, "let me tell you what David Hunter is up to."

Chapter 13 – A New Face

David Hunter stared at his image in the mirror. "Fuck!" he said.

"You don't like it?" asked the doctor. Her smile made the words a friendly query. Hunter liked her Lancashire accent, he decided. He'd never heard such a strong one before.

"Not sure," he said. "All that bruising. I look like a freak show."

"It'll go down in a few days. We didn't do all that much. Filled out the cheekbones with some padding, rounded the chin a bit, a tiny lengthening of the eyes and a straighter nose. Quite handsome, actually. I could fancy you myself if you weren't my patient."

Hunter laughed and flinched as the movement stretched the bruising round the eyes. "How much is reversible?" he asked.

"Just the cheek padding," the surgeon replied. "That's plastic and it will come out with just a snip or two. The rest, you're stuck with, but honestly, people would pay many thousands for the face you've got now."

Hunter studied himself again. "And you really think nobody would recognise me?"

"Most unlikely. We've got pretty good at this sort of thing. The idea is to do as little as possible so that there's no scarring and you feel comfortable with your new face, and enough to change the features so there's a different image."

"This sort of thing?" He looked across at her. "This is the sort of thing you do a lot? Who for? MI5, MI6?"

Her face was expressionless. "None of your business."

He knew when to change the subject. "So I can leave now?"

She nodded. "We've taken precautions. You're going out of here in an ambulance to a clinic in Stretford. We'll take you out in a wheelchair with your face bandaged so nobody can recognise you, and you'll stay in a private room at the clinic for a few days till the bruising has died down. Then you head off to wherever you're going."

"I don't think I want to know who you work for, Doctor."

She smiled and looked like a pretty young woman in a white coat with nothing more serious to worry about than her job as a young doctor and how to fend off hordes of young men. "No, you don't. Now, get dressed and bugger off. We need the bed."

"Another new identity to create?"

She stood up and walked to the door.

"Bugger off, David."

He took his clothes from the cupboard and dressed then sat and waited for the ambulance men to arrive to take him to a place called Stretford, somewhere in the area of Manchester.

* * *

His heart pounded as he slid his passport into the magnetic reader and stared into the camera. But nothing blew, no sirens sounded, no large uniformed men with hands twitching at their side arms appeared. He took his passport back and walked out to the Customs area. With just a small suitcase to haul along, he excited no interest and was outside in the public greeting area within minutes.

The fresh, beautiful morning air of Sydney met him as he walked outdoors. He took a deep breath and walked back in to find the railway link into the city. No expensive taxis or limousines, not now. *Stay under the radar, you're undercover*, he told himself.

An hour later, he arrived at the fairly cheap apartment block in Potts Point. The key that he had received in the mail while he was in Manchester fitted the lock and the door opened to a tiny studio pad. He closed the door and looked around. A minute kitchen area had a two-ring cooking appliance, there was an electric kettle, a grill and a tiny fridge under the countertop. The sink was barely large enough to wash a few plates.

A single bed was placed against one wall, and the surprising bonus was a wall to wall window looking out onto the Navy Dockyard at Woolloomooloo and across Sydney Harbour. Regretfully, he drew the curtain.

An envelope on the little circular dining table held

a lease in the name of Andrew Bedford, the same name as in his new passport with his new face and manufactured history. He hadn't asked, but he was sure that only the Australian Secret Intelligence spooks could have arranged all this so efficiently. He wondered how Charlie Simpson had managed to get that sort of assistance so quickly, together with the surgery in Manchester and how it could have been kept so secret. He suppressed the cold thought that if it hadn't been kept as hidden as he hoped, his life span was definitely limited.

Jet lag was starting to hit him. He had flown non-stop from London after taking the train down from Manchester. Economy class was a nightmare for the thirteen hours to Singapore and with only a couple of hours to stretch his legs at the amazing world of Changi Airport, he had been herded on board for the long overnight haul to Sydney. He hadn't slept in the completely filled economy cabin of the Singapore Airlines A380.

He stripped off his clothes, took a shower in the bathroom that was barely big enough to hold him and fell onto the bed as the blackness enfolded him.

It was noon the next day before he was up again. The day was beautiful and he dressed in blue jeans and a white t-shirt before strolling the short distance to Kings Cross. At that hour, it was a lovely quiet place, the pavements lined with coffee shops and souvenir shops, not the raucous, noisy, booze-filled circus it would become by evening. He found a newsagent and picked up the free copy of *"The Sydney*

Newsman," a little paper he had seen before but never read. He sat by the El Alamein Fountain, one of his favourite spots and ordered a coffee with bacon and eggs while reading the paper like any local. He noted down the office address in Newtown.

When he was done, he walked round to the subway, took the train into Central and changed for the Western Line, alighting at Newtown and finding the address he had noted. It was a small shop front and he walked in. Inside, things looked busy, but there was a counter set up for exactly his purpose. A stack of forms lay on the table and he picked one up and wrote out the advertisement he had been planning for weeks.

"I want to play the game," he wrote and signed it "Charlie." He took it to the counter and after a few moments, a young girl in her teens approached, read the paper, counted the words and stamped it with a red stamp.

"Eighteen dollars," she said, barely looking at him as he handed over the money. She quickly wrote out a receipt, handed it back, again hardly looking at him and walked away.

Hunter folded the paper into his wallet, found his ticket and returned to the station.

"The game's afoot, Watson," he muttered and sat down to wait for the train into Central.

The next day he repeated the routine. He walked up to the El Alamein Fountain, had bacon and eggs with a mug of coffee at the café and read the little paper, with an intense study of the personals columns.

When he saw his own advertisement, his heart skipped a beat. He was really into it now.

Another day went by and nothing new occurred. The paper had nothing in the advertisements columns that caught his eye.

But the next day, there was something. He stopped the motion of bringing his mug to his lips when he saw the notice. The heading said "Charlie." Underneath were a few words. "Provide contact details."

Hunter took a deep breath and resumed drinking his coffee. Maybe the trap had been set and the prey had bitten. Or perhaps he was the prey. This was a terrible game. He finished his breakfast, paid the bill and walked over to the subway to repeat the previous episode in Newtown.

"Charlie says the same place you met Jake," he wrote and handed the paper over to a different young person behind the counter. After he left the shop, he looked at his hands. They were trembling. He was well aware that he had walked into something that could easily kill him. He and Jack Savage had no idea who was the mole within the Police or what access they had to the real events going on.

But he knew that if he had it wrong, he could be dead very quickly.

At eleven o'clock that night, a young man in his late teens ambled along a couple of roads in Potts Point, dropping off advertising leaflets in the mailboxes of the numerous apartment buildings, including Hunter's new abode. A few moments later, he bent over the wall in the next apartment entrance, moved aside a brick by the dustbins and picked up an envelope, sliding it into his pocket. Another batch of leaflets posted, he walked a few blocks, collected his motorbike and drove off.

The following afternoon, Hunter found his way by three different buses to the pub where Robert Worthing had told him he had first been confronted by an unidentified young man. Despite the few words scrawled on the back of the leaflet in his mailbox indicating that somebody would be watching him there, the nerves crawled and twisted in his gut.

All afternoon, he sat in the bar of the pub. Nobody came near him. Several times, young men who could have been the ones who approached Worthing came into the bar, had a drink, sometimes two and left. One stayed over an hour, moving between the betting bar where Hunter saw him placing a couple of bets on the racing that was being televised from some country town, but he left and didn't reappear.

Hunter read his copy of the *"The Sydney Newsman"* and tried to keep his nerves under control. At six, he moved into the next bar and ordered a curry from the kitchen, waited till it arrived and forced it down together with his third schooner of lemon, lime and bitters.

Nobody approached him. In utter boredom, he reached the end of his patience at a little after nine-thirty and left, taking an hour to get home. Going under cover had never struck him as such a deadly boring process.

The next day was the same. When Hunter got home after ten-thirty, he scrawled a note, placed it in an envelope and went out. He could see nobody around and he moved to the dustbin area of the next block of apartments and slid the note under the brick.

It took a long time to fall asleep. As he had written in the note, he thought it probable that the game players had decided not to invite him to play.

On the third day, his nerves screaming at the boredom and sense of complete failure, he had reached the point of doing the crossword in the newspaper, having finished his meat pie and mashed potatoes that was his evening meal this time.

"Good evening, Charlie," said a voice behind him. His heart lurched and he sensed the hairs on his arms rising. He put the pen down on the table and stood up.

She looked about forty, he thought, neat, attractive but not eye-catching.

"I'm Charlie," he said.

"No you're not," she replied with a smile. "You're Andrew Bedford, you're unemployed, broke and you've just got back from England."

Holy Fuck, these people have connections, he thought. But under the shock was a sense of glee. *My mythical persona seems to be holding up. Those government spooks know what they're doing, all right.*

"That's right," he said.

"How did you know how to contact us?"

"Jake told me."

"Now why would Jake do that?" Her gaze on him was intense.

"We were talking here one night. He knew I was broke. I think he'd a drink too many."

"And when was that?"

"A few days before I went to Pommyland. I think he'd just got the first payment and he was feeling a bit loose."

"What else did he tell you?"

"Nothing. Just that it was a way to make easy money."

"And did he know that you had killed a kid when you were fifteen?"

Christ alive, these people can access the police computers! He wondered how Charlie Simpson had managed to get that fake record placed in the files. *But it seems to be working.* "No, he didn't. How the hell did you find that? Those files are locked away and I have no official record."

She ignored his question. "Why were you in England?"

"Looking for work. There's bugger-all here. But it was just as bad there, so I only gave it a few weeks till the money ran out."

She continued to stare at him for a few moments of silence. "You want to play the game?"

"Yes, I do. I need the money and I can do it."

"And you fully understand what it is you do?"

"Of course."

"So what's your sign, Andrew?"

"My sign?"

"Yes, what you leave behind and which we use to verify your claim."

"A lion."

"And after, you place a personal advert saying 'One Down' and sign it 'Charlie' again. Don't ever use a credit card. Always use that same paper."

"Got it."

"Then you wait for another advert. It will be headed with the name you've selected, 'Charlie' and will say 'Collection Time' and nothing else. Next day you come here and wait to be contacted."

"By you?"

"One of our people."

"I understand."

"Okay, Andrew, good luck. I wish you every success. Nobody's reached the five mark yet. But one thing. Don't do something as stupid as Jake did and tell anyone else, understand? We have our own selection processes. As it happens, you fit the bill and you check out clean, so we'll let you play."

He nodded.

"Now, one more thing. Be here again tomorrow, between three and five. Somebody will give you a package. There'll be some useful information and other stuff."

She stood up and he watched her walk away. He realised he was trembling.

Across the room, a young man who had been checking his telephone screen folded his device away and also left the bar.

David finished his drink and set off for home. He was in the game.

Chapter 14 – A New Player

The group studied the picture projected on the screen.

"We haven't identified her yet," said Bill Hamilton. "We're still working on it. But they seem to have swallowed the bait and in the process revealed that they have seriously strong contacts. They got to the locked files and found out that 'Andrew Bedford' had killed a kid when he was fifteen, a case that was completely hidden, as usual with minors."

"Who took the picture?" asked Rachel Norman.

"My elder son," said Hamilton. "And my younger son is handling the letter drops and leaflet communications."

"So everybody is at risk," chimed in Jack Savage. "If these people get wind of what's really going on, there's no knowing what they'll do."

"Shit," murmured Barrie Roche. "It's hard to realise that's David in that picture."

"MI5 used their best people," replied Savage. "Personally, I think it's a huge improvement."

"The conversation with the woman is a bit odd, isn't it?" commented Barrie Roche. "Very stilted."

"Very clever," said Savage. "You realise, she said absolutely nothing to indicate what was going on. Everything was based on David's understanding of what she meant. But nowhere does she say anything about killing people."

"Hell," said Rachel. "You think that they thought David might be wearing a wire?"

"Normal precautions, I imagine," replied Savage. "More likely, it's in case anyone accidently hears any part of the conversation. So far, they seem to have swallowed David's story."

The telephone ringing on the conference table prevented anybody replying. Hamilton pushed the button for the loudspeaker.

"Hamilton," he said.

"Bill, we've got one hell of a problem," said the voice of Charlie Simpson. "There's a body in the basement of a building near you in Surry Hills. The problem is that it looks like the fourth in the same series as before. Get your team round there. Chrysler Street, number fifteen."

The team stared at each other in shock.

"Jack, Rachel, with me," snapped Hamilton. "Barrie, somebody needs to stay here."

* * *

"Oh my god," said Hamilton. They stared at the body hanging from its wrists tied to a beam in the basement of the office building. It was a male, heavily built and some fat showing at the waist of the naked torso. Three stab wounds showed in the ample stomach. Blood lay in a thick pool under the body and drenched the corpse's trousers and shoes.

"But this is crazy!" said Rachel. "This is the same MO as before!"

"And there's a cross cut into the shoulder," said Angela Simpson. "It looks just like the other three, though this victim is a bit older and heavier than those. Getting him up there would have been an effort."

"So exactly the same MO that Robert Worthing used," said Hamilton. "Jack, are you sure you had the right man before? There's no way he could have done another one, surely, after that interview?"

"None at all," said Savage, his voice croaky with shock and tension.

"Have you checked the ID?" asked Hamilton.

"Not yet," said Angela. "That's my next step."

"No need," said Savage.

They all looked at him with curiosity.

"It's Robert Worthing," said Savage.

Back in the office at Taylor Square, they looked at each other.

"Do you think they know?" Rachel asked.

Savage shook his head. "David had an impossible situation. The only plausible way he could have known how to get into the game was to have been told by another player. He told the woman that Jake had suggested he try and get into the game, and that Jake, or Worthing as he was, had been a bit drunk."

"They don't mess around, do they?" said Roche. "They kill Worthing less than a day later."

"And you know what?" said Savage. "I don't give a shit. So we caused the death of one man who had killed three other men and should have been on trial and sentenced to life without parole. I don't feel guilty."

"What about his family?" Rachel looked distressed. "His wife and two kids?"

Savage shrugged. "This is easier on them. They'll believe Worthing was an innocent victim of a murder. Yes, tragic, very sad and all that, but a hell of a lot better than knowing he was a serial killer of young men he had picked up in bars, which they would have discovered fairly soon. This way too, they'll get Worthing's life insurance policy, which they wouldn't otherwise."

"Christ!" Barrie Roche looked stunned. "This is all very sick."

"Yes, it is," said Bill Hamilton. "I'll make sure David gets the news in this evening leaflet drop. He'll probably be upset also, but he'll see the reality. I doubt he'll have any sympathy for Worthing."

"Not after Debbie's murder, I agree," said Roche.

"Boss, why aren't we checking out that little newspaper that they use for the personal adverts?" Rachel asked. "We could go through all the back copies and find when the ads were placed. Maybe one of the desk people could remember who placed them?"

Jack Savage shook his head. "That's the last thing we want to do, Rachel. I know it's the *logical* thing to do, but these bastards are clever. They select a little paper that doesn't take credit cards for the adverts and there are a shitload of adverts every day. David commented in one report that the clerks are so rushed, they didn't even look at him, just counted the words, took the money, gave him a receipt and that was that."

Rachel sat back, looking annoyed. "And I suppose if we start questioning them, that will alert the players we're tracking them. Should have thought of that."

"And David will be dead soon after," said Hamilton.

"And the same with the paper in Melbourne," added Roche. "Same sort of rag, I suppose?"

"Something called *"The Yarra Gazette,"* replied Hamilton. "The Murder Squad down there went looking after we'd advised them. Identical sort of operation, small, scruffy offices, no credit cards, perfect camouflage. So for now, our hands are tied, we simply mustn't give any clue that we're tracking these people."

"The best we can do is pick up one of those papers every day and look for the adverts," said Savage. "Rod Hathaway's people in North Sydney are doing that already, so are the Melbourne crew. At the worst, we might get advance warning that a new killer has got into the game."

"This is seriously ugly," said Rachel.

"Right, so moving on," said Hamilton. He took a few sheets of paper from his briefcase and spread them out to the others. "The first is the new report of another murder, the second is the pathologist's report. Let me read the first one."

He picked up the first sheet, cleared his throat and began reading.

"Another in the series of killings that has erupted around Sydney and the suburbs has occurred. Police are investigating the death of an unnamed man in his fifties who was found in Centennial Park at dawn. Police will only say that the man was found stabbed, but will not release his identity until family have been informed."

Hamilton put down the paper and picked up the second.

"The medical examiner, Doctor Angela Simpson reports that the man was stabbed at the back of the neck, severing the spinal cord and he would have died instantly. A tiny puncture in his arm indicates that a drug of some sort was administered, but no toxic report has been completed yet. There was a burn mark on the back of the victim's neck. It was in the shape of a lion rampant, three centimetres high, one centimetre wide, a copy of the shape is attached."

He put down the paper and looked around.

"And when did this occur and why haven't we heard about it?" asked Roche.

Hamilton grinned. "In three days time and because it doesn't actually happen. During the night before, we will set up a tent in Centennial Park, Angela Simpson will arrive at five in the morning, she will examine a body and that will be carried out on a stretcher and taken to the morgue a little later."

"And the lion burn?" asked Rachel.

"This," said Savage, taking an article from his jacket pocket and placing it on the table in front of Rachel. She picked it up and stared at it. It was a flat metal shape in the form of a lion, exactly the dimensions stated in the report.

"Something I picked up in Singapore a few years ago," said Savage. "It's actually a stamp, can be used as a wax seal or a print image."

"And this is David's first fictional murder?" asked Roche.

Savage nodded. "And it's also our test run of how well this has been set up. We will definitely release a press report, there will be a quite real crime scene in Centennial Park, a real body will have been borrowed from the morgue and Angela will release a pathology report that very few people will see, but it will legally be entered into the computer."

"Christ, this is a risk!" said Roche. "If the people behind this realise it's fake...."

"David's dead, yes," said Savage. "That's the test. I think they can get to the computer records and see Angela's fake report and learn about the lion burn mark and that should confirm to them that David, or Andrew Bedford as they know him has killed his first target."

"But if they can access the morgue itself?" Roche looked nervous.

"Then they'll know that the body in Centennial Park was borrowed and that Andrew Bedford is as fake as this story and they'll kill him." Savage's face was without expression.

"And what do we do while all this is going on?" asked Rachel.

"Exactly what we'd do if the murder was real. We'll go and conduct house to house inquiries, and they'll turn up nothing because the nearest house is a long way from the area in the park. We'll check with the park management about when the gates were closed and what possible entry points could there be at night. We'll search the area for non-existent clues, write official reports and file them in the computer and generally we'll waste our time maintaining a façade of a real investigation. If we do it right, we'll convince the mysterious watchers and keep David alive. Do it wrong, arouse suspicion, and he's dead."

"And we can't have David come in and review the operation?" asked Barrie.

"Christ, no!" said Hamilton. "David may be being watched at all times. He must never show any signs of being anything other than what he is, an unemployed, broke, desperate loser. And blokes like that don't visit offices in blocks like this. No, our only communication with David is through the leaflets and his dead letter drop near his apartment building."

"No phone calls?" Rachael looked disturbed.

"Again, no, not any type of contact at all. If they see him make a call even through a public phone, it would be out of character and could arouse suspicions. He's not supposed to be able to afford a mobile phone and if he did have one, what's to say they wouldn't grab it off him some time and check the SIM card records?"

"So is that what we're going to do, sit here and twiddle our thumbs?" Roche was looking irritated.

"Not at all," Hamilton said. "For a start, we have to create a shitload of documents for the computer files to make it look like we're conducting a full investigation. So all your creative writing skills will be used here, but we have to work together to ensure coordinated reports. I reckon we need to spend the first two hours each day doing that before getting out there and doing those interviews and investigative things. But then we do have a major task."

"Which is?" Rachel looked suspicious.

"Genuine, painstaking, hard-grinding police work," said Hamilton. "It's a dead cert that these serial killings here, in Canada, Britain, the US and elsewhere are not the only ones. We're going to spend bloody hours at our computers hunting down every newspaper report of killings that might fit the same process. Almost all of them have websites."

"And if we find something?" Rachel's look had turned to interest.

"Document everything you can find and we'll have some review sessions to see if we agree these are really more cases like ours. If they are, we'll initiate very careful contacts with the police departments concerned and see if we can find confirming details, obviously the signatures."

"That's fine with English-language papers," said Roche. "What about the others?"

"For the moment, we need to keep it within this group," said Savage. "For anything other than English, it would mean getting in interpreters and possibly involving the embassies of other countries. We've got no idea who's involved in this thing and we can't take the risk."

"I can handle French," said Roche.

Hamilton looked at him in astonishment. "I had no idea, Barrie!"

"Bloody hell, Bill! Roche? My dad's a frog and he insisted I speak French as a kid."

"Well, good on yer, Barrie! That's a help! Okay boys and girls, we have a shitload of work to do. "We'll need to read the major papers from Britain, Canada, US and New Zealand. I've been told that the list should include *"The Guardian"* and *"The Telegraph"* from Britain, also *"The Scotsman," "The Toronto Globe and Mail"* from Canada and Barrie, look up the Montreal French-language papers. We'll read *"The Chicago Tribune," "The Washington Post"* and *"The Los Angeles Times,"* and any of the other regional papers you can find on the web. Barrie, find the best French papers you can see on the web."

"And if any other killings occur here?" asked Roche.

"Then we do the jobs we're trained for and investigate them," replied Hamilton.

Hunter sat in his tiny apartment. He decided to leave the curtains open so he could enjoy the sight of Sydney Harbour. There was nothing anybody could learn about him if they had gone to the trouble of watching him from another apartment and there were several that could provide a telescope view of his place.

The small package was fascinating. The young man had simply dropped it on the table by his copy of *"The Sydney Newsman"* and walked on before Hunter could see his face, but he wasn't worried about that. He knew that the kid with the telephone in his hands a few tables away had taken care of that.

"Wear rubber gloves," the single sheet of paper said. "Get a few sets of paper overshoes, you can get them from a good pharmacy or hospital supply shop. Put them on before moving to the action scene. Afterwards, burn both gloves and shoes."

That triggered an idea and he wrote a note for later deposit in the secret place near the rubbish bins.

There was a small vial of some liquid and five simple syringes. No words on the paper about them, but Hunter knew this was the sedating drug. That would be passed to Bill Hamilton with the note and Angela would find out what the drug was. Maybe it would provide a link to the supplier and the purchaser.

Meanwhile, he had two days with nothing to do. The scrawled words on the back of the leaflet he had picked up from his letter box read, *"It happens Thursday night."* They had been after the equally short note saying *"W was the victim of his own MO."*

He knew what that meant and felt neither surprise nor sympathy for Worthing. The woman's words had indicated there would be retribution. Like Savage, he realised that this way the family would avoid the horrors of learning just what Worthing had done as well as get a million or two from the insurance company.

He had no idea if he was being watched in any way. Better play the role to the letter, he knew and went for a walk down to the Cross where at a pharmacy he bought three pairs of domestic rubber gloves and a packet of paper overshoes.

That night he went to the bar and had a couple of beers before coming home again. He couldn't afford to spend big if he was to maintain his image of a desperate, unemployed loser ready to kill for a prize.

* * *

"His name is Colin Curtis," said Bill Hamilton.

The group studied the picture of the young man dropping the package by Hunter's left arm.

"So we know him, then?" asked Barrie Roche.

"Small-time crook," said Hamilton. "Began as a kid, some time in Juvenile Detention, graduated to some bigger stuff, bit of Break & Enter, couple of muggings, car theft, the usual stuff."

"So now what?" asked Rachel.

"When we find his place of abode, we'll start tapping his phone. If he doesn't have one, he'll have a mobile. We'll haul him in on something minor, hold him for an hour or two before letting him go with a grovelling apology, but after we've had a look at his phone records on his SIM card and got an address."

"Christ, won't that tip off the players?" asked Roche.

"Not if we play it right. Let's spend a little time on planning a good way to get our hands on the little bastard's phone and address."

"Any progress with the woman?" asked Roche.

Hamilton shook his head. "Nothing so far. Face recognition software hasn't come up with anything. Certainly no criminal record that we can trace.

* * *

"Okay, he's just leaving."

The voice rattled out of the loudspeaker in the patrol car sitting where it had been over half an hour. Its effect had been to slow down the traffic considerably though there had been no radar equipment on display. The dark van with no windows parked a few metres further along attracted no obvious attention. The road was not heavily travelled, but the pub was quite popular with the younger set because of the small rock group that played there a few nights each week. It had the advantage that most of the traffic came from the suburb nearby and thus the patrons returned home along the same stretch.

"Acknowledged," said the officer behind the wheel. He grinned at his female partner. "Showtime!" he said and they climbed out of the car. In just a few moments they had several plastic pylons laid out along the road surface. The dark van ahead of them also showed action as the driver climbed out, went to the rear and opened the doors to show a line of seats along each side wall.

Cars passed the breathalyser unit with drivers showing varying degrees of anxiety. The female officer waved one car down and directed the driver to stop by her colleague. The officer asked the driver to count from one to ten with his mouth by the detector.

"Okay, no problem, sir, carry on," he said to the

obviously relieved young man at the wheel and he turned his attention to the next one with the same result.

"This one, Garry," said the other officer who was closely watching the oncoming cars. She waved down the elderly Ford Falcon with another young man at the wheel who seemed undisturbed as he slowed and stopped by the male officer and wound down his window.

"Good evening, sir," said Garry. "Have you been drinking at all this evening?"

"Just a midi of beer," said the man.

"Okay, will you just count aloud from one to ten?" Garry said, holding the detector by the man's mouth.

He took the detector away and studied it, then took a second unit from his belt and plugged in a mouthpiece. "That shows you may have more than the limit, sir. I'll ask you to breathe into the tube, please, sir."

"But I've only had a midi," the young man said with alarm in his voice.

"Just breathe into the tube, please sir," said the officer, unmoved. "That'll show more precisely."

He stood up with the breath sample and studied the dial.

"Please get out of the car, sir," he said. "The reader shows you have an illegal level of alcohol in your blood."

"This is bloody insane," shouted the man. "I've had one single bloody midi!"

"Sir, if you don't get out of the car immediately, I'll arrest you for obstructing a police officer and that will get serious. Now, for the last time, get out of the car and stand up.”

“God almighty,” muttered the man, but obeyed and climbed out of the Falcon. Several cars went by, faces in the windows staring at the scene.

The third officer standing by the van door advanced on the group and took the man by the arm. “Come with me, sir,” he said and led him to the van and indicated he climb in and take a seat. Looking furious and alarmed, the man obeyed.

Meanwhile, the two officers had found one more middle-aged man wearing a suit and apparently displaying an excessive blood-alcohol level and he was also taken to the van. A brief nod between the three officers and the van door was closed and the driver carefully drove away.

A few minutes later, the two men were led out of the van into a police station. At the reception desk, both of them, now in a stunned silence handed over their wallets, mobile phones, took off their shoes and trouser belts and were taken to a holding cell. A few moments later, a doctor arrived and asked each of the men in turn to follow her into another room. Each man was then asked to breath into a tube attached to an instrument and returned to the holding cell where they were left alone again. Doctor Angela Simpson examined the instrument and the printouts and emerged ten minutes later, looking angry.

“You need to check your equipment,” she said at high volume, clearly audible to the two men in the holding cell where they sat with the door open. “Neither of these men has a level above the limit!”

"What? Hell, I'm sorry doctor, I've no idea how that happened. Of course, we'll check the gear. Jim, let them both out, please."

In an embarrassed silence, wallets, phones, belts and shoes were returned to the two prisoners.

"Gentlemen, I can only apologise! We'll run you back to your cars, of course," said the desk sergeant and waited while two very angry men were led out of the station to a waiting patrol car.

"Got it?" asked Angela Simpson.

"You bet," said Detective Sergeant Jerry Bowler, not in his customary snappy blazer and flannels but regular uniform. "Just as Bill asked. That's his address, assuming his licence is correct. And that's the list of calls he's made and received in the last few days on his mobile." He handed her a handwritten sheet which Angela folded and put into her bag of gubbins.

"And the DUI patrol, they're okay with this?" added Bowler.

"A nephew of my husband," replied Angela.

"Sounds safe enough," said Bowler with a grin.

"Thanks, Jerry," she said with a glowing smile. "That was easy!"

* * *

"Phone taps are in place in the apartment of Colin Curtis in Marrickville," Bill Hamilton announced to the group. "And we checked his mobile phone SIM card while we had him in the drunk tank. He's made three calls to a specific number and received eight from that same number. That number belongs to a Zoe Moreland, and we've tracked her to an apartment in St Leonards on the north shore. Taps will be placed on that line within the next few hours."

"Bloody marvellous!" said Barrie Roche. "Do we know who this bitch is?"

"Not yet," replied Hamilton. "We will soon. Meanwhile, David left a note with a good suggestion. As you know, his instructions were to buy rubber gloves and paper overshoes. Now many people buy rubber gloves, but not too many buy the paper shoes, and those that do will be hospitals and clinics that buy in bulk, not individuals. David suggests that a check on hospital suppliers and pharmacies might bring up something. Maybe somebody remembers a small sale of a package of paper shoes."

"I'll get the Plod onto it," said Rachel, making a note. "Hey, we might get really lucky and they have security cameras. I know my pharmacy does."

"Good thinking," said Hamilton.

"Shall I tell the guys in Melbourne about that?" asked Rachel.

"Christ, no!" swore Hamilton. "We've got no idea at all who might be involved in Victoria. We can't take the risk of alerting them."

Rachel nodded and went to the phone.

"And David's fictional murder takes place tonight?" asked Barrie Roche.

Hamilton nodded. "Andrew Bedford commits the first of his series of murders tonight."

"And we'd better pray that we really have fooled the people behind this and they're not doing the same as us, playing along until they find out the full extent of our operation." Jack Savage's face was without expression, but his voice cracked slightly.

With a weird sensation in his gut, David Hunter read the report of the murder in the Sydney Morning Herald. It had made page two and was accompanied a little further by a withering editorial blasting the ineptitude of the police force. There was a major killing spree going on in Sydney and the police seemed helpless, said the article. Also in the paper, above the fold on page two was an interview with Alan Kinsella. He was far less kind. For three columns, Kinsella fired blasts of rage against the authorities and their pathetic failure to save the good citizens of the city from this murderous wave. He didn't spare the Melbourne authorities either.

"Something's got up his bloody nose," muttered Hunter then re-read the report of the killing. It gave details of the discovery of the body by a morning jogger in the park and there was a picture of the white tent set up around the scene, even one of the stretcher being carried to the ambulance and to his delight, one of Angela Simpson coming out of the tent.

"Hi, sexy!" muttered Hunter to the El Alamein Fountain. The sound of the water hid his words.

"Police have not released the name of the victim until next-of-kin have been informed," said the stock standard paragraph. "But we understand it was a male, perhaps in his fifties and he had been stabbed in the back of the neck. They are appealing for anyone who witnessed any incident in the park to contact them immediately." There was no mention of a brand mark in the shape of a rampant lion on the body.

That evening, he took a seat in the local pub and watched the news reports all saying much the same, reporting the public anxiety and worry with the failure of the police to stem the killing tide. The channel owned by Kinsella's media empire was displaying far more fury. Kinsella himself appeared and his rage was palpable.

"This government is an absolute disgrace," he said, his voice dripping with contempt. "I have never seen such ineptitude and downright incompetence. The entire State Cabinet should resign and call for an election this very minute. And as for the police force, never in all my years have I seen such shoddy amateurism. Murderers and thugs are now wondering the streets with complete immunity, knowing full well there is nothing to fear from those idiots in blue who couldn't catch a cold in winter."

Startled by the raging invective in Kinsella, Hunter studied him. Kinsella was a small man, and though the camera stayed above his waist, the wheelchair was obvious and Hunter knew that the billionaire was a cripple, both legs stunted from birth. He looked fairly young, perhaps in his fifties, Hunter estimated.

"The little bastard will blow a brain cell if he keeps this up," he muttered. "That would probably improve the world no end." He knew how much his sister had detested the man. Later, he went to bed, nerves tight, wondering if the fictional murder would catch the right fish.

The next morning, he went to Newtown again. *"One Down, Charlie,"* he wrote. Not once had anyone behind the counter shown any interest in his advertisement beyond counting the words and taking his money.

Two days later, as David sat in his regular place in the Cross with his morning coffee, an advert appeared in the paper. David's heart lurched. *"Charlie – Collection time,"* it said. That was the call to get his money.

He wondered if he would live to spend it. He still had no idea which of them was the hunter and which of them was the prey.

Chapter 15 – Spook Watch

"Bugger!" said Bill Hamilton. He put down the phone and looked at the group. "Rod Hathaway's team in North Sydney have just caught another advert in the local rag. It said, 'I want to play the game' and it's signed 'Phillip.' Rachel, get onto the bloke tapping Curtis' phone, he'll be getting a call."

Rachel nodded and stood up, opening up her mobile phone as she walked out.

"There could be a message for that 'Phillip' person asking for contact details, first," said Barrie.

"Maybe," said Jack Savage. "But remember what David said, the woman told him they select their players themselves, so they'll probably know where to find this bloke already."

Barrie nodded just as Rachel came back into the room. Her face looked furious.

"The call was made three minutes ago," she said. "All she said to Curtis was 'make it this afternoon.' But there was no indication of where. It could be anywhere in New South Wales."

"Shit," said Bill Hamilton. "It's probably local, being such a small, local paper, but we still have no idea of where. Okay, Rachel, call Charlie Simpson, he's got access to some help. Tell him what's happened, ask him to get somebody over there to see if they can find Curtis and follow him. Let's hope to Christ we can find him before he contacts this 'Phillip' bloke."

Rachel nodded and opened her phone again.

"We can't do this ourselves," said Hamilton, his anger showing in his grated voice. "They know us."

"But boss, if we can stop this, we'll alert the top players that we're on to them." Roche's hands were twisted in frustration.

"I know, Barrie, but can we really leave the bastard to organise the murder of some innocent? God almighty, what a fucking mess."

David jumped on the bus, the first of the three that he took to get to the pub. Nerves twisted his insides. Was he going to get a package with $10,000 dollars as payment for his "murder" of a man in Centennial Park? If so, would that mean that the players behind this terrible game had been fooled? Or were they still leading him by the nose, knowing full well who he was and what he was doing? Because if the latter, he knew all too well that his entire team was at risk, including Bill Hamilton's two sons who were helping out as courier and photographer.

He sat and looked at the scenery of busy Sydney flowing by him. If the players knew what was going on, his life span was terribly short. It could end today. It would be easy, he knew. It could just be a needle with something lethal pushed into his body while he sat in the pub. Nobody would see it. Or it could be a single, silenced shot when he went out late at night to leave a message for Bill's son to pick up during his leaflet drop. He shivered slightly.

The bus pulled into Central and David walked out with the crowd, found the next bus stop and waited patiently until the bus arrived to take him over the Bridge to the North Shore. When it arrived he took a window seat in the middle of the bus so he could enjoy one of his favourite views, the Harbour and the Opera House. The bus gradually filled up but the seat next to him remained empty.

At St Leonards, as the bus slowed down approaching the rail station, a man got up from a few rows back and walked up to the middle of the bus to alight. He stood a few moments by David's seat as the bus slowed, and as he moved on to leave, he dropped a small package on David's right side then jumped off and vanished rapidly.

Startled, David picked up the package. The size and flexibility told him exactly what it was.

He'd been paid. The chances were getting better that the players had swallowed the whole story. But the delivery also told him an unpleasant fact. He was being watched, possibly all the time. He stayed on the bus until he reached Chatswood then alighted and caught the train home. When he got back to his apartment, he checked the package and found $10,000 in crisp new $100 bills.

The game had moved onto a whole new level.

For nearly an hour, he sat motionless, looking out at the Harbour. Then the loneliness and the fear and the grinding pressure of living every minute not knowing if he was hunter or prey, whether somebody would kill him at any time hit him hard.

He folded ten of the new bills into his wallet, tucked the rest away under the tiny fridge and walked out, heading to the Cross. There was a high-class brothel situated in one building. It was legal, licensed and he'd heard it had a population of beautiful women.

He badly needed the services of that establishment and he had no compunctions about letting a bunch of killers pay for it.

* * *

"So now that David got his ten grand, we know something more about the players," said Hamilton to the group.

"Yes, they can access the police files and see the post mortem reports, but they're not anywhere near the mortuary itself," said Rachel. "So they believe that David really did kill somebody, they read Angela's report, but they didn't see an actual body."

"That's how it looks," said Hamilton. "But I'm not totally sure. They could still be playing with him, maybe trying to find who his supporters are."

"They'll certainly know about this group, of course," said Roche. "We're the public face of the investigation."

"But they must never, ever get any idea that we're starting to trace them," said Hamilton. "If they get the slightest wind of that, David's dead and the game is cancelled. We'll never find them then. So we're putting out news items that really report no progress. We're getting crucified in the media and Simpson's taking a beating, but that's how it has to be."

There was a moment of silence round the table.

"Did anyone find Curtis?" asked Rachel.

Hamilton shook his head. "He seemed to vanish. No sign of him since that call was made."

"So he's probably contacted that 'Phillip' bastard?"

"Almost certainly," agreed Hamilton. "Meanwhile, we got some help from Spookland," he continued. "Charlie Simpson took the risk when he contacted the head of ASIO to help us get David's new identity established. We felt pretty sure we could trust him, even above any Cabinet Minister, and he's assigned a couple of his people that he's absolutely certain about. So they've investigated the woman contact, Zoe Moreland."

A stir of interest ran round the table.

"So here's what we know about her," said Bill Hamilton, reading from a single sheet of paper. "Zoe Moreland, née Zoe Whitelaw. She's forty-eight, divorced, two adult children, Christine aged twenty-two, Simon aged twenty-five, both living in the UK, not close in any way to either parent. Her husband walked out on her about fifteen years ago, he lives in Brisbane. The spooks are checking on him right now. She lives alone in a two-bedroom apartment in Chatswood, owned with no mortgage. She's a book-keeper for a private school in Lilyfield, drives a fairly new Toyota Camry, seems to have no financial problems of any sort."

"Not exactly the profile of somebody in an international murder gang," said Barrie Roche.

"And she gets even less likely as we go on," said Hamilton. "We've had her phone tapped for a week. She makes no calls that could be considered worth investigating. Those calls to Curtis on her mobile have not occurred since we started tapping her until this latest one."

"What about emails?" asked Rachel.

"Again, nothing to arouse suspicion," said Hamilton. "She chats on a couple of internet boards, but these are quite boring chat boards, comparing weather around the world with people in Europe, USA and Canada, mostly Canada, it seems. Sometimes they talk about pets, women's health issues, television shows, some jokes about men, generally dead boring. Nothing political, though she would seem to be vaguely right of centre in her views. She liked Howard, thought Bush was a dickhead, doesn't like the Labor Party, but that's about it."

"So if it wasn't for the fact that she recruited David to be a serial killer, she'd be of zero interest?" Rachel looked irritated.

"Odd, isn't it?" agreed Savage. "This is actually a superb cover she's got there."

"And yet she was quite open in contacting David, and Robert Worthing before that," said Rachel. "Wasn't that careless?"

"Not really," said Savage. "After all, if we believe Worthing told us exactly what she said, and David's report is accurate, she never actually said anything incriminating. Nothing about killing people and all her comments about being paid could equally have been talking about a betting circle or some sort of competition. And it's not as if the men she was talking to would want to report her to the cops."

"So how the hell is she getting instructions and reporting to the top people?" demanded Rachel.

Roche looked thoughtful. "How is David communicating with us? After all, nobody could tap his phone and find anything damning. He's been nowhere near any of us. And yet he's up to date with what we're doing and we're up to date with what he's doing."

"Because one of my sons is dropping advertising leaflets in all the letter boxes in the area, with just one specifically for him, and we have a dead letter pickup for him to leave us news." Hamilton was nodding vigorously. "Bog-standard spook stuff, and I bet that's exactly how she's doing it too."

"Oh crap," said Rachel. "We all know what that means! Can we get any help from the Plod?"

Hamilton shook his head. "Too dangerous. We just don't know who's in this thing and even a careless word could blow up in our faces, especially David's face."

"Okay," said Rachel. "I'll take the first watch starting this evening."

"That's fine," said Hamilton. "But if you see a leaflet drop into her letter box, do NOT go and look at it. She could come out at any time and if you're seen, we're fucked. What you should do is see if she comes out after dark and if she does, follow her and see if she leaves something anywhere."

Rachel nodded. "Let me have the address, Bill."

"Whoa! No!" said Savage. "You're thinking of parking somewhere nearby and sitting there and watching?"

"That's the idea," said Rachel.

"Not a good one," said Savage. "That's like running naked in front of the place, shouting "I'm watching you!" You'll stand out like a shag on a rock. It's too bloody obvious!"

"And the alternative is?" asked Hamilton.

"First, send your kid up there and reccie the area, see if there's an apartment placed right that's for rent. And check out the local estate agents, see if they have something. Then take up residence and watch from in there."

Hamilton nodded. "Let's hope we get lucky," he said. "I'll tell the kid this evening. I don't want to use the phone."

"God, it's like walking in nitro-glycerine," said Rachel. "We just have no idea where the leak could be or where it'll blow up."

"Good analogy," said Hamilton. "But how about we start to think about who the enemy is? Jack, have you had any thoughts yet?"

"Sure have," said Jack. "First thoughts only, but this is pretty obvious. First, it's a group. It's got to be, it's a game, after all. Players are competing to see who can have the most people killed. And based on how much they're paying their killers, these people are rich beyond normal standards of wealth."

"Reduces the odds a bit," said Rachel.

"Maybe, maybe not," replied Jack. "They could be anywhere in the world."

"But they'll have local organisations, won't they?" said Rachel. "Like our Zoe Moreland and Colin Curtis?"

"They'll have to, of course," agreed Jack. "The complication is that to have become as mega-rich as these people, they'll have that common megalomania that such people almost have to have to get there. The dividing line between that and the cold-blooded heartlessness and contempt for people that our players are demonstrating is quite fine."

"What if they inherited the wealth?" asked Barrie Roche.

"A good point. In that case, their childhoods will be the pointer. And they may well have the same profile as the standard serial killer."

"Refresh us on that, will you, Jack?" asked Hamilton.

Savage nodded and poured himself a glass of water from the carafe on the conference table. "Lonely, probably an only child, little or no warmth from parents, left alone most of the time. So inclined to be a day-dreamer, filling his or her head with wild fantasies."

"Her? Are there many female serial killers?" asked Rachel.

"Not a lot, it's mainly a bloke thing," replied Jack. "The actual figure is 88% of serial killers are male. So, the classic profile is a male aged in his twenties and thirties, nearly all Caucasian, with the sort of childhood I just described. The normal pattern is that the killers operate in their own immediate area, rarely travelling any great distance and they almost always have a very strict MO, they almost invariably kill all their victims in the same way."

"So very much the pattern of all the killings we're seeing around the world," said Roche. "And we only know one killer, at least we did, but he almost fitted the profile, but not quite."

"But the real perpetrators are the people behind the direct killers," said Rachel. "How does this fit in, Jack?"

"I believe that what we have here is a group of mega-rich people, constrained by their social position to be pillars of society, otherwise they would have become serial killers themselves, exactly like the classic profile. They've used that killer instinct in their professional fields and I'd say they're the classic examples of what somebody said, can't remember who it was, that behind every great fortune is a great crime. These people will be among the worst. When we find them, you can bet your life that they got to their positions by the most unscrupulous methods possible, quite probably even illegal methods."

"Even having people killed?" Rachel looked dubious.

"Possibly, not probably," replied Savage. "But in commercially destroying other people or corporations, they were, in their minds, killing them, even if they realised it or not."

"So what's different from the mega-rich who haven't gone about killing people in this game?" asked Hamilton.

"Most people who make it to the top retire cheerfully to enjoy their wealth," said Savage. "Though it's interesting how many seriously rich people you can meet who are not happy, for one reason or another. They always regret that extra million they didn't make, or be angry at the people who stopped them making that extra million. Or they could simply be hostile to those who have the billion or so more than they do.

"Let me give you an example. I dealt with one bloke in the USA, worth nearly half a billion at the age of fifty. He had all the toys, the waterside mansion in Florida with the fast boat, a fleet of cars in the garage, the penthouse apartment in New York. He wasn't a bad looking bloke either, but a bit plump and balding. His greatest anger was about the other hundred million he should have made in a deal where he got beaten to it by a competitor of his. Just what that difference the extra hundred million could have made to somebody worth five hundred million already, he couldn't say, but it was eating at his gut. The other thing that hurt him was the knowledge that all those Playboy Centrefolds and swimsuit models who surrounded him wouldn't be there at all but for his money. He was a very unhappy man.

"He's not untypical of the mega-rich. Delve deep into those psyches and I suspect you could find an impulse to kill."

"So is this what these people are doing? Killing others to make up for not actually having killed people before?" Barrie Roche looked almost amused.

"I think that's exactly right," said Jack. "Now they

can afford it, they're killing people like they always wanted to, but safely, they're living the thrill vicariously, through other people, but they're part of it because they have a competition going. They'll be people who are not just at the peak or very near the peak of their profession, but are still obviously striving hard to get even higher."

"These are very sick puppies indeed," said Hamilton. "But as you say, they could be anywhere in the world in this internet age. And these killings elsewhere would seem to point to that."

Before anyone could reply, the phone rang. Hamilton picked it up.

"Hamilton," he said. He didn't put the call on the loudspeaker.

"Yes, sir," he continued and listened for a moment or two before replacing the phone. He looked round to the group watching him intently.

"Rod Hathaway's team in North Sydney have caught another advert in the local rag. What they found this morning was another one from the same bloke. It said 'One Down.'"

"Oh Jesus Christ!" said Rachel. "He's already done his first."

"It would seem so." Hamilton was expressionless.

"So as we thought, it's somebody they sought out themselves," said Barrie. "They knew who to contact and where. That's why there was no request for contact details."

"Which means they have some sort of system of identifying killers," said Jack Savage. "All we can do now is wait for a body to be discovered."

"Shit," said Bill Hamilton.

"Shit," said Bill Hamilton. Barely an hour had passed since his last identical utterance. He, Savage and Barrie Roche stood silently as Angela Simpson worked on the pathetic corpse lying in the corner of a used car yard in the eastern suburb of Alexandria.

"Looks like a homeless old man," said Roche. "About as cowardly as a killing can get."

"Bloody oath," said Savage, an expression of disgust on his face. "There's blood on his face, but I can't see how he was killed."

"Stabs in the chest," said Angela Simpson, standing up and approaching the group. "Two, not expert by any means. But one looks like it got the heart. Lots of blood, so I think neither stab wound was immediately fatal."

"What are the marks on his face?" asked Savage.

"Swastikas, for Christ's sake," replied the doctor. "One on each cheek, but right-hand, not the standard Nazi left-handed ones."

"That's supposed to be a sign of good, isn't it?" said Roche. "And the left-hand is a sign of evil?"

"Right," said Savage. "So either the killer is having a good laugh at us or he's too stupid to know. My money's on the bastard being stupid."

"Probably," said Angela. "Anyway, this poor bloke is probably in his sixties, but the body's pretty wasted as you might expect. He could be anything over forty. I'll know more after I get him on the slab."

"No identification?" asked Hamilton.

"Nothing," said Angela. "You'll need to show pictures to all those groups in the area, maybe somebody knows him, but I think you'll have Buckleys of identifying him."

"So now we wait for an advert saying, 'Phillip – collection time,' I suppose," said Roche. "Then we'll know the bastard will be getting paid, but we won't know where or when."

"But we'll do our job, anyway," said Hamilton. "Let's get back to the office, we need to organise house-to-house inquiries again, the usual routines."

"I bet that sod Alan Kinsella will rip us another one tonight, too," said Roche. "I could really get to hate that bugger."

* * *

"She's leaving," the young woman called out softly.

"Okay, I'll get after her." The equally young man who had been reading a book, sitting in the armchair in the next room wearing a track suit and training shoes put down his book, stood up and switched off the light before opening the door. He didn't put on the light in the corridor and the room in which his colleague was sitting by the window had been dark.

She was still sitting at her place, the camera with the telescopic lens pointed at the exit to the apartment block across the road. She had taken several pictures as the woman walked out. "Moving west, look like she's carrying an envelope," she said.

The man said nothing, but opened the door and left the apartment, moving swiftly and silently to the front door of the block and stood motionless as he watched the woman walking away. With a good distance between them, he moved out into the darkness and carefully tracked his target, taking cover at every opportunity on the opposite side of the road. She seemed to notice nothing.

After ten minutes she stopped by another apartment block, moved to the array of letter boxes at the front and quickly slipped an envelope into one of the boxes. She turned and began walking back in the direction of her home.

"Definitely dropped something," murmured the man into the microphone clipped to his collar. "One of the letter boxes."

"Can you see which one?" asked the soft voice of his colleague in his ear.

"I think so." He moved across the road and checked the boxes. His excellent training had let him take a photographic image in his mind and he was sure he had the right box. He tried it, but it was locked. He reached into his pocket, extracted some useful implements and less than twenty seconds later, the box was open. The envelope lay alone in the box. He took it out, but it was sealed.

"Get the spooky stuff for opening letters," he said softly into his microphone and began to run back to the darkened apartment. On the way, he passed the woman walking back to her own apartment. She paid no attention to the man running along the road at two in the morning.

He walked into the apartment, put on no lights and walked into the kitchen where his partner was waiting. Only after the door was closed did they switch on the lights. Five minutes later, the envelope was open, the paper inside photographed and replaced and the envelope sealed again.

A few minutes after that, it was back in the letter box. The man noted the number of the apartment to which it belonged and ran back to the observation point.

"There's nothing of any interest, really, is there?" commented Rachel, looking at the copy of the letter taken from Zoe Moreland's dead-letter drop the previous night. "Looks like just a report of recent events. *'AB-1, paid; RW – contract cancelled; GS-1.'* I assume that means Andrew Bedford, our David and he's got his cash for his first killing. RW is Robert Worthing and they've killed him. GS must be the initials of the Phillip character, so at least we've learned something."

"But we blew it on the letter pick-up," said Hamilton, irritation in his face. "We assumed the apartment owning that letter box would be occupied, but it wasn't."

"And has the letter been collected?" asked Jack Savage.

"We'll have the spooks check that tonight," said Hamilton. "But I'll bet the kids' college fees that it has."

"No takers," replied Roche.

"Well, let's get the gap filled in, okay?" said Hamilton.

Two hours later, a local council truck arrived with

an elevated platform that lifted a worker up to the top of a telegraph pole opposite the apartment block where a letter drop had taken place. A worker attended to an apparent flaw in the wiring, but in the process installed a minute video-camera on the pole.

"How does it look?" he muttered into his lapel microphone.

"Spot on," was the reply into his ear-piece.

The man waved at the truck driver and the platform descended. The truck drove off.

Chapter 16 – The Game Gets Deeper

"I've discovered how Zoe's passing on messages," said Rachel with a smug smile to the group.

"I thought the dead letter drop was the way," said Hamilton.

"It may be one way, but there's something else going on," replied Rachel.

"You'd better tell us," said Hamilton and took a sip of his coffee.

"It's that boring chat board," said Rachel. "We thought it was just chats about weather and homes and pets and men and all that. So I started reading back through all her posts and I found something interesting. We know she posts as 'Gabrielle' and I noted down every comment she made and the date and time of it, and then I looked for every comment made in direct response to her posts. And then I went back through all the back copies of *"The Sydney Newsman"* and checked them against the personal advertisements."

"Christ, that must have been a drag," said Jack Savage with a look of intense interest on his face.

"Bloody boring at first," replied Rachel. "Then it got interesting. The day after the first killing in Surry Hills, Worthing placed his advert in the paper, saying 'One Down.' That afternoon, Zoe posted a comment that the Tiger in Taronga Park Zoo had had its first kitten. It was a true story and she even posted a link to the article in the Sydney Morning Herald. Quite innocuous, nobody would question that. Hell, I didn't myself!"

"And then?" asked Jack.

"There were four posts in response, all saying 'ooh' and 'aah' and 'aaaaw' and shit like that, because there was a picture in the link, but one comment was that their local zoo hadn't had any newborn yet."

"Who posted that?" asked Hamilton.

"Somebody called 'Jackie-Q,' replied Rachel. "She hasn't put any information about herself on the board and certainly no email address."

"Nothing there to set the policeman's nose sniffing," said Barrie Roche.

"Quite right," said Rachel. "So then I had a look at the date of the second killing. There in the paper was Worthing's personal advert saying 'Two Down.' And three hours later, Zoe posted on the chat board that her second daughter was heading off to the UK for a vacation. Problem is, she only has one daughter and she's already living in the UK."

"And the response from this 'Jackie-Q'?" asked Barrie.

"Just that she hopes the girl has a great time and that her own kids haven't travelled yet."

"All a bit of a stretch," said Hamilton, "but the fib

about her daughter is interesting, as well as the sequence of numbers. Any more Rachel? This is great work, by the way."

"Thanks, boss," said Rachel with a smile. "It gets a whole lot better. After the third killing, same thing. Zoe posts something about a cousin having had her third child. But then Jackie-Q chimes in, says something about a cousin of hers with two sons in Manchester, England being involved in a minor accident. I checked David's file and that was two days after the second killing of a schoolboy in Manchester."

"Holy Shit!" said Hamilton.

"It's just warming up," said Rachel. "Then yet another poster joined in. Her posting name is 'Allison' and she hadn't said anything I could find useful up till now, but she reports that she went on her first date with a guy in Chicago. She got the usual feminine squeaking about that, but a week later, she reported that she's been out with the Chicago guy a second time, three days later it was the third date. Her posts all followed within twelve hours of the three Chicago killings."

"Well, bugger me sideways," murmured Jack Savage. "What a bloody brilliant way of reporting to a group! Rachel, that's incredible police work, I congratulate you."

"Thanks, Jack. It's still going on. Jackie-Q has reported two episodes indicating the third and fourth Manchester schoolboy killings and a 'Florence' chimed in with reports of her dog having three puppies. That last one was within six hours after the third Canadian killing was reported. She says she's in Toronto."

"What about David's fictional episodes?" asked Barrie. "Did she post something?"

"Oh yes! Six hours after David placed his 'One down' personal advert, Zoe said on the board that her daughter's new boyfriend had got his first short story published in a magazine."

Hamilton sat up straight. "You've got all this documented, Rachel?"

"To the second and to the letter, boss."

"And where is this chat board hosted?"

"San Francisco."

Hamilton picked up the phone and pushed the numbers. "Charlie," he said. "We've got a hell of a breakthrough, courtesy of Rachel here. I'm sending you over some details. You'll need to get through to the FBI on this one. Also Scotland Yard and the Canadian Mounties. You'll understand when you see it."

He replaced the phone and looked around the group. "Okay, we'll get to the chat board host company and get the details of all those women, if they are women. In fact, we'll get everybody who posts at all on that board and make sure of who they are. Then the local cops can start watching them." He switched his gaze to Jack. "What the hell is this, Jack? International reporting?"

"No doubt at all," said Jack. "This sounds like the international coordinators in each country advising the game players of the running totals. It's brilliant! All quite innocuous, nothing to arouse suspicion."

"I wonder if there's anybody posting on that board who isn't part of this?" asked Barrie.

"I'm sure of it," replied Rachel. "There's oodles and oodles of utterly boring shit that sounds quite genuine. I think I counted over twenty regular posters on that board, but once the local cops have identified them, I'm dead certain most of them will prove unconnected, other than those I've found."

"Okay, this is good," said Hamilton. "I'd call it progress. Now we can watch with a better focus what happens. Here are the details, David has done his second one."

* * *

David Hunter read the Sydney Morning Herald with the same disconnected feeling he'd experienced the last time. The report was almost word-for-word the same as before.

"Yet another in the series of killings that has erupted around Sydney and the suburbs has occurred. Police are investigating the death of an unnamed man in his fifties who was found by early morning golfers at the Bondi Beach Golf Club at dawn. His body was lying on the Aboriginal carvings on the cliff. Police will only say that the man was found stabbed, but will not release his identity until family have been informed."

David knew exactly what the pathologist's report would say but this would not be made public. He could almost see the document in his imagination.

"The medical examiner, Doctor Angela Simpson reports that the man was stabbed at the back of the

neck, severing the spinal cord and he would have died instantly. A tiny puncture in his arm indicates that a drug of some sort was administered, but no toxic report has been completed yet. There was a burn mark on the back of the victim's neck. It was in the shape of a lion rampant, three centimetres high, one centimetre wide, a copy of the shape is attached."

David thought about this. On the nights of these fictional killings, he'd been in his apartment. So either his watchers weren't watching him at all times or they would know that he could not have killed two men. His nerves were stretching to breaking point, knowing he could be killed at almost any time.

Despite his visit to the brothel in Kings Cross some days ago, David felt the suppressed longing he felt for Angela Simpson and the sadness he knew he would always feel that she was quite unattainable. Her marriage to Chief Superintendent Charles Simpson was strong, he was certain of that and he was not a man to try and change that.

He finished his coffee at the café by the El Alamein Fountain and got up. He had a personal advertisement to place in the local rag.

* * *

"David's advert appeared this morning," said Rachel to the group. "It said 'Two down' of course, as we knew it would. I've got this computer switched to that chat board and I expect to hear from Zoe at any moment."

"Okay, I think we're getting somewhere," said Hamilton. "Rachel, stay tuned to that board, but both of you, I need you to keep checking the international papers. We're getting some help that we can trust. Charlie Simpson's daughter speaks excellent German, she's coming in to search through the German-language papers."

"Charlie has an adult daughter?" asked Barrie. "I wouldn't have thought Angela was old enough!"

Hamilton laughed. "Angela's thirty-seven. And Megan is just fifteen, but she's a cracker-jack German speaker."

"Is she as gorgeous as her mother?" asked Barrie.

"Even gorgeouser!" replied Hamilton. "She'll be here soon, you can judge for yourself. In fact, she appears to have arrived."

The buzzer at the office door sounded and Bill looked at the monitor on the table. It showed a young woman standing motionless. He pressed the security button and the door opened. All eyes turned to the lobby visible through the glass wall of the conference room.

"Ye Gods," said Barrie. "You were right, Bill!"

Hamilton waved at the girl to come into the conference room. She walked in and smiled.

"Hi," she said.

She looked like a younger version of Angela with the same presence and feminine glow about her. Rachel looked round the room and grinned at the male reaction.

"Welcome, Megan," said Bill Hamilton. He introduced each of the team and she seemed perfectly composed in the face of the police officers.

"My mother's told me all about you," she finally said. Even her voice sounded like Angela's.

"Okay, so you know what we need?" Bill asked.

She nodded. "Check the German papers, look for reports of multiple killings."

"Sorry to give you such a grim task," said Jack.

"My mother tells me all about her work and I've watched her in the morgue. I'm glad I can help."

Bill pointed at a desk in the far corner.

"Use that one," he said.

Megan waved at the group and retreated to her work area.

"How much will we tell her?" asked Rachel.

"Only what we're looking for," said Hamilton. "She knows nothing about David's mission and so she does NOT sit in our conferences when we discuss progress."

"Just as well," said Rachel. "Too risky. She may be Charlie's daughter and brilliant, but she's a teenager and not really part of the human race."

"That's what Angela said. We keep her out of the loop," agreed Hamilton.

"Oh my!" Rachel had pressed a button on the keyboard and was staring at the monitor. "Gabrielle, otherwise Zoe has just posted."

"Read it," ordered Hamilton.

"Good news at this end," read Rachel. "My daughter's boyfriend has had his second short story accepted by the magazine."

"Well, shit, eh?" said Jack Savage. "So she's reported to the international game-players. No responses as yet?"

"I'll shout when I see them."

"And that means she'll be sending something by the letter drop?"

"Right, Barrie," agreed Hamilton. "The spooks in the apartment opposite will be watching.

"Okay, stay with the chat board, Rachel. Barrie, you and I will get out to the BonD.I. Golf Club and start pretending to look for a murderer."

"What's been done there?"

"Much like Centennial Park. A team left a body in the area overnight and they were back there at dawn erecting the gazebo over it, closing off the crime scene. Two golfers really did discover the body, so we have a real crime scene."

"Angela's been out there?"

"She's expecting us. Let's go."

"She's coming out," said the young man at the window of the darkened apartment. The curtains, as before were only open wide enough for the camera to point out at the apartment block across the road.

"Okay, my turn for the night time ramble, eh?" said his partner, sitting half dozing in the armchair across in the far corner. She took the earpieces from their place, put the tiny player on the table and stood up. Both of them were dressed in tracksuits and running shoes. The woman carefully opened the door and moved to the apartment front door, closing the lounge door behind her so that no light could appear in the window and alert a suspicious watcher. She walked outside and began a gentle jog in the direction of the target. Knowing the probable location, she actually ran past the second apartment block and its array of post boxes and then stopped in the deep shadows of a bush-lined driveway, turning to watch.

The woman known as Zoe did exactly as before, walked to the letter boxes and slipped a letter into one of them. This time, the watcher didn't run back, but stayed and watched. She knew that the tiny video-camera was recording the scene, but her own curiosity and compulsion kept her there. Besides, there was a Plan B this time and she wanted to trigger it.

Her intensive training and conditioning kept her perfectly still in the blackness. She half-wished she'd brought her music player with her, but knew that the distraction could be costly. Her patience was finally rewarded when a car drew up at the apartment. A woman got out, but the hidden watcher was unable to be sure of her age and appearance as the car's internal lights had been switched off. The new arrival moved to the letter box, bent down and opened it, the tiny metallic sounds audible to the watcher a few metres away. Moments later, the car moved off.

The young woman in the tracksuit spoke softly into her microphone. "Toyota Corolla, blue or black, not sure, registration is...." And she dictated the vehicle's details. "Plan B, do you think, partner?"

Back in the apartment, the other watcher chuckled. "Plan B it is, kid!" He picked up his mobile phone and made a call.

The little Corolla was barely ten minutes along its route when the flashing lights of a police cruiser lit up the entire street.

"What the hell?" muttered the woman at the Corolla's wheel, but obediently slowed to a stop and wound the window down. She watched in the rear view mirror as a police officer climbed out of the driver's seat and advanced on her.

Her attention fully taken, she didn't notice the second police officer also leave the cruiser and stand by it, motionless.

"Good evening, Miss," said the male officer. "May I see your driving licence, please?"

"Officer, I have no idea what I did wrong," said the woman. "I know I wasn't speeding."

"No Miss, you weren't, but you swerved quite sharply back there and your driving seemed a bit unsteady. Will you speak into this and count from one to ten?" He held the device by her mouth.

"What, you think I'm drunk? Officer, I haven't had a drink in three days!"

"Yes, Miss. Unfortunately, this device seems to think otherwise. So I'll ask you now to breathe into this tube."

He produced a breathalyser unit and held it before the woman's face. She let out an exclamation of anger, but put the tube to her lips and blew into it. The officer took it back, looked at it and opened the car door. "Miss, I have to take you back to the station. This reading is above legal limits and I need you to be examined further."

"This is bloody preposterous!" she shouted. "I told you, I haven't had a drink in three days!"

"Yes, Miss, you did tell me. Sadly, technology is disputing you. Please get out of the car."

Displaying a furious face, the woman climbed out and moved back with the officer to the patrol car. The woman officer opened the passenger door for her and courteously held it while she took her seat.

"I'll drive your car to the station, Miss," she said with a pleasant smile which the furious woman ignored completely.

Half an hour later, an apparently angry Doctor Angela Simpson stopped at the police station desk.

"You need to check you equipment, Sergeant! There's no sign of alcohol in this lady's blood!"

A few more minutes passed while apologies were poured out to the outraged driver who stamped out to the front door where the same woman police officer was holding the door of the Corolla open.

"Really sorry about that, Miss!" she said and received no reply. She smiled at the receding tail lights as the car vanished into the dark.

"You got the letter?" asked Detective Sergeant Jerry Bowler, coming down from the front of the station.

"No problem," said the woman officer. "It wasn't even sealed, so I got a good picture of it."

"Great!" said Jerry and took the camera from her. "Jeez, I hope we don't have to do this again! I can't stand being back in uniform!"

"It's all in a good cause," said Angela Simpson, also walking out of the police station. "So who was this latest addition to the villain's gallery?"

"Jean Murray," said Jerry. "Lives in Marrickville. I suppose we'll find out everything about her in the next few days."

"I'm sure my husband is capable of that," replied Angela with a wide smile. "You all done good, kids!" Laughing at the expression of disgust on the young woman's face, she strode off to her car parked behind the station.

"Zoe has sent a text to Curtis," said Bill Hamilton. "It said, 'AB collection, first place,' which I take to mean that payment for Andrew Bedford, our very own David has been approved and will take place at the original contact point, the pub where Zoe first met him."

"So yet again, they've seen Doctor Simpson's fake pathology report, but not the actual body," said Barrie Roche.

"I hope to God that's the case," said Jack Savage. "We'll have Curtis trailed. It'll be interesting to see if he has to go to Zoe's place to get the money to give to David, or if he has a cache somewhere."

"And what did we get from the latest member of the cast?" Rachel pointed at the sheet of paper sitting by Hamilton's notepad.

"Nothing, or I'd have told you earlier," replied Hamilton, irritation written all over his face. "The page itself was just a summary of what we already know, the number of killings already committed in the UK, Canada and the USA. Though there is a number of two for Germany, but wherever these were, they weren't reported in any newspaper that young Megan has read so far."

"And who's the woman who was carrying that?" asked Barrie.

"Her name is Jean Murray," replied Hamilton, looking at his notepad. "She's thirty-nine, divorced, no kids, no record of any sort, lives in Marrickville, works as a clerk at a pharmaceutical distributor in Chatswood. There's absolutely no evidence of any connection to Zoe or to Curtis, no links to the police force that we can find, there's nothing suspicious about her at all except that she's acting as a courier for Zoe. One of our loaned spooks followed her this morning, she posted an envelope at the Marrickville post office on her way to work, so there's no way of finding out to whom or to where."

"These people have really got their arses covered, haven't they?" said Jack Savage. "We have no way of knowing how they identify their potential killers, those killers know how to cover their tracks. That chat board way of reporting around the world is quite brilliant! How the hell would any detectives think of looking there? I mean, shit, if we hadn't accidently found Robert Worthing with a cosh, we'd be still in the total dark."

"And the problem we face all the time is that we can't reveal ourselves." The tension in Bill Hamilton showed in the croaky voice. "We can't haul any of these people in for questioning. We can't go and question other possible connections."

"Like the casino," chimed in Jack.

"Like the casino, exactly," said Bill. "The moment we do, the players know we're onto the game and they'll shut it down."

"I suppose that if that happened, we could then haul in Zoe and Curtis and beat the living crap out of them until they tell us everything." Rachel's face showed some of the same anger and frustration they were all feeling.

"Nice to think of, Rachel, no use in practice." A smile eased Hamilton's face for a second. "The evidence would be useless, even if it told us who the top guys are. They'll be well protected. When we go for them, it has to be tighter than a swan's arse."

"I suppose so. Meanwhile, David is risking his life every minute of the day," said Rachel. "All we can do is keep watching everybody every second of the time and pray they stumble at some point, just like Worthing did. Our spooks are investigating this Jean Murray woman?"

"Thoroughly," said Bill Hamilton. "I've also had a full check done on every single person who has accessed the pathology reports since Worthing's first killing."

"Anything?" asked Barrie with interest.

"Absolutely bugger all," replied Bill. "Every one of them has a legitimate right to access those files for professional reasons. Now I'll turn the spooks onto them and dig even deeper."

"Any signs of unauthorised access? A copy of a legal sign-on?"

"Nothing like that, Barrie. Let's leave it to the spooks for now."

David sat at a table in the bar in which he had first met the woman known as Zoe. The instructions in the advertisement placed in *"The Sydney Newsman"* had been quite specific. *"Charlie – collection, original spot,"* had appeared that morning and he had taken the long trip by three buses, not knowing if he was being watched, but suspecting that he was.

He had been sleeping badly, still waking in a cold sweat two or three times a night, wondering who was predator and who was prey. It all *seemed* to be going his way, but he simply was not certain. The lack of real action was debilitating. He had taken on this role as a way of seeing the game in operation, and while some insights had been gained, he was terribly frustrated by the lack of solid progress. His regular posts written on the back of the advertising leaflets dropped in his mailbox kept him up to date with what the team was doing, but he knew that the longer they kept playing this game of fictitious murders, the greater the risk to his life.

The morning dragged along as several mornings had dragged in the past. David read the paper, drank two schooners of lemon, lime and bitters, went to the washroom a couple of times, and at one o'clock, ordered a pub lunch of chicken schnitzel and chips, washing it down with a midi of beer.

As he drained the glass, a young man walked past him, placed a package by his elbow and continued walking, leaving the bar through the betting area. David's eyes followed him, but it was not anyone he had seen before. *Probably they just pay some bloke to drop the parcel off,* thought David. *The bloke will know nothing, if asked. It's all well thought out.*

He tucked the package into the inside pocket of the loose jacket he was wearing and left for home, another $10,000 richer. He decided to treat himself to a bottle of the best single-malt scotch he could find and another evening at the establishment in Kings Cross. He deserved it, he felt.

Hamilton cradled his mug of coffee as if seeking comfort from the warmth. The worry showed in his face, there were lines there that hadn't existed before the serial killings had started and the already thin hair on his head had become greyer.

"These people have covered their tracks in a way I haven't seen before," he said. "Even if we nab all the people involved so far, we won't get the players. And even if we got their names, there's not a shred of solid evidence linking them to the game."

"The spooks have reported back?" asked Rachel.

"If you can call it reporting," said Hamilton and picked up a sheet of paper.

"Jean Murray," he began. "They entered her place in Marrickville and went through it like a mother looking for porno magazines in her son's room."

He ignored the small chuckle that ran round the room. "Sod all," he said. "Not a single reference to anything or anyone connected to this business. They got into the computer, she had no protection on any files at all, nothing. Any names and addresses they found referred to people we'd expect the woman to know, people of similar status, family, banks, utilities, so on and so forth. No multi-billionaire business tycoons, so if that's who she's posting her reports to, she's kept the details in her memory. Meanwhile, every single person in her file is being checked out, so something may come up."

"People in the pathology lab?" Roche asked.

"All clean," replied Bill. "We checked their bank accounts, no unusual payments, but if anyone is getting paid for information, it's probably cash. But again, nobody seems to be displaying unusual wealth in any way, no new cars, no new houses, nothing."

"What about the people on that chat board?" asked Rachel.

"Nothing yet," replied Bill. "Charlie has asked Scotland Yard, the FBI and the Canadian Mounties to check out all those posters, some thirty-two of them. They agreed, even though for now they don't know why. It will take a while longer."

He sat back, an air of defeat all over him. "Any suggestions?"

A short silence reigned and then Jack spoke up.

"The note I got from David last night says he's utterly jacked off with the game so far. Like you, he thinks we're getting nowhere and our biggest problem is that we can't let anyone else know what we've found. He's got a suggestion."

All eyes were fixed on him.

"David says we need to up the stakes. He wants to go and visit the other groups investigating these killings, see what they know and let them into the details."

A further short silence ruled before Rachel broke it.

"Christ alive, Jack! That's putting himself right on the front line! It only needs one leak through to the players, the game is closed down and David's dead."

"That's about it, Rachel." Jack's face was expressionless.

"What did you tell him?" asked Bill.

"I said go for it, if you're okay with it."

"Do I have any choice at all?"

Jack shook his head. "We all know we're blocked, getting nowhere. And the killings go on. We have to take the risk."

Hamilton sat upright, a decision clearly made. "One more killing for David, that'll give him another ten grand for cash if it goes through. Then I'll get Charlie Simpson to make the contacts and set up the visits."

"Good. Just Manchester, Toronto and Chicago," said Jack. "Something has to come out of those."

"God help him," muttered Rachel and to everybody's astonishment, made the sign of the cross on her chest.

Chapter 17 – International Horizons

"It's good to meet you at last, David."

The voice was pleasant and echoed strongly of the same accent that had pleased David when the surgeon had spoken to him after his operation. David decided he liked Manchester and its people.

"Thank you, sir," he replied.

Detective Chief Inspector Greg Robarts snorted. "Bugger the 'sir' bit," he said. "At least when there's nobody else around."

David took a deep breath. "Then I have to tell you, Greg, I'm scared shitless. Telling you the full story of what's going on could kill me stone dead."

Robarts stared at him. "You what?"

"I'm serious. This goes to very high places and if you let it out, I'm dead and so are a few other people."

Robarts continued to stare as if trying to pierce through David's skull. David looked calmly back at the tall, well-dressed officer. "I'm serious," he repeated.

"Can you brief the team?" Robarts asked.

"Do you trust everybody?"

"I'm pretty certain."

"Then I have to take the chance. We've hit a brick wall at home."

"But you've got further than we have, David."

"Only because of a lucky break. But it hasn't got us near the main villains."

"Lucky breaks are what solve a lot of crimes," replied Robarts. "Let's go and meet the team. I need to hear this."

He led the way out of his office and to a conference room that could have been a copy of the one where David had held so many meetings with his group. The group in there could have been similar copies, men and women of varying ages and appearances, dressed in jeans and sweaters or more formal jackets and ties. David counted six detectives. He couldn't help himself and laughed. He felt very much at home.

"All right, kiddies, this is D.I. David Hunter from Sydney," said Robarts. A chorus of greetings filled the room.

"G'day, everybody," said David and stopped as a wave of laughter erupted. He realised why.

"Honest, we really do say that," he said. "And forgive my own laughter when I came in, but you lot look so like my own bunch of malcontents, misfits and failures back in Sydney."

There was more laughter and David realised that he had been accepted as one of them. It would make his job much easier.

"I'm going to tell you a terrible story," he began. "And like I've already told your DCI, giving you this information may put a stop to any more killings, but it will almost certainly result in my being killed first."

He waited while the small murmur died down.

"You've had four schoolboys killed here, all the same Modus Operandi, so absolutely the work of a single killer. The same with the one I just heard about in Wales, but a different killer. We had a series of three young men killed in Sydney, all the same MO, then four women in North Sydney and you may have heard, that last one included my sister."

There was dead silence in the room.

"Three homeless men in Melbourne were all killed in the same way and just before I left, a new series of murders of homeless men started in Sydney. In Toronto, Canada, there's a series of middle-aged men, all killed by gunshot and a similar series in Chicago. I've been told that there are similar events happening in Germany and France."

He looked round the room at each of the faces. He saw blank incomprehension in some, utter horror in others.

"Let me tell you about three other killings in Sydney, where three men have been stabbed. That series is different, because I did them."

"What?" Several voices exploded and looks of utter shock were reflected round the room.

"Well, not actually," said David. "No such murders occurred, but the police reports contain the details, including the pathology reports. All are entirely fictitious."

Now the faces reflected confusion.

"Here's the thing about all these murders," he

continued. "As you know, your four schoolboys had their noses slit. The first three in Sydney had crosses cut into the shoulders. The ones in Toronto had their ankles shot, post mortem. Those in Chicago were all shot by bullets engraved with the Islamic sign of the Crescent Moon. All of them were signatures to prove responsibility to somebody as yet unknown. But here's the thing. It's a game."

He stared around the room again. Everybody was staring at him.

"It's a game," he repeated. "Somebody is paying $10,000 for each murder, with a bonus of $50,000 for the first one to reach five. Our profiler in Sydney, a man of huge experience and a hell of a successful record, says the players are people at the very top of their professions, immensely rich and they are competing to see who can have the most people killed. In a real sense, they are playing at being serial killers one step removed because they can't actually do the killing themselves."

"Good God!" said a lone voice from a young woman standing against the side wall.

David smiled at her. "Sick, isn't it? Now the reason I said I'd killed three people is because I went undercover and those killings were created in the police computer records. It was a hell of a chance, because we didn't know and still don't, just what access to the records the main player has. But it worked and I got my ten grand for each reported killing."

"But didn't they recognise you as a copper?" asked a middle-aged man in a tweed jacket.

David shook his head. "A few months ago, I was here in Manchester having some facial surgery from a doctor who works for the spooks. I looked a bit different before that, not a lot, but enough to work. I had a complete new identity created for me by our spooks back in Australia, what they call a 'Legend.' I'm travelling here on that identity which is Andrew Bedford, and I'll remain with that identity until this horrible game is over. So no, nobody recognised me and it all appeared to work, because I'm still alive. That means the player had access to the records on the computer, but not to the pathology lab where the fictional post mortems of my victims were carried out."

"But how did you get this breakthrough?" asked the tweed jacket.

"Sheer luck. We'd had an eye-witness to a car parked by the scene of the third killing in Sydney, total fluke, an old geezer working very late in his office. He got a couple of letters of the registration plate and the make of car. We checked out every possible combination, interviewed a lot of people, alibis all checked out, but then came the golden apple we all dream of. One of our patrol cars stopped one of those possible cars we'd identified, purely because of a broken rear light, and found a cosh on the front seat. We knew a cosh had been used to subdue one of the victims, so we brought him in and I gave him a somewhat informal interview."

He didn't smile as a laugh ran round the room.

"Actually, As you've obviously gathered, I beat the goddam crap out of the bastard and he finally told me it was a game and he'd been approached to play."

All smiles faded on the faces looking at him.

"Why was he approached?" asked Robarts. He looked perfectly composed.

"That puzzled us," said David. "A little later, we discovered that he was actually a killer. He'd stabbed a kid at school while he was a juvenile. Expensive lawyering got it labelled an accident and it was all shuffled away in secret files."

"Which means your killers have access to those files," said Robarts.

David nodded. "Scary, eh? We created a similar file for me, saying I'd done something similar as a schoolboy. And they sure checked that, because when I asked to play the game, they were deeply suspicious about how I knew how to apply."

"What did you tell them?"

"That Worthing, that was his name, the first serial killer, had told me in a pub."

"Apply? What does that mean, apply?" asked another young man at the back of the room.

"Here's how it works. And it's probably the same all over the world. Potential killers get approached, which means the players have some sort of knowledge base to find likely candidates. Worthing was approached in a pub, a young bloke gave him an envelope with the message. It said if he wanted to play the game and make lots of money he should put an advert in a specific local paper saying just that he wanted to play the game, sign it with some fictional name."

"And he did?" Tweed Jacket looked amused.

"He did. As he later confessed, he was in deep shit with a local casino and that was the stimulus."

"Is the casino involved in identifying candidates?" asked the young woman at the side of the room.

"Almost certainly," David said. "But you can see our problem. If we'd investigated the casino, the players would be warned off. We badly needed to know who was running this."

"At the risk of more deaths," said the woman.

David nodded. "A dreadful situation, you will agree."

She said nothing.

"What happened after that?" asked Tweed Jacket.

"Worthing was again approached in the pub, same young man and given a package with instructions. It included a syringe and a drug that would quieten the victim while still leaving them upright and obedient. It told him to get hospital overshoes, rubber gloves, instructions about not moving the body to another space and also asked him to state what his signature mark would be."

"Is this what happened to you?" asked Robarts.

"Almost identical. I put in an advertisement without having been approached. That made them suspicious and I was approached by a woman who has been the main controller so far. I told them Worthing had given me the details. Anyway, they must have checked my fictional record and I was approved."

"And Worthing?"

"He was found dead a day later, killed with the same MO as he'd been using himself."

"Holy shit!" said Tweed Jacket.

"A definite warning," David said.

"You said he was given instructions, David," said Robarts.

"Very clear ones. The game rules are that the killer must use the same MO every time, victims to be as much alike as possible and always in the same general area. After each killing, he has to place an advert in that same paper, saying, 'One down' or 'Two down' and so on. The players then check the details, especially the signature on the corpse and then place an advert saying 'Collection' and a little later somebody drops a package by the killer with ten grand in it."

"Have any of these people been identified?" asked the young woman.

"Very definitely. We got pictures of the young man and the woman who approached me. We know who they are, we know how she gives instructions to him and we know how she's reporting to the prime player. But that's another bloody problem. If we let them know they've been sussed out, that's the game over and all we'll get is a couple of minor players."

"This local paper, what's that about?" Another young man standing by the coffee machine chimed in.

"It's got to be a paper that takes adverts dropped into the office and accepts payments by cash," said David. "So not any of the main newspapers that only take adverts by email or phone and only take credit cards for payment. Again, we, the killers were instructed never to use a credit card, for obvious reasons."

"We've got a few papers like that," said Robarts. "We'll get all the back numbers and start going through them and read them daily as well."

"There's something else," said David. "One of my team discovered how the players are updating each other. They all have assumed characters on an internet chatboard and use simple code to report how many murders they have on their scoresheet. The one in Manchester posts as 'Jackie-Q' and we've already asked Scotland Yard to trace her identity."

Robarts reached into his jacket pocket and extracted a sheet that he waved at David then opened. "Amanda Fisher," he said. "Aged 48, works as an accountant for a tax company in Manchester, lives in Victoria Park, divorced, kids left home, absolutely nothing on her record to make us suspicious. She hasn't posted anything since the fourth killing here. I *wondered* what that was about when I got this from the Yard a couple of hours ago."

"See what I mean," said David. "These people have covered their tracks so well it's going to be bloody near impossible to know who's behind it all."

"We'll follow up on the newspapers and keep an eye on the website," said Robarts. "But you're right, this is well designed. We need a lucky break like you had with Worthing." He stood up and took over the meeting.

"You will now realise the risk David has taken coming here and briefing us. If one of you is a leak to the people who are playing this game, then David's probably got a day or two to live and then may God have mercy on your soul if I ever discover who it is.

But I don't think any of you are capable of that, so simply take this; you must not, absolutely NOT let any of what you've heard today go beyond this room. If you do, it's David who pays the price. But again, if one of you does make that mistake, believe me, you'll be out of this team in seconds flat and you will never work in the Manchester Police again. Does everybody understand?"

A chorus of consent ran round the room.

"Okay, so first of all, here's what we do. Get all the back numbers of every newspaper of the type David described and go through every advertisement back to three months before the first killing. Anything that looks like the things David talked about, record the date and time and check against our four killings. If you see anything that looks like a new applicant or an indication of a killing or a payment due, document it. Now, we've had no events anywhere but this region, other than the single event in Wales, which may or may not be one of these, so for now, it may be that nobody else is planning anything. That's good, because I don't want to let any other region into this, it would only multiply the chance of the thing falling apart. I've already requested the phone tap of this Amanda Fisher, landline and mobile, we'll see who she communicates with and we'll have a minicam installed by her house to watch her movements."

"Then I'll leave you to it," said David. "We all know how often a case gets solved because of some dumbfuck mistake by the crims, so let's pray for something like that now. I'm heading to Toronto tomorrow morning for a similar meeting to this."

The room erupted as everybody got to their feet and applauded. Confused, David looked at Robarts who finally let a wide grin crease his aristocratic features.

"You've taken us a long way, David," he said. "And everybody knows what it's cost you and the risk you're taking."

"I just hope you can build on it."

"Well, at least you've given us some foundations. We were totally in the dark till you came along."

"Then I'm glad I could help," said David. "I'm going to my hotel, I'm jet-lagged to death."

"I'll get a police car to run you there."

"That'll be good," said David, feeling the blackness settling around him.

* * *

"Detective Inspector David Hunter, this is Detective Sergeant Phil Coulsen who's leading this investigation." Captain James Ball sat down again after rising to greet Hunter.

"Pleasure to meet you, Sergeant," said David.

Coulsen didn't stand up and said nothing in response. David suppressed his irritation at the American's obvious hostility.

"The Inspector is from Sydney, Australia and he has some breakthroughs in these serial killings that may help us," continued the Captain with a thoughtful look at his sergeant.

"Captain, I said this before, we're on the track of these people and we don't need no foreign cops on our turf telling us what to do," said Coulsen, not looking at David at all.

"What people are those?" asked David.

Finally, Coulsen looked at him. "Look, Inspector, whatever sort of rank that is, we know what's happening and we don't need any help from you. It's just a bunch of Islamic crazies, the same gang as did those people in Virginia and we'll find them. Why don't you just get back on a plane and go home?"

"Well, let me enlighten you," said David, struggling to keep his anger under control. "First, the killings in Virginia may well be by a gang of Islamic crazies, but they have nothing whatever to do with those killings here. These have nothing to do with Islam or religion and everything to do with money and something else. Now, we've discovered what's really going on and if you want to learn about it, I suggest you swallow that silly pride and listen, *Sergeant*. And something else. Inspector is the rank of an officer, equivalent to a Lieutenant. Got it?"

Coulsen seemed to shrink back in his seat and said nothing.

Captain Ball grinned. "I think you've just been told, Phil. So listen up and we might both learn something."

David eased the tension. "Okay, I understand, I wouldn't want cops from somewhere else telling me how to do my job. But that's not what I'm doing, it's just that we had a very lucky break in our cases and we discovered something nobody else knows."

Coulsen remained expressionless.

"There's one thing more," continued David. "And you need to know this, but I'm taking a hell of a risk in telling you."

The tension in the room rose again.

"We've had several sets of serial killings in Australia. One of them, in Sydney got to a total of four when somebody killed my elder sister in a particularly nasty fashion. I don't know if that person knew who she was, probably not, but that's when I decided to do what I did. I went undercover and with the help of our spooks in Australia and the British spooks as well, I got a new face and a new identity and I'm travelling under that identity."

The Captain nodded. "I got a phone call from your Chief Superintendent, Charles Simpson explaining that. You can imagine, this has got me puzzled."

"And it's got me frightened, because if it turns out that somebody in your group leaks this, I won't get out of here alive."

For the first time, Coulsen looked interested. "Say what?" he snapped. "What the hell are you talking about?"

David smiled at him. "You see, Sergeant, this is a lot more complex than just some crazy terrorists. This is a world-wide problem."

"Christ, David!" The Captain's face displayed great shock. "Look, we arrested a guy this morning, just two hours before you arrived. We'd been able to get the rifling marks on the bullet that killed the last one and we'd traced the gun."

"You've got him here?" David slapped the Captain's desk with enthusiasm. "Well, bugger me sideway! That's exactly the sort of break that we had in Sydney. Has he said anything?"

"Not a peep, but he's obviously scared shitless. Do you want to see him?"

"Damn right I do, Captain. I'll bet the mortgage he'll tell us a hell of a lot once I'm done with him."

The Captain looked anxious. "Not planning on violence, are you?"

"No sir, but I have to tell you, that's what broke the case in Australia. I don't need to do it again."

"Just as well," said the Captain with a small smile and picked up the phone, pressed two buttons and spoke after a brief wait. "Larry, get Ronald Samuels to the interview room will you, and call the defender in." He replaced the phone, got to his feet and the other two followed. "So Phil, I want you two to go and interview this man. He's got a public defender standing by. Phil, you can start, but when David wants to take over, you let him, okay? I'll be watching from outside."

"One thing before we start, Captain,' said David. "Does this bloke have a record?"

"Bloke? What's a bloke?"

"Sorry, sir, Aussie slang."

"No, he doesn't," replied the Captain, not suppressing a grin.

"Here's a tip. Somehow go to the sealed records, get a court order if you need to, but I'll bet you that somewhere, there's a record that this character killed somebody in his youth, probably labelled an accident, but it wasn't."

Looking startled, the Captain nodded. *"Bloke!"* he muttered. "I like it!"

Coulsen didn't look happy about the order he'd received, but he led the way out of the office. The trio walked down the corridor, down a flight of steps and stood outside a large window of one-way glass. They waited a few moments until the door into the room opened and a uniformed officer guided in a young man dressed in ordinary jeans and a black sweater, his hands cuffed in front of him. The officer sat the man down at the interview table and retreated to the back of the room just as the door opened again and this time a middle-aged man wearing a blue suit walked in.

"Ronald," said the man. "I'm Nathan Plansky, I'm your public defender." He didn't offer to shake hands but sat down alongside the prisoner. "Now," he continued, "I must remind you that you don't have to say anything if you don't want to, but telling the truth is really your only option. Were you given your rights when you were arrested?"

Samuels nodded but said nothing. The fear in his face was obvious even through the window.

"Okay guys, showtime," said the Captain.

Coulsen turned and walked round to the doorway, followed by David and they entered the interview room. The lawyer didn't get up, but nodded as the detectives took seats across from them.

Coulsen switched on the recorder. "The date is November the eighth, 2011 and present in the room are Ronald Samuels, public defender Nathan Plansky, Detective Inspector David Hunter of Sydney, Australia and I am Detective Sergeant Phillip Coulsen. The time is 2:45pm. Mr Samuels, do you understand why you're here?"

Samuels looked at the table top and said nothing. The lawyer stared curiously at David, but also remained silent.

"Do you wish to say anything, Mr Samuels?" asked Coulsen.

"My client will reserve the right to silence unless he chooses otherwise under certain circumstances of his own choosing," said Plansky.

"Understood," said Coulsen. "Ronald, when you were arrested, you had in your possession a Heckler & Koch nine millimetre automatic pistol, is that correct?"

"My client concedes that," replied the lawyer.

"As a resident of Wilmette, are you aware that such a possession is unlawful in this Village?"

"My client claims that such a local by-law contravenes the Second Amendment and as such, his ownership is quite legal."

"That will be left to the court to decide at a later date. More important is the fact that the pistol still held seven bullets, each of which was carved with the insignia of the Crescent Moon. Can you explain those bullets, Ronald?"

The sergeant waited a few seconds. "For the benefit of the tape, Mr Samuels is not replying. Now, Ronald, identical bullets have been extracted from the bodies of three men in recent weeks. They all have the same rifling marks which identify them as having been fired by your weapon. Can you explain that?"

Again receiving no reply, Coulsen carefully took Samuels through the dates and times of the previous killings and asked him for his whereabouts, but each time, received no response. Finally, he turned to David, his tight features indicating irritation.

"Do you have any questions, Inspector Hunter?"

"I do," replied David but was interrupted by the lawyer.

"Sergeant Coulsen, what is an Australian police officer doing here?"

"Inspector Hunter is following up on similar events in other countries," replied Coulsen formally.

"Then I protest and demand that he not be present. There is no connection between the events for which you are interviewing my client and anything outside of the State of Illinois."

"Your protest is noted for the record as is your demand, which is denied. Inspector, please proceed."

David smiled to himself and decided he might get to like the sergeant after all.

"So, Ronald," he said pleasantly. "How much have you been paid for each killing? Is it ten grand, like it is back in Australia?"

The reactions were explosive. Samuels sat back in his chair in terror, his jaw dropped and he gasped loudly. The other two looked stunned.

"This is a disgrace," the lawyer finally shouted. "Sergeant, I demand, absolutely demand this interview stops! This is quite illegal. This man is trying to provoke my client."

David ignored all of them but stared at the man opposite who was starting to shiver.

"How was it done, Ronald?" he asked. "Somebody approached you in a bar and gave you a note saying if you wanted to make a lot of easy money, put an advert in some local paper saying you wanted to play the game?"

The room was deathly silent. Coulsen and the lawyer were staring at him, Samuels looked about to burst into tears, utter terror reflecting in his features.

"So you placed the advertisement in what, a tiny local paper that has an office where you can do it, cash on the nail, and nobody notices you, right? And you got instructions about how to avoid detection and you must leave a signature. Then you place an advert, saying "One down," yes? And then you get ten thousand. Am I right, Ronald?"

Samuels was breathing like an asthmatic, harsh, rasping breaths. The lawyer looked anxiously at him.

"Officers, I think we need a break and a doctor to examine Mr Samuels."

"I agree," said Coulter and David nodded his own agreement.

"Interview suspended at 3:17pm," said the sergeant and switched off the recorder. "There's a local doctor we use," he said. "He'll be here in a few minutes, but we'll take Ronald back to the holding cell."

The silent police officer who had been standing against the wall moved up and took Samuels' arm, leading him quickly out of the room.

"Mr Plansky," said David. "I need to caution you. You must not breathe a word of this interview to anybody, not your boss, not the District Attorney, *nobody,* because you'll be risking several lives if you do. Do you understand?"

The lawyer was white-faced, but he nodded. "I'll leave you until you're ready again," he whispered, clearly showing stress, and he walked out of the room. He was replaced by Captain Ball who took a seat at the table and both Americans stared at David.

"Holy crap!" said the Captain. "This is a global fucking *game?*"

"Is the intercom to outside still on?" asked David. "I don't want anybody to hear this."

The sergeant touched a button on the recorder. "It's off now. Sir, I must apologise. I had no idea about any of this."

"No need. Believe me, this tested the brains and sanity of my group when we discovered all this. Yes, it's a game. The killers get ten grand a death with a fifty grand bonus for the first person to reach five."

"And who the hell is playing it?" asked the sergeant.

"That we don't know. A very old friend and colleague of mine, the best profiler I've ever known has drawn up a picture, though. Jack said these are the very top achievers, industrialists, bankers, lawyers, god knows what, but top people in their field. Jack says that such people tend to be a bit psychopathic anyway and they run their professional lives as if they were killing people. So they destroy competition when they can, really ruthless bastards. If they hadn't made it big professionally, usually by having a wealthy start in life anyway, some of them probably would have genuinely become serial killers.

So now they're doing the killing for real, but one step removed, but the game is to see how many people they can have killed."

"And so this is why you went undercover?" asked the Captain. "You wanted to get into the game? How the hell did you do that?"

"Like I said, before all this, I got a whole new identity in England. New face, new name, new history, new passport, everything. Once I was ready, I went back to Australia, put in the advert, they responded, suspicious as hell because normally they make the first approach and invite you to play the game. But I survived, because as part of my fake history, there was a record of a killing I did as a youngster. Somehow, they were able to get to those closed records."

"And then what?" asked the sergeant.

"Once I'd been accepted for the game, my people documented three fictitious murders for me to claim," said David.

"Christ, how could you be sure they'd swallow it?" asked Coulsen. "Couldn't they have seen those records were fictitious?"

"It's what buggered my sleep patterns," said David. "I never knew whether they were playing me like a hooked fish or whether I was playing them. But I got paid for all three murders, so it looks like I was the fisherman, after all."

"So what the hell happens now?" asked the sergeant.

"I'd say the game's over," said David. "There's no way you can release this Ronald Samuels the way we released our guy. He'd be dead in days, once the players realise he's been pulled in. Did you get any data from the FBI about a character posting on an internet chatboard?"

"Yes, we did, but I had no idea what that was about."

"He or she is the local controller."

"It's a she, somebody called Marion Fitzwilliam, lives in Winnetka, nothing suspicious about her at all."

"Pull her in, Captain. She's the one who does the recruiting of killers and organises them. That chatboard is how she reports to the other controllers on progress."

"Jesus Christ, David!" The Captain picked up the phone. "Larry, get a patrol car out to that Winnetka address I gave you yesterday and bring in Marion Fitzwilliam. Tell her we need her to help us with our inquiries, don't arrest her unless she plays hard to get." He put the phone down. "And this is going on all over the world?"

"Canada, Britain, Germany, Australia and here," replied David. "Possibly France and Germany also."

They were interrupted as a young man stuck his head in the door.

"Jim, I've given him a sedative, it'll calm him down. You should be able to talk to him in about ten minutes."

"Thanks, doc. Does the attorney know?"

"He's with him. Looks like he needs a dose of the same stuff. What the hell did you do to those guys?"

"Can't tell you, doc, not yet."

"Okay!" The doctor closed the door.

"So how do these players select their killer?" asked the Captain.

"Still a key part of the puzzle," David replied. "There was nothing that could have identified our bloke, Robert Worthing as a killer, except for that highly secret fact that he'd killed a kid when he was young."

"And when they've identified one, what happens then?"

Quickly, David took the two Americans through the processes, his experiences of placing the advert, being approached by several young men who were clearly messengers and the interview with the woman identified as Zoe Moreland. He told them how he was obviously followed at times and how he received three packages of $10,000 after his fictitious murders had somehow been verified.

"So they never saw any corpse?" asked Coulsen.

"That's the crucial part," said David. "Believe me, I was bloody terrified after the first murder was announced. If the players had realised then this was a put-up job, they'd have known I was undercover and I'd have been dead within hours. When that Zoe Moreland woman talked to me, I'd told her that Worthing had given me the details of how to apply. He was dead in a day, killed with the same MO he'd used for his three murders."

"Christ on a crutch!" said Coulsen.

"Let's have the man in again," said the Captain and picked up the phone.

The police cruiser drew up outside the pleasant

two-storey house in the wealthy village of Winnetka, north of Chicago.

"Any idea why we're bringing in this woman?" said the officer in the passenger seat. He was in his early twenties and found his job exciting beyond measure.

The older officer at the wheel was fairly placid. "No idea," he said. "The Captain says bring her in, we bring her in. Don't force the issue unless she plays hard to get, he said. Let's go."

They climbed out and put their caps on. The younger man walked to the front door and rang the bell. The senior man waited by the front gate, carefully looking around. Some bad experiences had fine-tuned his sense of danger.

No answer came to the bell ringing and the officer applied the door knocker with some enthusiasm but with equal lack of success.

"I don't think she's in, Steve," he called down to his partner.

Steve advanced up the drive and headed round to the rear of the house.

"I know she's there," called a woman's voice.

Steve looked to his right to see a young woman standing by the back door of the next house.

"I was just talking to her about twenty minutes ago," she said. "And somebody just called round, I saw the car stop and a man went in through the front door."

"Thank you, ma'am," said the officer. He moved round to the rear of the house and peered in through the kitchen window.

"Oh shit!" he said and reached for his radio.

The phone on the desk rang and Captain Ball picked it up. He listened quietly, and David watched as his face tightened in anger. The Captain put down the phone.

"My guys went to Winnetka to bring in this Fitzwilliam woman. They just found her body in the kitchen, bullet between the eyes."

David felt cold and began to shiver. "I think I need to send some emails," he said. "The other investigators have to know this and they'll try and get to the local controllers before the players do."

"My office," said the Captain, stood up and led David back to his office and gave him the seat before the computer screen. He leaned over David as he logged into the system and switched to the internet. "All yours," he said. "Come back to the interview room when you're done."

David nodded and went to his email system.

Twenty minutes later, he returned to the interview room, still feeling shaky. The suspect, Ronald Samuels was back at the table, his attorney sitting next to him, looking anxious. Captain Ball had stayed at his seat, the sergeant had taken another one at the side of the table. David took the third chair opposite the prisoner.

"For the benefit of the tape, the interview has started again at 4:53pm," said the Captain. "Present are the same people as before, plus Captain James Ball."

David looked with interest at the two men opposite him. Samuels had his face fixed firmly on the table and had slumped, looking hopeless. It niggled at David's mind until he remembered where he had seen this before. Robert Worthing had looked like this after all the life and bravado had been knocked out of him. Samuels had given up.

But the lawyer was more interesting. He looked severely disturbed, his face had lost colour and he appeared badly frightened. David's mind, attuned by months of worrying about the problem and the fear of just how powerful were the forces he was tackling, clicked into high gear.

"Captain Ball," he said. "When was Mr Samuels arrested?"

The Captain looked at him for a few seconds before replying. "At 9:15 am today."

"And when did you first hear about the possible connection of the serial killings with Marion Fitzwilliam?"

"Inspector Hunter," said Ball, some anger showing in his face. "This is not a subject for discussion here."

David was watching the attorney and saw the shock in his face. "Bare with me, Captain, please. When did you hear about Marion Fitzwilliam?"

"Yesterday morning," replied the Captain. "You will be explaining this, I hope Inspector?"

"So if anyone knew about the arrest of Samuels, they'd have wanted Marion out of the way immediately, correct?"

"Yes, Inspector, they would." The Captain had obviously realised something was happening for his anger had been replaced by interest.

"But somebody called at her house just minutes

after you ordered her to be picked up. Just minutes after we had taken a break for Mr Samuels to receive medical attention, which left his attorney free for a while."

Both Americans turned their attention to the attorney who now looked terrified. There was a cold silence for a few moments before the Captain broke it.

"Mr Plansky, how did you get assigned to this case?"

Plansky swallowed nervously. "We're on a roster as well you know. It was just my turn."

The Captain nodded at Sergeant Coulsen. "Check that, will you, Phil?"

The sergeant picked up the phone, referred to a printed guide by the side of it and dialled three digits. He didn't have long to wait.

"Hi, Alice," he said. "Would you have a look at your roster for public defenders for today? Who was scheduled to be here?"

A few seconds silence passed. "Thanks, Alice," said Coulsen and replaced the phone. "We were supposed to have Jim Gilson and Erika Nordstrom here today. Apparently Mr Plansky called the office at 9:30 and said he'd be at the precinct here anyway, so he'd handle the Samuels case."

"I'd like to see your cell phone, Mr Plansky," said the captain, holding out his hand.

"No way," said the attorney, standing up. "I'm leaving."

The Captain looked briefly at the police officer who had been standing silently throughout the interview. He moved forward and placed his hand on the attorney's shoulder, gently pressuring him to sit down again.

"Mr Plansky, I'm detaining you on suspicion of involvement in the killings in this region. The formal arrest will come a little later and I'll read all your rights and all that stuff, but for now, consider yourself a suspect. Now, hand over your cell phone."

The Captain again held out his hand and this time the attorney reached into his pocket and placed it on the desk top. David watched the move and saw the drops of sweat on the table where the man's hands had touched. The Captain opened the phone and found his way to the record of calls placed.

"Phil, what time did we end the first stage of the interview?"

"3:17, sir."

"Okay, note these numbers, Phil. At 3:22, he dialled a number in his memory listed as "AB." And that number is..." He switched to the phone's directory and read out the digits. "Then he called.... Ah, okay, that's the public defender's office two minutes later. Just those two, it seems. So find out who that AB person is."

Coulsen stood up and left the room.

The Captain looked at the attorney. "Unless you want to tell us yourself, Mr. Plansky?"

The lawyer shook his head, now looking as hopeless and frightened as his client.

"Maybe you don't know just what happened as a result of your call, Mr Plansky," said David. "Assuming that the AB person is the key player in this business, he or she reacted rapidly. Marion

Fitzwilliam is dead, shot just minutes after you told your contact that she'd been identified and the rules of the game uncovered."

Plansky looked like he'd been punched in the gut, his mouth opening and closing as he gasped for air. Next to him, Samuels lifted his head and focused his eyes on David. There was nothing but resignation in his expression.

"They told us that if we followed their instructions, we'd never be found out," he muttered.

"They were stringing you along," David said. "There was always an excellent chance you'd be caught, but they didn't care. They just wanted gullible killers to play their game for them."

The Captain took charge again. "Ronald, we're going to have somebody come and take your statement and then you can sign it and we'll get another public defender to come and work with you. So just sit there and we'll leave you alone in a few minutes. You, Mr Plansky, you're going to be taken to a cell after one of my officers has read you your rights and let you make a phone call." He nodded at the officer at the back of the room and stood up. "Let's get back to my office, David," he said and led the way out of the room.

Back in his office, he sat down heavily behind his desk and waved at David to take the seat opposite.

"Jesus tapdancing Christ, David! Does this sort of stuff happen everywhere you go?"

"Not bloody likely!" David laughed and wondered if there was touch of hysteria in his voice. "In Manchester, they were certainly gobsmacked when I told them everything, same in Toronto, but you're the ones who had a real live suspect freshly arrested."

The Captain waved to somebody outside the open door and Phil Coulsen walked in, taking the second seat at the Captain's desk.

"There've been three phone calls for you, sir," he said to David. "Your office in Sydney, the police in Manchester, England and the Toronto Police. They all said much the same, they've got the women in custody and under protection. And your guy in Sydney said he's advised the cops in France and Germany to do the same."

"Thank god for that," said David. "It took a lot longer for the word to get out to the other players, it seems."

"It should give you the break," said the Captain. "They must surely know who the players are."

"I hope so, but those bastards have put so many barriers in the way, I won't believe it till I see it."

"And that phone number, Phil? Any luck?"

"Arthur Berriman," said the sergeant.

"Shit!" said the Captain.

"That's what I thought," replied the sergeant.

David raised an eyebrow. "And he is...?"

"One of the most powerful men in the country," said the Captain. "Personal friend of the Governor, power broker in State and Federal politics, industrial tycoon, worth several billions."

"And therefore untouchable?"

"Most would believe so."

"How about you?"

The Captain smiled. "Why don't we go and see? Want to come along?"

"Try stopping me!"

All three men stood up. "Phil," said the Captain. "We'll take a police cruiser. And we'll take a second one. Get four SWAT men in the other and tell them to stay close."

"You think we could have trouble?" asked David.

"You've seen more than most just how these people behave. Let's take no chances."

The ride was very short. Arthur Berriman lived just a few miles further up the shoreline of Lake Michigan. The police vehicle, driven by Sergeant Coulsen and closely followed by a second vehicle, stopped at the gates of a sizeable estate.

"Police," said Coulsen to the grille on a post by the drive. "Captain James Ball to see Mr Berriman."

"I'm afraid Mr Berriman is unable to see any police officers," said the voice on the intercom. "Please make an appointment."

"This *is* the appointment," said Coulsen. "We can come in now by car or we can come in by helicopter in half an hour. Your call."

The silence lasted a minute before the gates swung open without further discussion.

The Captain smiled. "This could be interesting," he murmured.

The two vehicles proceeded slowly along the driveway which curved through perfect lawns and ended at a parade-square sized area before the pillars of the mansion.

"How the other one percent lives, eh, Phil?" the Captain said and climbed out, followed by the other two. He gestured at the second vehicle and the SWAT team members got out. They were dressed in full protective clothing with helmets and visors covering their faces. Each of them carried a heavy automatic rifle. They spread out to the edge of the area before the house and stood motionless.

A man was standing at the entrance to the mansion. He was quite young, looked very fit and David's expert eye saw the beautifully cut suit hung well, despite the shoulder holster under the man's left side. He looked at the armed men, then at the Captain.

"Come with me, please sir," he said and turned and led the way inside. The hall in which they found themselves was enormous, big enough to contain a medium-sized house and leave room to spare. White statues of Greek and Roman style lined the sides with fern trees and assorted plants placed at intervals on the black and white tiled floor.

"Evidence that great wealth doesn't bring great taste," muttered the Captain.

"Early Queen Victoria Mausoleum," replied David and the Captain chuckled.

They were led to a doorway and the guide opened the door and stood back to allow the officers inside. They entered to find a large study, walls lined with bookshelves, a huge desk on one side with a luxurious leather executive chair behind it. Four armchairs sat around a circular coffee table and in one of them sat a man. He didn't rise as the officers came in. He was dressed in black trousers and a yellow golf shirt. His hair was white and David estimated he was a good six foot tall, probably in his late fifties.

"Good evening, gentlemen," he said in a pleasant, baritone voice. "Now that you've bullied your way in here, please explain why you are interrupting my business."

"Good evening, sir," said the Captain and took the armchair across from Berriman who seemed annoyed at the liberty. David nodded at Coulsen and they took the other two seats, receiving an irritated glare from Berriman.

"I'm sorry we had to be pushy about this, but homicide cases take precedence over courtesies."

"Homicide, Captain? What on earth would I have to do with a homicide case?"

"That's what we've come to find out, sir. This afternoon, a woman called Marion Fitzwilliam of Winnetka was shot in her house."

"And so?" Berriman looked uninterested.

"Shortly before she was shot, an attorney in our offices made a call to this house."

"Captain, I imagine many attorneys call this house during the day. My many business and political connections make that inevitable."

"Yes, sir, I'm sure they do. But this attorney is a public defender, not a top corporate lawyer, and he was defending a man suspected of three murders. He had just learned that we knew about Fitzwilliam and her involvement in those murders."

"Again, officer, what does all this have to do with me?"

"Why would a public defender working with a serial killer call this house?"

"Really, captain, you're wasting my time. It's time you left."

David caught the swift look the Captain gave him.

"So how are you doing in the game, Mr Berriman?" he asked.

Berriman didn't look at him. "Who is this man, Captain?"

"Didn't I introduce him, sir? So sorry. This is Inspector David Hunter of the New South Wales Police Force Homicide Squad. He's investigating a whole series of killings."

"So why is he asking about some game?"

"Because you're playing a global one," said David, amused at the way Berriman was trying to ignore him. "It's very competitive and quite a lot of people are dead now as a result."

"Captain, you're wasting my time with this nonsense. It's time you left and took your foreign guest with you."

"Of course, Mr Berriman," said David, "you must know that you're well behind in the game. You've only got three, your opponent in Australia has at least seven so far, probably more by now."

Berriman finally turned to stare at David. "My understanding, Inspector, is that you have in fact resigned from the police force and left to go travelling. You are no longer a police officer."

David felt a small current of excitement at this serious error by the American.

"Really, sir?" he said. "Now just why would that be

your understanding? What possible reasons could you have for knowing the events of a police station in Sydney or my status with the Police Force?"

For a moment, David saw a look of quite frightening hatred on Berriman's face.

"Most of your competitors seem to have scored about three, the same as you," David continued. "Though like I just said, the one in Sydney had seven, the last I heard, though he could be over ten. So you're a bit behind, aren't you? I bet you don't like that and you're not used to it."

Berriman seemed to regain control of himself and sat back in his armchair.

"My Australian colleague asked an interesting and crucial question, Mr Berriman," said the Captain. "Just why would you be familiar with the events of a homicide investigation in Sydney and the history of one detective there?"

"Captain, you do realise that I could pick up the phone and your career would be over in minutes?" Berriman seemed relaxed again.

"Yes sir, I do realise that. But I'll probably retire soon, anyway and I'm financially independent, so to be honest, that prospect doesn't bother me much. But you, on the other hand are facing something horrible. As the word of this game of yours gets out all over the world, and the hints are delicately dropped about your involvement, it could get quite embarrassing, especially as you aren't even the winner. As Inspector Hunter has pointed out, your three killings don't match the seven in Sydney or similar numbers elsewhere. You're a loser, Mr Berriman!"

That pressed the button with Berriman. His lips drew back and he literally snarled, something David had never seen anyone do before.

"Here's the thing, mate," David said, no longer caring about courtesies. "The cops in the UK, Canada, Australia and Germany, we're all onto your sick little game. Now I admit we've got some stuff still to find out, like how you select your killers and hell, we don't even know who the other players, your competitors are and we can't yet pin it onto you. But I have to tell you, it doesn't matter how powerful you are and what connections you have, the spooks in all those countries really don't like shit like this going down and they're not always so concerned about legal niceties, like proof, and courts and trials and stuff. And if you think your political connections will save you, forget it. Politicians can't afford to have themselves connected in any way with mass murders. It's really bad for their image."

Berriman wasn't looking at him, but David was watching closely and the American was sitting rigid, staring into space.

"Well, I think that's a good point at which to leave Mr Berriman to his quiet evening," said Captain Ball and stood up. "Let's go, guys."

They walked out of the room, across the giant hall and Coulsen opened the large doors to the outside. As they reached the bottom of the steps, the leader of the SWAT team came up to them.

"Anything, Frank?" asked the Captain.

"There was a man on the roof with a rifle," replied the armed man. "And we saw two more moving in the trees, both carrying weapons."

"Good thing I brought you along, then," said Ball cheerfully. "We might have lost David by now, otherwise."

With a chilly feeling on his back, David thought the Captain was quite correct.

"In the car before one of those idiots make a mistake," said Ball and David gratefully climbed into the police cruiser. They were well away from the house before the SWAT team left their positions and also drove away.

"What now, David?" asked the Captain as they pulled onto the main road.

"Time for me to go home, I think," said David. "There's work to be done."

Chapter 18 – Coming in From the Cold

"David! What the hell are you doing calling me? We agreed!"

"Oh shit Jack, my cover's blown anyway. You can bet your life somebody in Manchester learnt about my visit and told whoever is behind their killings. Same with Toronto and Chicago. Anyway, I went with the Chicago Captain to visit their perp. That was entertaining, I assure you!"

"You went to see... Holy crap, David, what have you been up to? Who was it?"

"A bloated American plutocrat, exactly as you forecast. Anyway, there's no point in my being out here anymore. I'm coming in."

"The gang will be delighted to see you."

"If they recognise me!"

Jack laughed. "They've already seen pictures. It shouldn't be too much of a shock!"

"See for yourself tomorrow," said David and disconnected.

* * *

"The game won't stop now," said Jack Savage.

"Explain why," said David. He sat at the conference table with the rest of the group. It was his first day back and the others were still looking curiously at him as they tried to get accustomed to the face that was a lot like their old boss's but not quite.

"These people see themselves as the Masters of the Universe," said Jack. "They've been at the top of their hills for many years now and they got there by destroying anyone who got in their way and stayed there the same way. Now they have powerful connections as well, in many cases, they *are* the power connections, the source of political, business and social power for maybe the whole country."

"So they see themselves as immune?" asked Bill Hamilton.

Jack nodded. "Exactly, Bill. They believe themselves like the Gods on Mount Olympus. The rest of us are mere mortals, we do not even have the right to *question* their actions, never mind try and make them accountable. And even if they're found out, they know very well that they can control enough of the system to make sure there'll be no prosecutions that touch them. The junior cast of characters, they don't care a shit about them."

"So you think this Berriman guy I met in the US, even though he knows that we know he's the player, he'll carry on?" David looked angry, sensing what Jack's answer would be.

"Count on it," said Jack. "You've probably even challenged him to kill more people. He'll recruit another controller, he or she will find more killers, there'll be more bodies found soon. And anyway, he hasn't won yet, you told him he was behind on the scoring and he *cannot* stand for that."

"But that means it will go on and on," said Rachel. "None of them will give in because every one of them wants to be ahead."

"There'll be a time limit," said Jack. "Because it's a game, so they'll have set rules. Some of them we know about, the MO, the rewards, and so on, so there'll be a time limit as well."

"But we can't just sit here and watch the bodies pile up!" said Rachel, considerable distress in her face.

"And just how deep is that pile?" asked David. "I've been out of real communication for a while.

"Deep," said Hamilton. "We had the three by our guy, Worthing. The four in North Sydney hasn't changed. The Melbourne total is five, the other Sydney series of homeless men has risen to three. Two in Perth. The group in Toronto reported they were up to five, Manchester's had no more but there's been an outbreak of four in Birmingham. Angela's daughter, Megan found four likely serial killings in Germany, around Bonn and six in Stuttgart. Barrie found three likely different sets of killing in France. And another German paper has reported something similar going on in Moscow."

"Christ!" said David. "It's like the Black Death. And despite all our progress, even knowing one of the players, Jack reckons we haven't even slowed it down, never mind stopped it. Is there any good news at all?"

"We got the killer of that woman in Alexandria," said Bill. "Turns out she'd started dating a bloke through an internet service. He wasn't what he said he was and when she tried to dump him, he shot her."

"Jesus," muttered David. "Okay, one success, a hell of a lot of mysteries remaining. So as Rachel asked, what the hell do we do?"

"Come at it from the other side," replied Jack. "It looks like that bloke Berriman was exactly the profile we'd worked out. Let's get down to working out anyone else we can identify with those same characteristics. Then we can start chasing up the connections."

"Okay, but first, what about those women that were taken into custody around the world as controllers?" David asked. "What's happened to ours?"

"We've picked up all three players so far," replied Hamilton. "We collected Zoe Moreland at her house. When we told her that her opposite number in Chicago had been shot dead, she literally begged us to take her into custody for her safety. The same with Colin Curtis, the bloke who does the legwork. And we also took in that second woman, Jean Murray who passed on the messages from Zoe."

"Well, she must surely know where's she's mailing them?" said David.

"These people are careful," said Bill Hamilton. "All she had was a post office box number. We checked that out and it had already been closed down. The original booking had been made with cash. There's just no record of who might have opened it in the first place and nobody has any recollection of seeing somebody go to the box. It's a dead end, David."

"Where was the box?" asked David.

"North Sydney."

"Good choice," said David with a nod. "Very busy, no chance of anyone being spotted. So has the Moreland woman said anything?"

"Nothing," said Jack. "She's scared shitless, so I think she must know who's behind all this."

"Okay, I'll interview her this afternoon. Jack, can you run us through as detailed a profile now as you can?"

"No worries," said Jack and stood up to refill his coffee mug. "Now, let's start with the standard profile of the serial killer. We've covered this before, but it's worth repeating."

His mug filled, he returned to the conference table. "So far, the killings have been close representation of a standard serial killer. One of the best studies done in the USA says that eighty-eight percent of serial killers are male, mostly in their twenties or thirties. Some eighty-five percent are Caucasian, that is, white European. They mostly kill strangers and over seventy percent of the killings are in a specific, quite small area."

"That last part fits all our killings in Australia," said Hamilton. "They've all been very localised."

"Same with the others in the UK and North America," said David. "And our two killers identified so far have certainly fit that profile."

"And the rest," continued Jack. "That whole signature thing, the cut cross, the cut off ear lobes, all those post-mortem marks, those are standard features of a serial killer."

"So it sounds like the game players knew all this, or at least the one who made up the game," said Rachel. "Or could they have drawn up the rules without realising they were following a profile?"

"An excellent question," said Jack with a nod at her. "And I don't know the answer. It could be either. But the sort of person who'd behind all this is almost certain to have done their research, so I suspect they designed the game around that profile, probably as their own way of laughing at the investigating cops."

He sipped his coffee thoughtfully for a moment. "Anyway," he finally continued. "One of the most common characteristics is a seriously dysfunctional family background. Usually, it's sexual or physical abuse, drugs, alcoholism, severely overbearing and authoritarian parents with little or no capacity for affection. The result is often disorganised thinking, bipolar problems, huge resentment towards society, sexual problems and all those ugly things. It commonly leads to intensive day-dreaming, compulsive masturbation and isolation."

"But we're looking for people at the very top of their professions," said Hamilton. "Can people like that come from those backgrounds?"

"Most certainly," said Jack. "Nothing in that background prevents very high intelligence. And that intelligence will let the person develop highly sophisticated day-dreams, which could involve killing those who have hurt him, plus complex and quite workable plans for those killings. Not a big step from developing those sorts of plans to business strategies and tactics for destroying the competition. And the main reason for that compulsion is to prove to their parents, usually the father, that they really can succeed beyond the level the father achieved. If not the father, then society in general, or both.”

“But you said something about disorganised thinking?” said David.

“Sometimes, not always,” replied Jack. “The serial killer will be intensely focused in many ways and equally driven to prove their point. These characteristics are really quite useful if somebody wants to get to the top of their particular tree. They usually see themselves as dominant, controlling, powerful persons and many become exactly that. They need to hold the power of life and death and if they don’t have that in their professions, they certainly hold the power of success or failure over corporations or organisations and also of individuals. So they perceive themselves as God.”

“It sounds like the line between becoming a serial killer and a Master of the Universe is very fine indeed,” said Barrie Roche, his first words of the meeting.

“Probably depending on the life the person had a child,” said Jack with a nod of agreement. “I think that the Master of the Universe type would have come from the high socio-economic strata and who would have been able to subjugate his drives into business or law or something equally competitive. The killers tend to be from low socio-economic origins.”

“So can we summarise just what we’re looking for?” asked David.

“Let’s start with looking for the top of the tree in

business, politics, law," said Jack. "Identify those who have reputations for absolute ruthlessness, those with the really domineering management style, feared rather than respected by those who know them. If you can find those, try and get into their histories, find out if their childhoods were anything like I described."

"We'll still have a problem with proof," said Rachel. "These bastards have put some high walls around them."

"And as I saw with Berriman in the States, even if we find them, they believe they're immune," added David.

"Almost certainly," agreed Jack. "But that may be their downfall. They think they're God, so they can't be touched. They might get careless or even let something drop deliberately to boast of their genius and invulnerability."

"All right, then we need to get to work identifying these possible players," said David.

"David, remember that you're at horrible risk," said Jack. "They know who you are, what you look like, where you live. They know you fooled them and took thirty thousand dollars from them and they know that you've let loose the dogs on them all over the world. You've killed their game and they'll want you dead."

"I'm not hiding," said David. "I've got to play a part in the hunt. So now I'm off to talk to this Moreland woman."

"Are you armed, David?" asked Hamilton.

David nodded and patted his shoulder holster. "Always," he said and walked out of the office.

The interview room was the same one in which David had first encountered Robert Worthing and given him the beating that provided the breakthrough in the serial killings.

He sat silently as he waited for Zoe Moreland to be brought in from where she was being held in protective custody. The door opened and a police woman walked in, followed by Moreland and a second woman officer. Moreland was not handcuffed and she wore her normal clothing, not a prison garb. She didn't look at him as the officer led her to the seat then walked out of the room, leaving the other one to stand silently against the wall.

"Are they treating you well, Zoe?"

Finally she looked at him. "Don't I know you?" she said.

"You should. Last time we met, you admitted me into the great game of murder."

Her eyes opened wide and she brought her hands to her mouth. "Oh my God! You're Andrew Bedford! What...?" Her voice tailed off as understanding came to her.

"Detective Inspector David Hunter."

"Oh my God," she whispered again, the shock robbing her of any strength.

"Thank you for the thirty thousand dollars, but I have to tell you, I got the money under false pretences. I didn't kill anyone."

Her face was white and David could see the trembling in her hands.

"Then how...?" She seemed to be struggling for breath.

"False post mortem records in the computer," David said. "Some excellent scene-setting at the sites of the murder and a few spare bodies used for colour. You all fell for it."

She stared at him, her face looking a lot older than when she came in.

"Then it wasn't Robert Worthing who told you?"

"Indeed it was, but in this room, after I'd beaten the living shit out of him. We'd got him for carrying a cosh, the bloody idiot, and we'd had an eye witness to his car at one of the murder scenes. He broke fairly quickly and told us everything."

She stayed silent, but tears appeared in her eyes.

"Okay, Zoe, time to clean this up. Who's behind it?"

"I don't know."

"Bullshit! How did you get involved? Where does the money come from to pay the killers? Who gives you your orders?"

She shook her head, saying nothing, but the tears were now rolling down her cheeks.

"We learned a lot about all this while I was undercover," David continued. "But what we still want to know is how you selected the killers. Any ideas, Zoe?"

She shook her head again. David began to feel frustrated.

"We also learned that while you could access restricted police computer records, like the one they implanted about Andrew Bedford killing a kid when he was fifteen, you couldn't actually get into the post mortem laboratory and see real bodies. So, once more Zoe, who's the chief player in this game?"

She hid her head in her hands and burst into tears.

"Zoe, let's get straight on this. You will be charged with aiding and abetting at least four murders, those committed by Robert Worthing and then the murder of Worthing himself. If we connect you to the other killings around Sydney, which we certainly will, that all gets added and you'll never see the light of day again. You'll die in prison, Zoe. Nothing's going to save you, so you might as well let us have it all."

The woman opposite seemed not to hear him. She had curled up, her arms round her knees and her face in her lap. David sighed and looked at the police woman by the wall. She shook her head. He was not going to get anything further from Zoe Moreland.

"Okay, take her out of here," David said. "We'll keep her in the cells here rather than put her in the Detention Centre so we can keep an eye on her and I'll talk to her again later."

He watched while the other woman officer entered the room and the two women led Zoe back to where she was being held.

"Shit!" said Detective Inspector David Hunter.

Chapter 19 – Closing in on the Prey

That evening, he got another break.

"David," said the voice on his telephone. "Rod Hathaway. I've got fantastic news."

"Rod! I need some good news. What have you got?"

"We've had a lucky break. Unfortunately, it had to come from another killing in North Sydney, same MO as the rest, woman in her forties, same profile as the others." Detective Inspector Hathaway paused. "Sorry, David, but much like your sister."

"No worries, Rod. Go on."

"And this time, the killer made a mistake. We got some DNA material from under the victim's fingernails. We ran it through the system and we got a hit!"

"Good God!" David's heart leaped. "Who is it?"

"A bloke called Jeremy Wood. He did time for GBH a few years ago, clean since, but of course we had his DNA on file."

"Rod, that's bloody fantastic. Can I get over there and see this bastard?"

"Not tonight, mate, we're all knackered over here, we've been hunting this piece of shit for three days and we just got him. Get here at eight, eh?"

"Eight it is, Rod. Shit, mate, you've certainly improved my day."

"No worries, David. Always good to help out a mate!"

Hathaway's chuckle was still echoing as David replaced the phone.

He got very little sleep that night.

The drive over the Harbour Bridge was slow and David was beating on the steering wheel in frustration on the approaches to the Bridge before things speeded up in the two lanes heading north. On his right, the majority of lanes were set for southbound traffic into the City and they were just as slow.

"Sometimes I hate this bloody place," muttered David as he turned off the express way onto the Pacific Highway into North Sydney and found the police station.

"D.I. Hathaway asks for you to go to his office, sir," said the desk sergeant and David walked briskly along the corridor, knowing exactly where to find his friend.

"G'day, mate!" said Hathaway with a broad grin as David entered. He stood up and the two men shook hands.

"Bloody well done, Rod," David said and took a seat.

"Well, we all know how it works, don't we?" replied Hathaway. "Ninety percent of police work is pure grinding detail slog, but sometimes we get a lucky break when the perp does something immensely stupid, like not wearing gloves when he's killing somebody."

"Or carrying a bloodstained cosh in the car," said David in full agreement.

"Here's the file on this Wood bloke," said Hathaway, handing over a manila folder. "All copies for you, so keep the file."

"Great." David opened the file and began reading.

"Coffee?" asked Hathaway, rising to his feet.

"Please," said David, already absorbed in the sheets before him.

Jeremy Wood was twenty-eight, a labourer, lived in a rooming house in Chatswood. He had served four years in prison for Grievous Bodily Harm after attacking a man in a pub for some perceived offence and had been released two years ago. Before that, there was series of petty thefts, some drunk and disorderly arrests without being jailed, the usual litany of miserable behaviour patterns. David had lost count of the number of similar histories he had read.

The report by the prison psychiatrist was not particularly illuminating. Wood had a recorded IQ of 95. "Some tendencies to sociopathic qualities," wrote the psychiatrist. "But these are not severe and do not constitute a threat to others in my opinion." The doctor's signature was not easy to read, but the document held the printed name. Simone Whitelaw, said the report.

Hathaway re-entered with two mugs of coffee. "Jeez, you can't even get somebody to get an Inspector a coffee, these days," he said in mock complaint and put the mugs on the desk. He nodded at the file. "Anything useful there?"

"Not really," said David. "Just your common or garden dimwitted thug. It's hard to know how or why he was selected to be approached by the players. Have you interrogated him yet?"

"Couldn't get a lawyer from Legal Aid till now," said Hathaway. "So no, we haven't."

"Okay, something that may help." David reached into his breast pocket and brought out an envelope from which he extracted two pictures. "This one is Zoe Moreland," he said. "She was the controller for the killings in Surry Hills and almost certainly those here in North Sydney too. The other one is Colin Curtis, the kid that did the running around, made contacts, paid the money over."

"Thanks," said Hathaway. "I'll confront him with these at some point, see if he recognises them."

"So can I watch?"

"Sure, of course. But I can't let you do the interview, David."

"I understand, it's your case."

"No, I just don't want you beating the living crap out of this one," replied Hathaway with a broad grin. "His lawyer's here now and I can't get her out of the way for you to do your unique interviewing style."

David laughed. "But you have to admit, I got results!"

Hathaway got to his feet. "You did, but I reckon it's a good thing he's dead or your career would be in the crapper. Let's go and talk to the bastard."

* * *

Wood was nothing exceptional to look at. About 180 centimetres, slight build but looking very fit in blue jeans and a black tee-shirt that fitted tightly against a muscular chest and flat stomach. He had light brown hair, sported no facial hair, no tattoos, no jewelry and little expression. He looked up with disinterest as Hathaway entered the room.

The lawyer sitting next to Wood was a young woman, David estimated she was in her late twenties. Her name was Jocelyn Babcock, he'd been told as he took his position outside the observation window and she had been assigned by the Legal Aid Commission. She looked neat, attractive, dressed in a dark blue trouser suit and a white shirt open at the neck. A tall police officer stood against the far wall.

Something started to nibble at David's mind. He ignored it and concentrated on the scene in front of him.

Hathaway took his seat at the table opposite the other two and switched on the recorder.

"The time is nine fifteen am on Tuesday, the thirteenth of December, 2011 and this interview is taking place at the North Sydney Police Station at 273, Pacific Highway, North Sydney. Present are Detective Inspector Rodney Hathaway, Senior Constable Kenneth Green, Legal Aid lawyer Jocelyn Babcock and the defendant, Jeremy Wood who has been informed of his rights."

He leaned forward and placed his elbows on the table. "Jeremy, last night you were charged with the murder of Catherine Hall, aged forty. Anything you want to say?"

Wood sat motionless, staring at the table.

"You were arrested because under the fingernails of the deceased were traces of human skin where she scratched her attacker. The DNA we obtained from those traces match the DNA records that we have on you from your time in prison."

Wood moved his left hand and covered up the scratches on his right. Both Hathaway and the young woman watched the move.

"Yes, those scratches," said Hathaway. "That evidence is enough to put you back behind bars for many years, but the fact is, you also killed four other women of very similar appearance with exactly the same *Modus Operandi*. That's enough for a real life sentence. You'll come out of prison in a coffin."

"Please stick to this case and don't go fishing, Detective Inspector," said the young lawyer. She had a clear, musical voice. Hathaway grinned at her.

"No problems, Miss Babcock. Now, Jeremy, let's get back to this one as your lawyer said. Did you get your ten thousand dollars, or has your contact not appeared yet?"

Wood jerked as if hit with an electric prod. Finally, he looked up and stared at Hathaway.

"Ah, pressed a button, did we?" said Hathaway. "You see, we know all about the game, Jeremy. We know how you were approached and invited to kill people at ten thousand dollars a pop. We know how you placed an advert in the little paper in Newtown, what your signature was, cutting off the earlobes after you'd killed them, how you placed more adverts saying "One down," or "Two down," and all the rest. And we know that with this fifth killing, you were in line to get the fifty thousand dollar bonus. Sadly, you won't get that, nor the ten grand for that fifth killing."

Hathaway looked at the lawyer. Her expression was one of utter horror as she stared at Wood.

"You didn't know about that, did you Miss Babcock? I'm sorry to have to deal you that hideous card, but we couldn't reveal this information before."

The young woman took a deep breath. "Are you charging my client with those murders?"

"Not yet, no."

"Then I repeat what I said before. Stop fishing. Stick with this case."

"I believe I am, Miss Babcock." He turned back to the man. "Jeremy, anything you want to say about those other four murders?"

Even from the other side of the observation window, David could see the man's hands shaking. The irritating presence in his mind was starting to bite harder. *What the hell's the matter?* he thought.

"She said we'd be okay," Wood mumbled. "Nobody would catch us."

There was a moment of silence in the room before the lawyer broke it. "Jeremy, I advise you to say no more!"

Wood seemed not to hear her. "She said if we followed instructions, we'd be okay."

The lawyer was about to speak, but Hathaway got in first.

"I believe your client is speaking voluntarily, Miss

Babcock. I suggest you let him. Now, Jeremy, when you say 'she,' do you mean this woman?"

He slid the photograph of Zoe Moreland across the table. "For the record," he said, "I am showing Mr Wood a picture of Zoe Moreland."

Wood looked at the picture for a few seconds. "That's her," he muttered.

Hathaway looked sideways at the window, though not able to see David and grinned before turning back to Wood.

"And were you first approached by a man to sound you out about earning easy money?"

"Yes."

"This man?" Hathaway slid a picture of Colin Curtis across the table. Wood barely glanced at it.

"Yeah," he said.

"For the record, I have shown Mr Wood a picture of Colin Curtis. Let's get back to you, Jeremy. This man, Curtis, did he tell you to place an advert in the paper, saying, 'I want to play the game,' which you did?"

The grilling continued, but David was distracted by a call on his mobile phone.

"Hunter," he said.

"David, it's Jack. Zoe Moreland was found this morning in her cell. She'd been shot. We're all back in the station."

A cold, ugly sensation slid down his body and into his gut. "I'll be right over," said David and folded away the mobile phone. But despite the shock and rage at this new event, the persistent niggle in his mind refused to go away. *Something in the file he'd been reading...*

"How the hell did this happen?" demanded Superintendent Charlie Simpson. His rage could be felt through the room like the heat of an open wood fire, but it was not a friendly warmth. He had been summoned from a staff meeting in the City and was clearly furious after facing rush hour traffic for so long, even with a police escort clearing the way as much as possible.

"Either one of our cops did it, or somebody let in the killer," said Bill Hamilton.

"I don't like either answer," snapped Simpson.

"It's not popular with anybody here," said Jack Savage. "But it's all we've got. Nobody can get through to the cells without a pass key."

Simpson glared at him. "Has my wife examined the body?"

"She has, sir," David replied, attracting Simpson's furious glare away from Jack. "A nine-millimetre bullet through the back and into the heart, death would have been instantaneous. The shooter fired through the hatchway when Moreland was sleeping, curled up with her back to the door. The blankets hid the blood and there wasn't much anyway, because she died immediately."

"What time did it happen?"

"Some time between midnight and two," replied Hamilton.

"During the night shift, then." Simpson had calmed down and become his normal, thoroughly professional self. "You've got the list of all officers who were here?"

"We do, boss," said David. "We'll get onto it at once. They've all been called in."

"Grill them," said Simpson. "Like a bloody steak. Burn them, if necessary."

He walked out the room.

"You heard what the man said," said David. "Jack and I will do the interviews. Bill, Rachel, Barrie, you watch them like a snake watching a mouse. Any twitch, anything at all, note it. Somebody must have let a killer in here."

The group headed for the interview room.

The desk sergeant was the first. He looked unwell, bleary-eyed and distressed.

"What's going on, sir?" he asked as he was led into the interview room. "I'd been asleep for just about an hour when I got hauled out of bed and back to the station."

"Nobody has told you anything?" David Hunter didn't feel like being his usual easy-going self. Somebody had murdered a prime witness in his own station and he was furious.

"No sir," replied the sergeant.

"Right. Sergeant, tell me exactly what your movements were during your shift."

"I logged on at seven pm, sir. That's in the log. I was at the desk right through till midnight when I took a half hour meal break, and that's in the log also."

Watching carefully, David could see that the

sergeant was intensely irritated by this process, but was displaying no fear at all. This was not the culprit, he was pretty certain.

"On your break, who was in charge of the desk?"

"Senior Constable Patrick Wilson, sir."

"Did anyone come into the station at any time during that first session?"

"Nobody."

"And after the meal break?"

"I returned and relieved Patrick for his own break. I stayed at the desk from then through till seven a.m. which is the end of my shift."

"Any breaks away from the desk?"

"Yes, sir. Ten minutes for a coffee at 2:30, once for a toilet visit. I logged that, but I can't tell you the exact time now, sir."

"Did you leave the desk empty in those times?"

"No, sir, I did not." The sergeant was clearly annoyed at the question. "Patrick again replaced me for the coffee break and I asked WPC Beryl Austin to take over while I went to the washroom."

"A probationary police constable?"

"It was just a few minutes, sir."

"Still against the rules. Consider yourself disciplined. Okay, Alan, go home and go back to bed."

"Sir, what's happened?"

"Zoe Moreland was shot dead in her cell during the night."

"Good God!"

David was sure now. This man had nothing to do with the crime. The shock was extreme and genuine.

"Go home, Alan."

Without a further word, the sergeant walked out.

"It's not him," said Jack.

"I agree. Guys, what about you?"

The other three watching through the glass had heard the entire conversation through the speakers.

"He's clear," said Bill Hamilton.

"Okay. One of you get Patrick Wilson, will you?" Something from the morning's visit to North Sydney was still chewing at his mind but he had to concentrate on these interviews.

The tall, skinny frame of Senior Constable Patrick Wilson entered the room and looked with uncertainty at the two seated men, unsure if he could sit down.

David gestured at the seat on the other side of the table. "Sit down, Wilson," he said.

With obvious relief, the younger man did so.

"Take me through your schedule last night," said David.

"I came on at seven, sir," said Wilson. "I did an immediate check of the cells, but we only had three people in there, so that only took five minutes."

"Were they all awake then?"

"The woman, Zoe Wilson was, she was reading. The other two blokes, they were in for drunk and disorderly from an incident that evening, they looked out cold."

"And your next cell check?"

"Midnight, sir. All three were asleep at that time."

"And then?"

"I replaced the desk sergeant at one and when he came back half an hour later, I had my own meal break for thirty minutes. I was doing paperwork till about half past two, I had some arrest reports to check and file, then the sergeant called me to take over the desk again."

"And you did?"

"Yes, sir. For about twenty minutes."

"Twenty minutes? You're sure?"

"Er, yes sir."

David went to full alert. The sergeant had said it was ten minutes and there was something in the constable's tone that indicated something wrong. He glanced quickly at Jack Savage and saw a tiny shake of the head.

"After you were relieved by the sergeant again, then what?" David continued.

"All paperwork except for the scheduled cell checks at three and four."

"And all was normal?"

"Yes, sir. The two blokes were obviously restless, but the woman was quite deeply asleep. She was curled up, facing the wall, not moving."

"Let's get back to that twenty minute period at the desk, Wilson. Are you absolutely sure you were there the whole time?"

He was sure about it now, Wilson was distressed. "Wilson, some time last night, Zoe Moreland was shot dead in her cell. When you checked her at four, she was probably dead. Somebody came in and killed her. Now, about that twenty minutes?"

Wilson's face had gone white. "Sir...." He began.

David waited.

"Sir, it was only supposed to be ten minutes, but Sergeant Barker said he was ill and was puking up. I'd promised I'd call my girlfriend during that time, she's a nurse on the nightshift at Paddington General, so I asked Beryl Austin to take over so I could make the call. She gets very upset if I don't call her during her break."

"So you left a probationary woman constable alone at the desk for ten minutes?"

"Actually sir, it was nearer fifteen minutes."

"Wilson, you're a fool. There's a reprimand going on your record, that was a bloody stupid thing to do. Now go home and go to bed."

He waited until Wilson had left.

"It's the woman, Jack."

"No shit, Sherlock," replied Jack. "Now we have to find out how they got to her."

It didn't take long. As soon as the young police woman came in, it was clear to David that she was terrified. David gestured to her to take a seat then went in with all guns blazing.

"I don't know how good a copper you are, Austin, but you're a lousy actress. You're scared shitless and I know why. So start at the beginning and let's have the whole story."

Her face was the colour of wood ashes, David thought, watching her seem to shrink in her chair then burst into tears. He gestured at the watchers outside to bring in a mug of tea for the girl and waited while she calmed down. He said nothing until Rachel entered and placed the mug on the table and then again gestured for her to take the seat next to the young woman.

Rachel understood and began stroking Austin's shoulder to calm her further. "Take your time," she murmured gently. "But we need to know exactly what happened last night."

The police woman sniffed loudly a few times and took a sip of tea.

"Somebody came into the station last night, Austin," said David. "It looks very likely it was while you were on the desk for some fifteen minutes. Is that right?"

She nodded. "I got..." her voice choked and she took out a handkerchief and blew her nose. "I got a call during the evening before I came on shift. A woman, she said she was with the Public Prosecutor's people and someone needed to talk to Zoe Moreland. She said it had to be done then, because people were out to silence Zoe, so secrecy was essential. She said it would only take a moment."

"And then what?"

"While I was on the desk, a bloke walked in. He showed me his card, it was clearly an ID for the Office of the Director of Public Prosecutions, I've seen them before, lots of times."

"Can you describe him?" asked David.

"Quite short, about fifty, black hair, big ears that stuck out a bit. Long upper lip, he was sweating a bit. Brown suit, it didn't fit well, as if he'd put on weight recently and he had a double chin and quite a paunch. His shirt was white, his tie was some horrible green and yellow, tied in a terrible knot instead of a Double Windsor and he had the cuffs buttoned, no cuff links."

Despite the situation, David grinned. "That was a hell of a good description. If you survive this, consider the detective division once you're up to Senior Constable. So, what happened?"

"He came in, said his name was Harold Murchison."

"Is that what it said on his ID?"

"He flashed that too quickly for me to read. He said he needed just a moment with Zoe Moreland. I took him through to the cells and unlocked the gate."

"Did you stay with him while he was in there?"

"No sir, I had to get back to the desk."

"Was he carrying anything?"

"A briefcase, sir."

When you got the call earlier, was that to your mobile phone?"

"Yes, sir."

The girl seemed calmer now and spoke confidently.

David reached out a hand and the girl opened her handbag and extracted her phone. David opened it, checked the "Calls Received" section.

"What time was the call?" he asked.

"About eight."

There was a call listed at three minutes before eight. David noted down the number and handed it to Rachel. She knew what to do and left immediately.

"That bloke left soon after?" he asked Austin.

"Just a few minutes. It seemed awfully quick for a conversation. Did Moreland say anything about it?" She lifted the mug to her lips and sipped at the tea.

'Constable Austin, that man you allowed in was

carrying a gun, obviously an automatic pistol with a silencer. Zoe Moreland is dead."

There was a crash as the mug fell to the floor. Beryl Austin stared in utter horror at David and seemed catatonic.

"Constable Austin, you've been a bloody fool and this will go on your record. But a lot better officers than you have been fooled by these people. We'll work out what to do with you later, but right now, go home, go to bed and stay at home. You're suspended until further notice."

He waited while the young woman raised herself from her seat like a cripple and walked out unsteadily.

"Poor kid," said Jack. "She'll make a good cop one day. I hope you give her the chance."

David got no chance to reply as Rachel returned.

"It's a woman called Simone Whitelaw," she announced.

"Whitelaw? Holy shit! That's the prison psychiatrist!" David thumped the desk in glee. "I saw her name on the release certificate for the other killer."

"So now we know how they're finding their killers," said Jack.

And just then, David realised what had been eating at his memory since the morning. The memory rose up in his mind of another sheet of paper from the files of all the events since he'd left for the UK and gone undercover.

"Whitelaw! God damn, Zoe Moreland was a Whitelaw before marriage! Those two are related!"

"Well, bugger me sideways!" said Jack Savage. "It all falls into place!"

But David didn't hear him. He had the phone jammed to his ear. "Get a car to the prison immediately. And call the prison, tell them to hold Simone Whitelaw, the psychiatrist until the car gets there. Find her home address and get a car there, too. Whichever car finds her, arrest her and bring her in."

He put the phone down. He thought for just a second then picked it up again.

"Get me the Office of the Director of Public Prosecutions," he snapped. He waited a few seconds. "This is Detective Inspector David Hunter," he said. "I have a description of somebody who may work there. Put me in contact with somebody who can help me."

He waited for a few moments and grinned at Jack. "Bloody marvellous people there," he said cheerfully. "Dead clever, seriously motivated and there's one group that specialises in prosecuting VIPs and people like that. I reckon we'll have a real juicy case for them in little while. Hey, Lorrie? You're in Human Resources? This is David Hunter of the Sydney Homicide Squad. Look, we've got a description of somebody who may work in your place."

He read his notes from the woman officer's description of the night time visitor. "Is that anybody there?"

He listened a moment, then gave a thumbs up to Jack. "That's Hugh Ireland? Lorrie, you're a sweetie. I'll be round there in about five minutes. Keep it quiet, but please let Old Grumpy know."

Jack laughed at hearing the nickname of the popular Director of Public Prosecutions.

"Let's go," said David.

But before he could leave, the phone rang. He pushed the loudspeaker button and the voice of the desk sergeant came up.

"Sir, the prison reports that Miss Whitelaw is not at work today. She should be, she has therapy sessions scheduled."

David felt a sinking sensation in his stomach. "And her home?"

"No report so far, sir."

"Okay, get me on my mobile as soon as you hear. And have a car for me as soon as I get downstairs."

He replaced the phone and the two men raced out.

"It's a bloody barrister in ODPP Chambers," David said as they went down the elevator. "His name's Hugh Ireland. Christ alive, a bloody *barrister* shooting people in prison!"

"It all goes to confirm what we already know," said Jack. "Whoever's playing this game is very high up, very rich, very well connected and very powerful. We're on dangerous ground here, young David and I have to think we're both at risk of becoming a bit dead."

"You think?"

"These people see themselves as gods. We're throwing stones at them. I expect they'll want to do to us what they did to Zoe Moreland."

"Goes with the territory, Jack. But you've done what we asked you, old man. We're nearly home. If you want to head back to the farm, it's fine with me."

"No way, kid. This job has turned you crazy. You need me to look after you."

David slapped Jack on his shoulder. "Let's get another of the little people then," he said. "But this one may be a bit higher up the slopes of Mount Olympus than the others."

The ride to the building housing the office of the Director of Public Prosecutions was only a few minutes from the office suite in Taylor Square. David and Jack jumped out and were followed by one of the uniformed officers. The elevator took them up several floors and the three men advanced on the reception desk.

"Hugh Ireland, please," said David, displaying his warrant card. The receptionist displayed no surprise. Police officers were a common visitor to the Director of Public Prosecutions and his departments. She picked up the phone and dialled, but after a few moments said, "He's not answering his phone, Inspector. Hang on, I'll try his secretary." After a few seconds, she spoke again. "Wendy, is Hugh there? He's not answering his phone." She replaced the phone, looking puzzled.

"He's not been in today," she said. "He should be, he's got several briefs he's working on."

The two men looked at each other.

"He's done a runner," said Jack.

"No doubt." David pulled his phone out and punched the digits. "Bill, get the hunt going for Hugh Ireland. See the description... you've got it, well done. He must have flown out early today, all domestic and international… yeah, you know the routine. Thanks, Bill."

He looked down at the astonished face of the receptionist. "Tell Old Grumpy that Ireland has gone permanently and needs replacing. And tell him also that they'd better review all of Ireland's cases. They could be unsafe. I'll call him later and explain."

Jack had already pressed the call button as soon as David had started his phone call and the elevator arrived in time for the two men to leave without further explanation.

"Shit!" said David in the privacy of the elevator.

"Probably," said Jack.

His phone rang and David answered. As he listened to the voice of the sergeant at the other end, he experienced that same cold horror he'd felt when told of the news of Zoe Moreland's death earlier in the day. He closed the phone.

"Simone Whitelaw's dead. Shot with a nine millimetre pistol, probably during the night."

Jack showed no emotion. "To be expected," he said calmly. "The gods are angry with us."

"Shit!" said David.

"That too," replied Jack.

Chapter 20 – Spotting the Enemy

"So it was Simone Whitelaw who identified potential killers and passed them onto her sister, and she organised the recruitment?"

Charlie Simpson looked outraged.

"That was the procedure, boss," David replied.

The entire group had returned to their regular location and were back in the familiar conference room. The coffee machine bubbled and a number of the regular crew sat around, some carrying mugs, others drinking from water bottles.

"But *why?*" exploded Simpson. "Why the hell did these two women connive at so many murders? And was Whitelaw feeding names to the rest of the country?"

David had never seen such distress in his Superintendent's face and body before.

"That we can't answer yet," Jack Savage replied. "The crews are searching both those women's houses right now, hopefully we'll find something that tells us more. We may even get some pointers to whoever has been organising this. And we've sent an inquiry to the

Melbourne prison authorities, asking them for a quiet check on their psychiatrists, seeing if any of them might be suspect."

"Christ, let's hope we get something," Simpson replied. "So what's the next step?"

"We're still trying to find out who leaked the faked reports of the pathologist's reviews of those murders David is supposed to have committed," said Rachel.

"Any luck?" asked David.

Rachel shook her head. "I'd say it's a dead end, boss," she said. "Whoever it was is fairly low on the totem pole, probably got just a few hundred dollars each time, cash only and there's no way of finding out."

"And there's a good chance they had no idea why they were doing it," added Jack.

"Then let's leave it," said Simpson. "We've got bigger animals to trap. What's next, David?"

"Jack laid out the precise profiles we should be looking for," David said. "And all these very bright boys and girls in this room have been busily searching for every top dog in the country who might fit it." He smileded at the burst of laughter and applause than ran round the room. He was delighted at how much the department's spirits had risen on his return and the discovery that he had not left the Police Force after all.

He gestured at Barrie Roche. "Barrie has been a particularly clever little boy," he said. "He developed a measuring system. Barrie, tell us what you did."

Barrie Roche stood up somewhat self-consciously. "Quite simple, really," he began and smiled at the laughter that ran round the room. "Jack had listed a number of characteristics that would indicate the sort of bloke we're looking for."

"Only blokes?" interrupted the Superintendent.

"No sir," replied Barrie. "Once we had the measuring scale, we'd apply it to everybody who seemed to fit."

Simpson nodded and waved at Barrie to continue.

"So things like overbearing, tyrannical parents, lonely childhoods, they're all critical factors, but we began with the business profiles, people renowned for being ruthless, aggressive executives, people with little empathy for others, reputations for severely sharp business or professional practices. With those, I set up a scale of one to ten, with ten being the worst. Then we set everybody to researching every top dog in the country and applying that scoring system, rating each character we identified. Then, if you multiply the rating by the score and add up the totals, the higher the score, the more likely the individual is to be who we're looking for."

"Not hugely scientific," said Jack Savage, "but a clever way of identifying the first round of suspects. Barrie, that was a beaut job you did there."

"And what did you come up with?" asked Simpson.

"Twenty seven names," replied Roche. "Every one of them is considered to be a real bastard, in one form or another. So that's when we got onto the hard part, researching their families, their histories, school days and so on and applying the same scale of one to ten to each of those personality factors that Jack's identified."

"How the hell did you get those details?" asked Simpson. "I can't imagine it was easy."

"Actually, sir, you made it quite simple," said David with a laugh.

"I did? How the hell did I do that?"

"The spooks. You'd set up the contacts initially, so we asked them. You'd be amazed at how much they know about these people. Our guy in Canberra said it was essential to know them inside out because of the influence they have on the government."

"Good grief!" said the Superintendent. "I would never have thought of that. And what did you get?"

"Five names stand out from the rest," said Barrie. "They all scored high on every one of the factors Jack identified."

"Let's have them," said Simpson.

"Okay," said Barrie. "Starting at number five, Janet Hawthorne. She's the CEO of a chain of hardware stores all over Australia, New Zealand and South Africa and she's starting to branch out into South East Asia."

"A woman!" exclaimed Simpson.

"A woman," agreed Barrie. "And considered to be a grade-A, five star, first class horrible bitch by everybody who knows her, but a top-notch business brain."

"Married?" asked Simpson

"Four times," said Barrie. "Four divorces, leaving wrecked, shattered, destroyed men behind her each time."

"So what's new?" asked an unidentified male voice and the laughter took a moment to subside.

"Number four, Gerald Hornsby," continued Roche. "President and owner of several chemical plants around the country. Has a Ph.D. in Chemistry and insists on being called *Doctor* Hornsby."

"Definitely the sign of a high grade wanker," said Jack Savage. "Seriously, kiddies," he continued into the laughter, "anyone other than a medical doctor who calls themselves Doctor something is a wanker and highly suspect in my professional opinion."

"Aren't you a doctor?" asked the young sergeant Jamie Patterson, hiding his grin.

"I've got a doctorate, yes," said Jack. "Two of the bloody things, if you must know, but if anyone tries calling me Doctor Savage, I'll cut their balls off."

The room descended into wild laughter and David realised there was touch of hysteria in the merriment. He decided it was most likely the sense of progress that the group had made and shown the rest of the world just how well they had worked, as well as the relief at seeing him back with them.

He let the noise run for a few moments, thinking this was a good way to let off steam then raised his arms for silence. He nodded at Barrie.

"Three," said Barrie. "James Elmore Cartwright, Senior Counsel, defends only the biggest corporations against charges of fraud or whatever, feared by everybody in his Chambers, as well as the State's judges, believed to follow some highly unsavoury practices in getting evidence against his opposition, up to and including blackmail, but nobody has ever had the courage to come up with statements. He's stinking rich, worth several hundred million, but the rumour is that he's got much more in illegal offshore accounts and assets."

Much shaking of heads around the room. David didn't think he'd heard of Cartwright, either.

"He keeps a low profile," said Barrie, noting the blank looks.

"Probably a good survival strategy," said Rachel and received murmurs of agreement.

"Two," said Barrie. "Wong Li Chang, adopted name Peter, originally from Hong Kong, lived in Australia since 1972, owns and runs a massive haulage firm, a shipping company, several other operations and has major holdings in a number of areas. Little known, keeps a low profile, but considered a nasty among nasties, probably a member of one of the big Tongs, those Chinese crime rings. Rumoured to have had people killed when they get in his way, an absolute bastard to work for, but pays so well, people will put up with the shit he throws at them."

"Christ, but we have some turds walking around the place," muttered Rachel. "Thank God I didn't go into business like my father wanted. I'd hate to have to work with people like this."

David smiled at her. "And lastly, Barrie, who do you have for us as our King Shit?" He knew the details on Barrie's list, but he wanted Barrie to have his turn in the limelight.

"You're going to love this," said Barrie. "None other than the bastard who has been flinging crap at us seven-twenty-four in the newspapers and on television for many months now, but the lovely and talented Mr Alan Kinsella."

Silence rang loud in the room. Every single one of the detectives present had suffered from the abuse Kinsella had thrown heavily and for so long at this department.

In the silence, a tap came on the door and a woman constable walked in, carrying a folder. She walked up to Charlie Simpson and handed it to him and just as quietly, walked out again. With the whole room in a state of shock at hearing Kinsella named as the prime suspect in the hideous crime spree of recent months, all eyes focused on Simpson. He read a single sheet and studied a picture and got up. He walked over to David and handed him the papers.

David studied them as the silence got deeper and tension in the room rose. Somehow, everybody knew that those two pieces of paper were to do with this case.

Finally, David looked up. "This is a report of the search of Simone Whitelaw's house. There was evidence that the woman's family was connected with one of the names Barrie has just listed and there's a picture here of her family at a university graduation ceremony when Whitelaw got her medical degree, with the man who apparently supported her through her studies."

David took a deep breath to control his own sense of shock.

"It's Alan Kinsella."

His words fell on silence. David looked round the room and saw varying degrees of shock on his group's faces. It lasted only a few seconds before cheers and yells broke out in the room.

David and Jack looked at each.

"Well, bugger me sideways!" said Jack. "We've got the bastard!"

"Not yet," said David. "Now we have to get past his army of defenders. How about we go and talk to him?"

"What a splendid idea," said Jack.

* * *

"This is Detective Inspector David Hunter of the New South Wales Police. I wish to interview Mr Kinsella and I will be at his home within half an hour."

There was a moment's silence from the male speaker at the other end of the line.

"I'm afraid Mr Kinsella is not at home, sir."

"What is your name?" asked David. "And who are you?"

"My name is Dennis Kershaw. I'm one of Mr Taylor's private secretaries."

David could hear a sudden note of nervousness in the man's voice.

"Dennis, I've already checked with the television offices and they assure me that your boss is at home, because they have already talked to him there. So here's your choice. You can let your boss know we're coming and I'll be really nice about things. Or we can arrive with a warrant to inspect the premises and if necessary, force our way in with a shitload of noise and broken gates and stuff like that, and when we do, you'll be arrested for obstructing a police inquiry. Your choice, Dennis. What do want to do?"

David struggled to avoid laughing at the expression on Jack's face.

"I'll let Mr Kinsella know you're coming, sir," said the thin, tense voice in David's ear.

"Good call, Dennis," replied David and put the phone down. He beckoned at Bill Hamilton who grinned with delight.

"Let's go," said David and the three men headed out of the door.

"Very imposing," said Bill Hamilton as the car stopped at the high gates to the Kinsella property in Point Piper in the Eastern Suburbs, one of the richest locations in Australia.

"We're being watched," said Jack, pointing at the camera that was focused on the car.

"What a way to live," said David and pressed the button on the wall by the gates.

Nobody spoke through the grille, but the gates swung open silently.

"We seem to be expected," said Jack and smiled broadly.

"Not the warmest of welcomes, I expect," said David and drove through the gates. The ride to the front door was short, perhaps fifty metres, most unlike the lengthy ride along the curving road to the house of the American business tycoon, Berriman.

The house was less imposing too, but the value of this place was in the startling views across Sydney Harbour that David could see from the side as he pulled up. The location was high up on the hillside and from just the few seconds that David stood to breathe in the sea air, he saw that the view extended from the Harbour Bride and the Opera House all the way round to the Heads, the entrance to the Harbour from the ocean.

"Nice pad," said Jack with an approving nod. "I think I'd rather be home at my place, though."

They hadn't knocked, but the large front door opened and a young man stood there.

"Detective Inspector Hunter?" he asked, uncertainly eyeing both men.

"Me," said David, producing his badge. "This is Jack Savage."

"Mr Kinsella is on the back deck," said the man. He moved inside to allow David and Jack to enter then closed the door behind them. David was carefully watching him and could see the anxiety in the man's face and body stance.

They walked through a lobby that to David's eyes had been decorated by the same person who had done Berriman's house. What was it about the mega-rich, he wondered, that led them to fill their house with tiled lobbies, large ferns and Greek statues? He resolved to ask Jack later.

They walked out onto an enormous deck that gave full justice to the beautiful view of the Harbour. It was perhaps twenty metres long, David estimated and ten metres deep, no railings but a glass front to avoid spoiling the view when seated.

Alan Kinsella was seated, not in a wheelchair as he was normally seen, but in an upright seat. His upper frame looked thin but strong, though his shoulders were narrow. He wore a golf shirt and a sweater. His legs were covered by a blanket despite the warm day. David knew that Kinsella was fifty years old, but the man before him looked a lot older than that. His face was devoid of any flesh, heavily lined and the mouth was set in a permanent expression of disapproval, the thin lips turned down at the ends in a set groove. He did not look like a man who enjoyed his wealth.

"You threatened me with a search warrant, possibly even a violent entry, Hunter," he said. "You cannot be attached to your job." The voice was the strong baritone that David had heard on the television and the anger was evident.

"Oddly enough, your colleague and competition in the States, Arthur Berriman said something like that when the police visited him," David replied and took a seat across from Kinsella without being asked. Jack did the same and stared hard at the man.

Kinsella looked uncertainly at Jack. "And you are?"

"My name's Jack Savage. I'm a profiler."

"A profiler?"

"Yes. I work out just what sort of insane psychopath could organise a game which involves murdering people using third-party killers."

Watching him carefully, David saw a tiny flinch in the way Kinsella held himself. He was definitely nervous, David thought.

Kinsella resumed his glare at David.

"Berriman, you said? Who the hell is Berriman?" he demanded.

David ignored the question. "Explain why Simone Whitelaw has selected at least two, probably four or even more killers to carry out your insane killing spree," he said.

"Just what are you talking about, Hunter?"

"Simone Whitelaw. Friend of your family, it seems, judging by the pictures of you in her house. And she seems to be rather well paid by you, judging by her bank statements which we've been reading the last few hours. We traced the Singapore account where you've been paying it, by the way, so no point in denying it."

"There's no law in supporting someone who has worked her way up," said Kinsella. "And I'm sure you've already found out that I supported her through University, too."

"Indeed we have," said David. "Though I don't know why, given the wealth of her parents."

"That's my affair," said Kinsella. "Her parents have been friends for many years."

"So it must have distressed you to have both Simone and her sister killed?" said Jack.

Kinsella looked at him. "I'm distressed at their deaths, yes. I hope you catch whoever did it, though judging by the competence I see here, that seems unlikely."

"How interesting," said David. "The news of their murders has not yet been released."

"I'm a newspaper and television station owner," said Kinsella with a supercilious smile. "You think I don't have contacts everywhere?"

"I'm sure you do. But you really seem quite untouched by these two deaths."

"That's your opinion," replied Kinsella.

"Who designed the game, Kinsella?" asked Jack. "You or one of your minions?"

Kinsella looked briefly at him then back at David.

"Do either of you fools know who you're dealing with? I can pick up the phone and in five minutes I'll have more police here, but to arrest you both, charged with assault, libel, entering under false pretences, you name it, I can have you charged with it. The story of your insane accusations will be all over the newspapers and television by tomorrow. Your reputations, if you ever had any, will be destroyed."

David was unmoved. "Quite possibly. On the other hand, when it gets out, as it will, that Australia's richest man, owner of numerous television networks around the world and any number of newspapers and magazines has been playing a game where he and his friends compete to see who have the most people killed, I suspect that your fall from the heights will make mine look like stepping off a pavement."

Kinsella resembled a lizard in his absolute stillness.

"I reckon it was one of his minions," said Jack with a broad grin.

"What was?" asked David.

"Whoever designed the rules of the game. I don't think this joker has the brains. After all, his wealth came from his parents, he never did anything to get it himself. All he has ever had to do is hire people to do his business planning for him. His father had already made the millions, so had his mother. This little twerp doesn't have it in him. Same with killing people. He gets other people to do it. He doesn't have the balls to do it himself."

David watched as the fury grew in Kinsella's face. But the man stayed silent.

"Same with sex too, eh, Kinsella?" Jack continued. "You can't do it yourself, so what do you do, hire other men to fuck women for you? Or do you just rent dirty movies?"

That finally blew Kinsella's control.

"You think I couldn't organise some silly game like this one?" he snapped. "Don't be a fool! I set up the whole thing, the chatboard system, the walls between the people involved. Sure I did it! And it was better than anything my parents could have set up. I've had eighteen people killed, far more than any of the other losers. And you two idiots think you can pin it on me?"

Or a moment, David was stunned at hearing the blatant admission from Kinsella.

The older man looked at him in utter contempt. "You think you've got me, Hunter? Are you wearing a wire? Well, let me tell you, it'll do you no good. I've got the police in my pocket, I've got the ODPP in my pocket, I've got the whole fucking *government* in my pocket. They daren't cross me. And you insignificant little puppies walk in here and think you can frighten *ME?* Get the hell out of my house before I have you thrown off the deck."

Jack laughed out loudly. "He's really rather good, isn't he?" he said. "What do you think, David?"

"Bit of a bloody ham actor, I'd say," David replied with a smile. He looked back to the billionaire.

"You see, Kinsella," he said. "You might have the government in your pocket, even some of the police and the judges, but I seriously doubt you have the ODPP. And anyway, not all of us are smelly little turds like the ones you own. There are many ways to skin a cat, that's you by the way, and going through legal processes is only one of them. I advise you to enjoy your power and status and money for as long as you have left, which isn't long. You're going down, you nasty little poison dwarf and the move from Point Piper to the prison cell is not going to be pleasant one."

He stood up. "Jack, let's leave this murdering little bastard to his dreams of glory."

Kinsella's face was ugly. The lips were curved in a rictus of sheer hatred and the lines on his cheek and neck were deep. His skin looked grey and ill.

"Don't expect to have your jobs, either of you, by tomorrow morning," he said in a harsh croak.

"And you, you little toad, don't expect to have all this," - David waved generally around the deck and the view of the harbour - "by next month."

"That long, eh?" said Jack and the two men walked back into the house and to the front door. They were met by the same man who had admitted them. He looked nervous and uncomfortable, with sweat on his neck staining his collar.

David smiled at him. "My advice, mate, would be to start looking for another job. There won't be one here pretty soon."

The man swallowed but said nothing as he opened the door.

Twenty minutes later, David and Jack walked into the office to be met by the desk sergeant.

"Superintendent Simpson says you're both to go straight to his office," he said.

"Surprise, surprise," murmured David.

"I'd say the poison dwarf has been on the phone already," said Jack as they walked along the corridor.

Charlie Simpson's door was open and Charlie was behind his desk. He beckoned the two men in.

"Shut the door," he commanded, harsh tension in his voice.

"Uh-oh," murmured Jack. They took their seats across the desk and looked at the Superintendent.

"I've just had the Commissioner on the phone," said Simpson. "He's raving mad. He ordered me to pull you both off the case, to stop harassing Kinsella and to place you, Hunter on suspension. You're to wait while the Commissioner prepares charges of illegal action, slander and conduct unbecoming an officer against you. His instructions are that your career in the Force is over. You, Savage are to leave and go home immediately."

"And what did you tell him, sir?" David asked.

To his utter astonishment, Simpson grinned cheerfully.

"I told him to go fuck himself," he said.

The silence in the room rang like a bell. Simpson sat back in his seat, pulled open a drawer and brought out a bottle of scotch and three glasses. David's heart was beating rapidly as he watched his boss pour three slugs of liquor and slide two across the desk.

"Good health, gentlemen," said Simpson and sank the entire contents of his glass.

"And yours, sir," said David with an echo from Jack and took a more cautious sip. This was something he had never seen in his boss.

Simpson smiled a little sadly. "Look, David," he said. "I know the hell you've gone through and the price you've paid. I've put thirty years into the Force, but if this is what it's become, some sort of obedient puppy to slime balls like Kinsella, I don't want to stay. That's what I told the commissioner while he was still struggling for breath."

"Anything else you told him, Charlie?" Jack asked.

"Actually, yes. I told him he could have my resignation any time, but if he enforced this bullshit I'd be in front of the Police Integrity Commission by the afternoon and I'd call a press conference to tell everybody how our police commissioner was doing what he'd been told by Alan Kinsella."

David finished his scotch. Simpson slid the bottle to him and David refilled his glass.

"Not the single malts you like, I know," said Simpson. "It'll have to do."

"It's doing very nicely, thank you, Charlie," replied David, his heart still racing and a slight sense of sweat in his thighs and behind his knees.

"Oddly enough," Simpson continued. "The Commissioner has withdrawn his demands. Jack, how will that affect Kinsella?"

"Badly. This will be to him like a slave uprising against the Emperor. Look at Ghadaffi in Libya, look at Assad in Syria, this is how supreme authorities, which is how these people see themselves, react to opposition. He'll want to kill, very badly indeed."

"What, do it himself, or get others to do it?" Simpson looked startled.

"We goaded him, Charlie," said Jack. "We told him he didn't have the balls to do his own killing and he was a dismal failure compared to his parents. This was simply the most awful thing he could hear from somebody. He'll get help, he has to, but he'll badly need to do the killing himself, so long as there's no risk to his own precious little body."

"Shit!" said Simpson. "Okay, David you go home in a patrol car with armed cops. You're carrying as well?"

David nodded. "My Heckler & Koch nine millimetre."

"And you wait for a patrol car to bring you in tomorrow morning, got it? Jack, same for you. Where are you staying, anyway?"

"I still own an apartment in Coogee," Jack replied. "The family uses it when we come down here."

"Then you get armed escorts to and from home. Both of you, take the usual precautions. Once you're home, stay there till the next morning. Keep the curtains closed. Don't open the door to anyone."

"Christ, how long does this go on?" Jack looked as unsettled as David had ever seen him.

"Until we bring down the bastard," said David.

* * *

That routine worked well. David rode home in a police patrol car. Two armed cops escorted him to the front door of his apartment building and waited till he was inside.

He spent a quiet, boring evening, refusing to watch the television and instead reading a thriller and sinking a few more scotches.

The following morning, he was greeted at the front door by a different group and brought to the office. He knew there was one unpleasant visit he had to make.

The Whitelaws were in a state of utter grief. They had lost their two daughters, both murdered, in the space of a few hours. The news had been broken by specialists in that awful business, but David and Jack were still faced with two parents fighting to avoid being overwhelmed and falling apart.

They were a good looking couple in their late fifties, David estimated. The house was an up-market, expensive home in a wealthy north-shore suburb. He knew that Nathan Whitelaw was a successful business executive, Australian head of a large American chain of engineering shops. Diane Whitelaw was a professor of Mathematics at Sydney University. The wealth showed in their deportment and elegance, but right now, they were two distraught parents who had lost their only children in brutal fashion. They sat together on a large, expensive leather couch, holding hands. Diane Whitelaw had been crying hard and her face looked a mess, red-eyed, mouth turned down in grief. Nathan was not much better off, occasional tremors rippling through his body like the aftershocks of an earthquake.

"Can we talk about just what this relationship was

with Alan Kinsella?" asked David as gently as he could. "Do I understand that Kinsella had paid for both girls' schooling?"

"Just Simone," said Nathan.

"But why?" asked David. "It looks like you could have well afforded the best for both girls, why only Simone?"

He watched carefully and knew that Jack was doing the same. He thought that he saw some reaction, perhaps a small shiver, perhaps a tightening of their hands.

"Zoe didn't have the same academic drive that Simone had," replied Nathan. "She never had any interest in going to University. Simone had wanted to be a doctor all her life."

"But again, why did Kinsella do this? You have no financial difficulties that I can see. How did you meet him, anyway?"

"We owe him a lot," Nathan replied. David was sure now, there was something in the undercurrent. The tension in Nathan Whitelaw was rising.

"We were going through a bad patch about ten years ago," continued Nathan. "Simone was in her first year at medical school and I lost my job. Diane was just a lecturer then and frankly, our financial situation got really bad."

At his side, Diane stirred and looked at her husband with anxiety. "Nathan, please don't," she whispered.

David and Jack looked at each other. Something was definitely coming out of the woodwork and David was certain it was not going to be pleasant.

Nathan gently stroked his wife's hand. "We have to, honey. It's time all this came out and if Kinsella's had something to with all this, then I want it to be out now."

He turned back to David. "Kinsella came to see us. He said he's seen Simone at a University drama and talked to her afterward and was most impressed. He said it would be a tragedy if she had to give up medical school. He offered to pay her expenses and fees as long as it was necessary. Then he made me another offer. He said he had a friend in the USA who was opening up a company here. He needed a man who could run it. As it happened, I was qualified, it was what I'd been doing before, I have an MBA from Harvard and an engineering degree, so it was not unreasonable for me to apply. Kinsella said he'd make it happen. So I met this American, bloke called Arthur Berriman from Chicago..."

David and Jack looked at each other briefly. The pattern became clearer.

"..and the next thing I know, I've got the job at a very generous package, far more than I was getting before. A month later, Diane gets a promotion to full professor and tenure just another year later. It was incredible."

"And all this, for what? asked David. "Why this amazing generosity? Did he want something in return?"

Diane rose to her feet with a sob and ran from the room. Her husband looked after her with an expression of resignation but didn't follow her.

"It gets ugly from here, doesn't it?" said Jack softly.

Nathan took a deep breath. "It was fine for just over a year," he said. "Kinsella had us all over for dinner at his place in Point Piper, he came to the house-warming party we threw when we bought this place, never anything but friendship. Mind you, Zoe couldn't stand him, thought he was a horrible little creep and said he was lusting after Simone. I couldn't see it, but Diane said she agreed with her, but she only said that when we were alone. She didn't really like him either."

"And Simone?"

"Simone is... was... a deep person. She kept her opinions to herself. She was always pleasant to him, well aware of how he had affected her career."

"So what happened?" asked Jack.

"Kinsella came round one night for a small gathering, just a few friends. In the middle of things, he asked me for a private discussion. He said he had something he needed to raise with Diane and me."

Nathan's face had turned grey, almost as if he was ill. "I called Diane over and we went into my study. He sat down as if he owned the place, took out a cigar and lit it, even though we'd made it plain that we didn't permit smoking in the house. Diane asked him to put it out and the little bastard just smirked at her. 'You know,' he said, 'you only got your promotion and tenure at the university because I offered them a ten million dollar donation. It was a condition. The same with your job, Nathan. I asked Berriman to give it to you. You were qualified, so it was no skin off his nose to give it to you and you've done okay, but I only have to call him and your job's done. You're in the unemployment queue again.' The little bastard was laughing at us."

"So what did he want?" Jack asked.

"He said he wanted Simone. Not all the time, she could do her job, live in her own place, but when he called her, she was to go over to his place and *service* him. God almighty."

Nathan looked quite sick, almost ready to throw up.

"And he said if he didn't get what he wanted, Diane would lose her position and have such a scandal thrown at her, she'd never work in a college again and I'd be fired with similar results. We had no choice. We went and talked to Simone and she wasn't quite as shocked as we expected. She said she knew the miserable little bastard was lusting after her. She certainly hated the idea but she said she'd do it, anything to keep the family together and financially stable."

"And how long has this been going on?" asked David. He felt a tinge of nausea himself at this story.

"Five years," Nathan replied. "From before she qualified as a psychiatrist. And I think Kinsella got her the job with the prison system, too, for whatever goddammed reason of his own."

"You're right about his reasons," said David. "He needed somebody in that position for his own sick purposes. I can't tell you yet what they were, we have to get everything wrapped up legally first. But I can tell you that he was using Simone for something more than sex and he'd got Zoe tied into his games as well."

"Jesus Christ!" said Nathan and put his face in his hands. "I hope you kill the bastard."

"We'll do far worse than that," said David. "We'll bring him down to rock bottom and destroy him. I can promise you that."

Nathan was now weeping noisily, the deep anguished sobs of a man driven to utter despair and loss.

Quietly, Jack and David rose from their seats and found their way out of the house.

As they entered David's office, Barrie Roche appeared at the door.

"Boss," he said, "we've tied in the Melbourne murders to Simone. We heard from the Melbourne prison people. It seems Simone had filed official request forms for copies of all prisoner psych reports in Victoria, said it was for a research project. It wasn't all that unusual and she got the approval quickly. She must have been feeding likely killer profiles down to her organiser there."

"Another piece in the jigsaw," said David. "Thanks Barrie, sterling work, mate. Get every name that was sent to her and give them to D.I. Feeney in Melbourne. He can follow up. And get this to all the cops around the world who've been having the problem. It's probably the pattern everywhere."

"Sure Boss," said Roche. "They should nab all the buggers fairly quickly with those details."

He waved, grinned and departed.

"Well, bugger me sideways," said Jack. "I think we may have broken the bastards and their game."

Chapter 21 – The Point of Death

"Shit!" said David. He stared down at the section of his fridge where the beer was normally kept. It was empty. He remembered the last time he'd drunk one and how he'd realised then that he needed restocking. The pressures of the last couple of days had driven the thought from his mind.

"Bugger it," he said aloud. "I really need a beer tonight! Sod the rules, I'm going to get some."

He found his door keys and walked out of the apartment and to the elevator section. The bottle shop by the pub was only a couple of hundred metres away and he had his gun in its shoulder holster. *I think I'll be happy if one of Kinsella's goons try something*, he thought to himself. *I'd enjoy putting a bullet into him almost as much as I'd enjoy putting one into the poison dwarf himself.*

He reached the basement car park, which was the shortest way out to the road. There was a man walking from where he had parked his car to the door and David politely held it open for him. Too late, he saw the second man standing against the wall, the first one moved fast and David felt a thump on his head.

A cosh, he said to himself as consciousness faded.

* * *

Arthur Berriman picked up the phone, puzzled. This was the phone reserved for only a small number of selected people, state and federal senators, some judges, the state governor and very few others.

"Berriman," he said.

"Well g'day there, Arthur," said the rarely heard voice with its Australian accent.

"Kinsella! What the hell? You weren't supposed ever to use this number. Are you fucking insane?"

"Never felt saner," replied the Australian.

"God dammit, man, do you realise what you've done? Now there's a record of our contact. We agreed, dammit, we agreed never to contact each other, any of us."

"Ah well, Arthur, all good things come to an end. I heard the cops in Illinois were onto you and they're onto me here. I thought I'd give them something to play with."

"Kinsella, you're a fucking lunatic!" Berriman felt panic rising in his chest. "You're destroying the whole thing!"

"Well, Arthur, I reckoned that I've won, anyway! I got eighteen, how many did you get?"

Berrriman slammed down the phone. He knew that the whole structure was about to collapse on all of them. The wonderful game they'd developed, the incredible thrill of hearing about the deaths that they had caused to happen, all was about to come crashing down, despite the series of protective barriers they had designed to keep them apart from the actually killers.

Why the fornicating hell had Kinsella done this?

* * *

Detective Chief Inspector Greg Robarts stared at the computer screen. "Holy Clucking Duckshit, Batman!" he said loudly then emitted a shout. "Will!" he roared. "Get your arse in here!"

A moment later, the startled face of Detective Sergeant Will Carter appeared in the doorway.

"A massive breakthrough from our friend in Australia," said Robarts. "Get onto the prison service. Find out the name of every psychiatrist who meets prisoners. Find out every prisoner they've ever interviewed and get the names of any of them who've been released at any time before this shit started. Okay, don't just stand there like a stunned rabbit, get the crew to work!"

* * *

Captain James Ball opened his emails and quickly scanned the long list with a sigh. *The usual pile of administrative garbage,* he thought to himself. *Christ, I could save an hour a day if only the important stuff came though.*

But one email caught his eye and he opened it. A few seconds later, he ran out of his office and into the general area where his team worked in an open plan location.

"Everyone, listen up! Our pal in Australia has cracked it!"

He rapidly informed the team of the contents of the email from Sydney and got a loud yell of applause. His sergeant, Phil Coulsen grinned widely.

"Yer gotta hand it to that damned Aussie, he's got balls!" he said. "Tell you what, Captain," he added. "Why don't I check and see if that bastard Berriman has had any calls from Australia?"

Captain Ball nodded. "Why don't you do that, Phil? Okay, the rest of you, you know what to do. I want the name of every shrink the Illinois prison service has used in the last five years, the name of every con they've interviewed, a copy of that report and which of those cons has been on the streets since that interview and I want it all by yesterday. Go!"

* * *

The phone rang in the luxurious study of the mansion house on the border between Cheshire and Lancashire.

The man in the armchair, dressed in his silk dressing gown and sipping a glass of single malt scotch looked up startled. This was his hot line to a very few of his colleagues, two government ministers and just a handful of the most rich and powerful people in England.

He stood up and went to the phone, looking down at the little screen. A shock ran through him like a kick in his guts. He picked up the phone.

"Kinsella, what the fuck are you doing calling me? You know we agreed never to do this?"

"Ah well, old chap, things change," said the Australian tones in a poor imitation of an upper-crust British accent. "It's all coming to end, so I wanted to let you know I won!"

"What do you mean, won? Do you realise the risk you're taking here?"

"I got eighteen," said Kinsella. "I think you only got nine, right? Four each in Manchester and Birmingham and one in Wales?"

"Jesus Christ, Kinsella, are you mad?"

"Never saner, old chap! I'll expect the prize money any day."

The call was disconnected. The man in England resumed his seat and sat staring at the fireplace without moving.

What the hell had Kinsella done and why?

* * *

Detective Sergeant James Clancy looked at his computer screen, saw one that triggered a wave of interest and opened it. Two minutes later he got on the phone and has his team assemble in the meeting room. This was going to blow their minds, he knew.

* * *

The dinner party in the rich suburb of Forest Hills in Toronto was well in progress. Six very suave men in tuxedos, all accompanied by women of great elegance in gowns that would have cost a year's wages of any secretary sat round the long table in the enormous dining room. Three ice buckets of Krug champagne sat at strategic places and several bottles of the very best wines stood in the middle of the table. Conversation flowed like the wine.

A phone rang, barely heard and was picked up after only two rings. A few moments later, a young woman appeared in the room looking anxious, approached the man at the head of the table and spoke into his ear.

For just a second he looked frozen.

"You're sure of that name?" he said softly.

"Yes, sir," she replied. "He said he's calling from Sydney, Australia."

The man took a deep breath. The woman sitting at the far end of the table looked curiously at him.

"Darling?" she said as he passed her chair.

He touched her shoulder. "Just a business call," he said, but she knew him very well and she could detect the tension in his voice. Her worried eyes followed him as he walked out of the dining room.

* * *

David Hunter felt sick. His head pounded like a bass drum between his ears and he tried to lift his hands to try and stop the thunder, but he couldn't. Slowly he regained consciousness and realised he was tied to a straight wooden chair, his hands roped behind him and more rope round his feet. Blood had trickled down one side of his face and was now dry, leaving his left eye partially obstructed.

"David, can you hear me?" a voice drifted to him from out of a dense fog. It seemed familiar.

Angela? What the hell was Angela doing here? Why was he tied....? With a sickening crash, his memories returned. The cosh, the vague recollections of being carried out of his basement. Where the hell was he?

He looked up. He was in a spacious and well furnished room, it looked like a male study or rec room, or similar.

"David?" said the voice again and he turned his head.

"Angela?" he croaked. "What the hell...?"

"It's Kinsella," she said, her voice tight with fear. "His thugs grabbed me about an hour ago when I was out for a morning run. You were here when I was brought in, but you've been out cold the whole time."

David was struggling to absorb all this. Slowly, his mind cleared and the pounding in his head receded.

"What time is it, do you know?" he managed to say.

"About eight," she replied. "I went out about six, I was half way through my route when they grabbed me. It was about an hour's ride, though my head was covered the whole time."

Eight? thought David. *It was only about nine last night that I was coshed. I must have been drugged to be out for so long.*

"Good," he said. "So Charlie will know you're missing and my guardians will know it too. The shit will be hitting the fan already."

"Oh God, David, what's he going to do?"

He looked at her. She was dressed in a white tee-shirt and blue shorts with running shoes. Her hair was in a ponytail. She looked gorgeous, he thought, despite her white face and expression of fear.

Before he could answer, the door in front of him opened. One large man entered, looked around then signalled to somebody outside. Kinsella appeared, wheeled in sitting in his wheelchair and pushed by the man who had first met David and Jack on their visit to the mansion in Point Piper. Any consideration David might have had for that man's future vanished like mist on a summer's day. He was a part of Kinsella's operation.

So we're in the little bastard's house, thought David.

Kinsella stopped about two metres away from the prisoners. He muttered something to the man behind him and he walked into an adjoining bathroom, emerging with a wet cloth and wiped the blood away from David's eyes before remaining behind him. The second man moved to stand behind Angela.

"You underestimated me, Hunter," said Kinsella.

"No I didn't. This takes no organisational skills. A ten-year old could have arranged it."

Kinsella didn't move but David saw a flicker of rage cross the man's face.

"That's not what I was referring to," replied Kinsella. "You and that idiot shrink of yours got it quite wrong. You said I couldn't handle a woman, for a start."

"Ah yes, Simone," said David. "We didn't get it wrong. "You think that beautiful woman would have come to your bed of her own accord? Don't be daft! We know all about the blackmail you applied there."

"Well then, you bastard, consider how far you're wrong when I kill both of you!"

David heard the sob of fear from Angela and almost let out a gasp of shock as well, but struggled for self-control.

"And that's supposed to prove what a hero you are? God, what a stunted little poison dwarf you are, Kinsella! Shooting two bound prisoners is something heroic?"

"You'll still be dead," retorted Kinsella. A look of ugly delight ran across his face. "And that's after I've had a play with the delectable Angela. Just think what Charlie is going to think when he discovers that!"

David looked across to Angela. Tears were running down her face and she was breathing hard.

"You really are a fucking maniac, aren't you Kinsella?" said David. "We've been here, we know where you are, we know just *what* you are and what you've done. How long do think it will take before the Tactical Operations Unit gets here?"

"You're a fool, Hunter," replied Kinsella. "You didn't listen to me. I've got the cops in my pocket, I've got the courts in my pocket, I've got the fucking *government* in my pocket. You think your playmates back at the station can get a court order for a Tactical Operations Unit to come *here?* There's not a judge in the land will allow that!"

David stayed silent. The chords of madness in Kinsella's voice had become stronger since the meeting at this house a few days before. He suspected the cripple seriously believed in what he was saying, that he was above the law and beyond retribution. The trouble was that he thought Kinsella could be partially right. For a start, Charlie and Jack didn't know where he and Angela were and after that, it could take a while to authorise an armed attack given the absence of any genuine cause and evidence. The sickness in his stomach got worse. He fought for control of his voice.

"You really are quite mad, aren't you, Kinsella? You think the cops are going to let you get away with this? You may manage to kill us here, but what happens after that? The long-range sniper bullet in your head while you sit on your lovely deck? Dead easy! How about the pistol shot to the head while you're at some function? A needle in the back as you get out of your limo? All of them possible. And you think you've got the government in your pocket? How long do you think that will last as the rumours come out about this little episode?"

Kinsella nodded and the man behind David stepped round and swung a fist into his face. It almost sent David back into the blackness as he heard a suppressed scream of horror from Angela, but he hung on, despite the dizziness and pain. He concentrated on deep breathing for a few seconds and scrambled back to some sort of clarity.

"Like I said, you little turd," he mumbled. "You need other people to do your dirty work. And Simone said you were a dead loss in the sack. She had to struggle not to be sick all over you."

He sensed the man about to swing another blow at him, but Kinsella stopped him with a gesture.

"Turn him to face the woman," Kinsella ordered.

Oh Jesus Christ, what's the little bastard going to do? thought David in anguish as the two men hauled his chair round ninety degrees.

"David!" Angela cried out, her throat hoarse with panic.

"Kinsella, for Christ's sake, stop it!" David shouted but might as well have stayed silent. Kinsella moved his wheelchair to the side of Angela's wooden chair and reached underneath her tee-shirt, grinning widely as he fondled a breast.

Angela went quite still and expressionless but David could see her jaw clamped in disgust.

"Don't you wish this was you, Hunter?" said Kinsella, looking back at David. "Everybody knows how much you lust for this bitch. And it's me, not you who's getting her!"

He tried to reach behind Angela and loosen her bra strap but the ropes binding her prevented him.

"Can't even undo a woman's bra, you little fuck?" said David, struggling to keep his voice under control. "Shit, Kinsella, I was doing that at sixteen!"

David had never actually heard anyone snarl before he'd heard Berriman in Chicago, but now Kinsella did it also. Kinsella snarled, a growl of rage and switched his attention to Angela's legs. He placed his hands on her thighs and massaged them up to the groin.

David felt the sickness getting worse but he kept taunting Kinsella.

"Look at you, you little dwarf!" he shouted. "Can't get a woman unless she's tied up or you're blackmailing her parents. This is supposed to make us admire you?"

Kinsella ignored him and kept stroking Angela's thighs. But suddenly she turned her face to his, just a hand's width away and spat firmly in his eyes.

Kinsella snarled again, his face going almost purple with rage. He backed away from Angela as one of the men moved quickly to the bathroom and came back with a wet towel, handing it to his boss. The little man wiped his face slowly as he regained control.

"I'll leave you two losers to think about what happens next," he said, spun his wheelchair around and waited till one of the men came up and started wheeling him out. All three men left, switching off the light as the last one walked out.

David knew very well what Kinsella intended to do next.

Life was running out.

Chapter 22 – Facing the Dark Angel

The atmosphere in the conference room was bleak.

"He didn't show up when his escorts came for him," said Bill Hamilton. "We've got to assume he's been nabbed."

"I don't get it," said Jack. His face was pale. "He knew bloody well not to go out, but he must have done for some stupid reason. It was obvious they'd be waiting for the chance."

"He had a gun, he probably thought he could handle anything," said Bill. "Hell, knowing David, he was probably hoping for a chance to damage somebody."

Rachel and Barrie sat silently, the bleakness reflected in their faces.

The door opened and Charlie Simpson walked in. He was unshaven and his hair was a mess.

"They've got Angela," he said and sat down heavily at the table.

Silence hung over the room like a heavy blanket for a few seconds.

"Oh Jesus Christ!" said Hamilton. Rachel hid her face in her hands and Barrie Roche stood up abruptly and went to stare out of the window.

"Tell us what happened, Charlie," said Jack.

Simpson stood up and went to the coffee pot. Jack watched him carefully as the Superintendent poured himself a mug, his hands trembling slightly then returned to his seat.

"She went out for her usual run about six," Simpson began. His voice was cracking with tension. "She's always back by seven and I had breakfast ready for her."

He took a sip of coffee but Jack could see tears in the man's eyes. Simpson put down his mug, some drops falling from it as his hands shook.

"Oh Jesus, Jack, I don't know what I'll do..." Simpson turned away but it was too late to hide his distress. He began openly weeping, huge sobs shaking his body.

The others could only watch and share his grief.

* * *

In the darkness, David could hear the suppressed weeping of Angela. He felt terribly helpless amid his own desperate fear.

"I'm so sorry, Angela," he said. "We thought something like this could happen, but we assumed he'd go for me, not you."

He heard her struggling for breath and control. "I know," she said. "That's what Charlie said. Actually, he did say I should have somebody watching me and I was the one who told him that was silly, so...." Her voice broke into another flood of weeping. "Oh God, David, what's he going to do?"

David took some deep breaths again, desperate to keep his own control and somehow help Angela.

"I don't think he's got the guts, Angie," he said. "Jack thinks the same, he's all bullshit and no courage."

"Oh God, I hope so," she whispered through her tears.

I hope so too, Angie my love, thought David. *Jack, for God's sake, work out that Kinsella's brought us here and persuade Charlie to bring in the heavy guns. We haven't got long.*

He realised Angela was speaking again, so softly it was difficult to make out the words.

"I know you always liked me, David," she whispered.

He seized on the chance to keep her mind away from the probability of their deaths in a short while.

"I couldn't hide it too well, could I?" he replied.

"No, but I liked it. You did my ego good, the way you looked at me."

David realised that she was trying to talk about something, *anything* that would stop her thinking about the next hour or two.

"But you caused me a problem," he said, grasping at the chance to keep hysteria away. "I just couldn't get excited by another woman. They all seemed so dull compared to you."

"Did you know that sometimes I had little fantasies about you, David?"

"You did?" Despite the situation, he was startled and pleased. "Do I have anything I need to apologise for?"

"Nothing at all. I used to imagine you and I could fly off to Tahiti for a dirty weekend or something. I imagined you were a wonderful lover."

"I would have been with you, Angie. But I always knew you'd never leave Charlie."

"No, but a girl can dream."

He heard her breathing become choked again.

"Tell me what you dreamed about," he said softly, struggling to keep her mind off the terrible possibilities of the next hour.

"I thought about sitting over the ocean in one of those lovely thatch roof cabins in Tahiti and having a wonderful seafood banquet and cold champagne and watching the sun set before we went inside and made wild, wonderful love all night."

"How lovely! I had my own fantasies about you too."

"Tell me what they were, David."

"I just imagined you doing a strip tease for me in my apartment while I drank my favourite scotch and then when you were completely naked, you'd come over to me and I'd make love to you on my carpet."

It didn't work. He heard the sobs rising in her throat and she let out a cry of utter terror.

"And now it can't ever happen! Oh God, David, I'm so frightened."

And then she broke down into a full flood of terrified weeping and there was nothing David could do but try and control his own fear.

* * *

"Jack, where's he taken them?"

Simpson had recovered his self-control. The marks of the tears remained on his cheeks and his eyes were red but his voice was that of the commanding officer again.

"To his house in Point Piper," replied Jack.

"You're certain? Why?"

"It's where he feels safe. It's his castle. It confirms his total belief that he's in control of everything, the government, the police, you, me, *everything*. He reigns supreme, nothing can touch him there."

"And what's he going to do?"

"Charlie, he's going to kill them, there's no doubt. It's his last chance to prove he's capable of doing it himself. He probably knows deep down that he's through, we'll get him in the end, but he's not letting himself believe it."

"Will he have done it already?" A small tremor ran through Simpson's body.

"I doubt it, Charlie. If he picked up Angela sometime between six and seven, it would take an hour to get to his place, tie them both up and hold them for a time. He won't want to do this too quickly. He wants to savour the power he has, he wants them both to recognise that power and he wants to watch them be frightened."

"How long?"

"Probably another hour or two. Can you get a Tactical Operations Unit there?"

"I doubt it, Jack." Simpson looked calmer than the situation warranted.

"Why not?" Jack almost shouted in his frustration.

"First you'd have to find a judge who'll grant the warrant," chimed in Bill Hamilton. "I don't know how many we can trust. And frankly, all we have is suspicion. Even an honest judge would have difficulty granting a heavy weapons raid without any real evidence, especially against someone like Kinsella."

"Christ, Charlie, we can't just sit here and wait for Kinsella to kill them!" Jack was standing up in his anxiety.

"Indeed we can't," said Charlie. "Bill's quite right, going through channels will take too long. But hey, I've already told the Commissioner to go fuck himself once, my career's probably over and I'm not sure I care too much."

He picked up the phone.

* * *

She hadn't said another word since that last terrified outburst. David estimated it had been twenty minutes or more since then and the silence had been broken only occasionally by a muffled sob. The room was completely dark, not even a gleam from a window or light from under the door.

"David?"

Her voice sounded almost like a little girl's.

"Yes, Angela?"

"Do you think Charlie knows where we are?"

"I'm dead certain of it. Jack and I were here only a little while ago and Charlie knows of that visit. I'll bet

Jack has told Charlie to get an armed team here."

Before she could reply, the door opened into the room and light flooded over the scene. David felt his insides lurch and fear ran through him, making his hands clammy and sweat ran down his neck and inside his thighs. His life might be just minutes in duration. He heard an indrawn gasp of horror from Angela.

As before, Kinsella was preceded by a silent man who looked round the room then nodded for the second man to push Kinsella's wheelchair into the space in front of the two bound captives. David turned his head and saw that Kinsella held an automatic pistol in his lap. The crippled man was grinning widely.

"Showtime!" said Kinsella.

David struggled for control of his voice and turned to stare at the other two men.

"At this stage, you'll get about ten years for taking part in a kidnapping," he said. "You could be out in six. You let this happen and it's life for murder and there'll be no doubt that you were part of all this little bastard's other hired killings. That could mean a whole series of life sentences. You'll die of old age in prison. This is what you want?"

His words had no effect.

Kinsella laughed. "You don't listen, do you Hunter? I told you, I control everything! They do what I tell them. Like this."

He nodded at one of the men who advanced on Angela taking something from his pocket. Horrified,

David saw it was a box cutter, the blade as sharp as a scalpel.

Oh God, is he going to cut her throat? David thought for a dreadful moment, but the man simple bent behind Angela and cut the ropes round her chest. Then he moved in front of her and sliced her t-shirt away.

Kinsella let out a gasp of erotic joy and wheeled himself to Angela who shrank back. He held out his hand and the man placed the box cutter in it. Kinsella placed the blade at the front of Angela's brassiere and sliced the join apart.

"See, I don't need to learn how to undo a woman's bra, Hunter, I take the direct route. Now, don't you wish this was you?"

Moaning softly to himself, Kinsella began to fondle Angela's breasts.

"You filthy little pig!" she shouted at him.

Kinsella looked irritated. "You shut your face, bitch or I'll slice these off," he said. But the reaction seemed to have killed the enjoyment and he moved his chair back.

He picked up the gun and examined it lovingly. "You'd know very well, it's illegal to own one of these in Australia," he said, smiling at David. "Just goes to show you, Inspector Hunter, the law doesn't apply to me."

David felt as if an icy hand was squeezing his heart and Angela was weeping freely again.

A slight thump echoed from upstairs. All three of the captors looked up.

"What was that?" asked one of the unnamed men.

"Nothing," said Kinsella. "Probably just a delivery truck arriving with more stock for my wine cellar. So, David, which one of you shall I shoot first? Would you like to watch your girlfriend die? That'll prove just how wrong you've been. I really can kill somebody. Then when you see that, it'll be your turn to die."

He pointed the gun at Angela and David watched his finger tighten on the trigger.

One of the men moved suddenly and walked from behind the captives' chairs to Kinsella's wheelchair. The small man looked up in astonishment as the man reached down, gripped Kinsella's right hand and pulled it upward.

"I won't be part of this," he said.

For a second, Kinsella was motionless, as if stunned by this sudden turn of events.

"You what?" he said, his voice hoarse with shock.

"I'm not going to be part of murder," said the man. "I've helped you so far, but I've realised just how insane you are. It stops here."

Deliberately, Kinsella brought the gun to bear on the man's face.

"No, it doesn't," he said and pulled the trigger.

The man's face seemed to dissolve and the head exploded in a shower of blood and brain matter, some landing on both David and Angela.

Just at that moment, the heavy door to the room was shattered by a battering ram and fell inward onto the carpet. Several armed men in the full protection of a police Tactical Operations Unit raced in, shouting loudly.

"Police! On the ground! On the ground!" Kinsella appeared totally stunned as one officer placed the barrel of his rifle against his head and yelled, "Drop the weapon!"

Kinsella dropped the gun into his lap and the armed officer took hold of it, checked the magazine and removed it, placing the gun and the magazine in one of his pockets.

From the dust of the shattered doorway, a familiar figure advanced.

"Well, bugger me sideways," said Jack Savage. "Got yourself in a spot of difficulty, did you, you silly bastard?"

"Took your bloody time, didn't you?" said David, feeling hysteria threatening to swamp him.

"Traffic," retorted Jack and began undoing the ropes round David's wrists. As he waited to be freed, he saw Charlie Simpson rush to Angela and place his arms protectively round her. She collapsed against him, sobbing and when her hands were free, she wrapped her arms round her husband's neck and hid her face against his chest. Wistfully, David watched them for a few seconds. He knew that his conversation with her had been just fantasy in the face of death but it still hurt to see that confirmed.

"Kinsella shot his own man," said David. "Can you cover him up?"

One of the TOU officers searched the area and found a blanket in a storage cupboard to one side. He draped it over the corpse but it didn't hide all the debris from the man's head.

Kinsella was still sitting motionless, seeming to ignore everything going on around him. David nodded at him.

"What's going on there?" he asked Jack.

"Catatonic shock," replied Jack. "He's failed and he just can't cope with the fact."

"Get the cuffs on him," said David. One of the armed men advanced on Kinsella and placed handcuffs on the small man who offered no resistance.

"I'm taking my wife home," said Charlie Simpson.

"A good idea," said David. "I'll write up all my statements back in the office, Angie can do hers later when she feels up to it."

He watched as Charlie almost carried Angela out of the room. She didn't look at David at all. He realised that he was nauseous, almost ready to throw up and trembling in every limb.

"Christ, Jack," he said. "That was all a bit too ugly and a lot too close."

"We pushed him over the limit," Jack said. "He reached the point where he had to kill somebody to prove that he wasn't the weakling we'd called him."

"But I think he knew it was all over," David said, still trying to control the waves of panic that shook him every few seconds.

"Did he now?" replied Jack, looking thoughtful. "In that case, he'd need to tell all the other players that he'd won the game. David, I bet he has a separate line somewhere. Find it and get it checked. It's a dead cert he's called the other players."

"Holy shit!" said David. He reached for his mobile phone and realised he hadn't taken it with him when he left his apartment. "Give me your phone," he said, extending his hand to Jack. A few seconds later, he was instructing his office to follow up. "We might get all the bastards this way," he said to Jack.

To his amazement, Kinsella spoke.

"You think you've got me, Hunter? You fool, I'll be out of your hands in a couple of hours. Do you think anyone in this country will convict *ME?*"

David stared at him.

"He's quite insane," Jack said softly. "He really does believe he's immune. Just ignore him."

David nodded and began to walk out of the killing room, the trembling in his limbs making it a major effort of self-control. Kinsella was still muttering with a grin on his face.

"I own everything," he babbled. "I own the government, the police, everybody. I'll be back here in a couple of hours. You think you can get *ME?*"

David and Jack walked out of the room.

Chapter 23 – Closing the Net

The black Toyota SUV rolled quietly along the driveway to the huge imposing house. Two others followed a few car lengths behind and all three vehicles stopped in front of the pillars that shielded the enormous front door.

Captain James Ball and Detective Sergeant Phil Coulsen stayed in the lead vehicle while the several armed men climbed out of the following vehicles and fanned out round the house. After a few minutes, a voice crackled in the loudspeaker by the Captain.

"Clear, sir," it said.

"This should be fun," said the Captain opening the door and the two men advanced on the front door. It opened as it had the previous time with an anxious young man standing there.

Coulsen moved up to him.

"I'll take the gun, please," he said quietly. "There's a high-powered rifle pointing at you, if you decide to play silly games."

The man looked alarmed and didn't resist, slowly pulling his pistol out from his shoulder holster and handed it to the sergeant. Coulsen looked at it and removed the magazine, checked the barrel for one bullet in there, found none and put the weapon in his pocket.

The man still didn't speak but turned and led the police officers into the hall, decorated with ferns, black and white tiles and Greek-style statuettes, to the same room as before.

Just as he had on that occasion, Arthur Berriman was sitting in an armchair, dressed in dark slacks and a white golf-shirt.

"Don't you people learn?" he said, his voice cold with anger.

"About what, sir?" said the Captain. He remained standing while Coulsen walked round behind Berriman. The seated tycoon twisted round in irritation to stare at him then returned to glare at the Captain.

"About keeping your job," snapped Berriman. "What the hell are you doing here?"

"Ah! That! Yes, sir, as I said, I don't really give a rat's ass about keeping my job, it's got boring. But I have to say, moments like this do add a certain oomph and pizzazz to my day. Arthur Berriman, would you stand up, please?"

"You what? Ball, do you have any idea who you're dealing with?"

"I do believe so, sir. Would you stand up, please so I can arrest you for conspiracy to commit murder, acts of terrorism and a few other things we'll work out later?"

The rage in Berriman's face was almost radiating and the red tinge to his cheeks indicated a possible heart attack. He picked up the phone on the side table next to his armchair, pressed the loudspeaker button and dialled just two digits.

"You might as well listen to this, you two bastards. Listen as your careers go down the shit hole, because that's what's about to happen."

Only two buzzes came from the loudspeaker before the phone at the other end was picked up.

"The Governor's office," said an educated male voice. "What can I do for you, Mr Berriman?"

"Get me the Governor, now!" said Berriman, almost shouting.

"I'm sorry, Mr Berriman, the Governor is unavailable."

"What do you mean, unavailable? This is Berriman. Put him on this minute."

"Mr Berriman, I know who you are," said the cool voice. "The Governor has given strict instructions that your calls are not to be put through to him."

Listening carefully, Captain Ball decided that there was an echo of amusement in the man's voice. He decided that the young man had probably been on the wrong end of some abuse and insults from Berriman and was enjoying the tycoon's fall.

Berriman's face was becoming a dangerous colour.

"Listen you little turd!" he raged. "Do you know who you're dealing with? You tell that little squirt that he talks to me *NOW* or that's the last dime he gets from me! Do you understand me?"

"Very clearly, Mr Berriman and I'm sure the Governor will regret the loss of your support, but the order was quite clear. I wish you a very good day, sir."

The call was disconnected and Ball watched the man's face as it slowly changed from massive rage to puzzlement and finally understanding.

"You see, sir, the Governor was briefed on the details yesterday," said the Captain. "Like we told you last visit, once the authorities are faced with clear evidence of what you've been up to, they'll withdraw their support for their own political survival."

Berriman sat slumped in his chair.

"We know it all, Mr Berriman," chimed in Sergeant Coulsen. "We know who your controller was, we know who the prison psychiatrist was and how he was finding killers for your sick little game. We've got everybody, apart from the woman you had killed."

Captain Ball nodded at Coulsen who moved round to stand by Berriman.

"So now, sir, will you stand up?"

With no evident spirit left, Berriman rose to his feet. Coulsen moved in front of him and snapped the handcuffs on his wrists.

"Read him his rights, Sergeant," said Captain Ball and waited while Coulsen recited the standard phrases. Then he turned and led the way out into the hall and to the front door. The young man was still standing there. Ball pointed at him.

"You," he said. "I think you'd better come with us. You've got a hell of a lot of questions to answer. You can ride in the back with your boss and the Sergeant."

A few minutes later, the cavalcade left to return to Chicago.

* * *

The opening of the latest art show in Manchester was well under way. Three young artists were surrounded by the normal ring of admiring patrons, the smell of money was overpowering, many hundreds of thousands of pounds-worth of jewellery flashed and glowed in the bright lights and the walls were surrounded by framed canvases of many kinds.

Detective Chief Inspector Greg Robarts stood silently with Detective Sergeant William Carter just a few feet away from him. Instinctively, both men studied every individual in the colourful scene before their attention was brought to the front of the room where a small stage had been set up. A woman of extraordinary beauty in perhaps her early forties climbed the single step onto the stage. Robarts recognised the well-known face of one of Lancashire's richest and most famous titled women.

She rang a small handbell on the little table in front of her and smiled brilliantly at the room.

"Ladies and gentlemen, it's wonderful to have such a magnificent crowd here tonight. These three young artists are quite brilliant, as you can see and it's good to know that have already sold quite a few of their works this evening. My foundation works hard at supporting local talent and I believe our efforts have paid off superbly here! Now I'd like to introduce our biggest patron, Sir Peter Collingwood. As you know, Sir Peter is Chairman of several major corporations and of a number of similar foundations and a great patron of the arts, so please welcome him to our evening of great colour, genius and dedication!"

She moved backward, applauding as the crowd followed suit. A short, elderly man, white-haired and with a neat goatee beard, dressed in a tuxedo moved onto the stage, smiling broadly.

"Now, I think, Will," said Robarts and began moving forward through the crowd.

"You bloody drama queen," said Carter and Robarts grinned cheerfully.

They reached the front as Collingwood began speaking. The two detectives stood directly in front of him, arms folded and stared at him.

"Lady Helene, Patrons, ladies and gentlemen..." began Sir Peter. He glanced round the room and finally down at the two detectives standing staring at him.

"I think you should stop there, Sir Peter," said Robarts. "This is going to be embarrassing enough as it is."

The man's face had gone white and his jaw had dropped. The beautiful and elegant Lady Helene moved to the front of the stage.

"How *dare* you!" she shouted. "How dare you interrupt this? Who the hell are you?"

Robarts struggled to restrain his laughter as her accent seemed to have lost its perfect, refined tones and fallen into pure Manchester back streets. Both detectives flourished their identification cards and the woman fell back in confusion.

"Time to come with us, Sir Peter," said Robarts. "You know why."

In absolute silence, the three men walked out of the gallery. At the front door, they stopped.

"Read him his rights, Will," said Robarts.

* * *

The unmarked police car pulled up before the gates of the mansion on the Bridle Path, the most exclusive road in the most exclusive suburb of Forest Hills in Toronto. Two other similar vehicles arrived at the same moment and disgorged a number of men in plain clothes. All of them seemed to be fit, powerful young men with well-cut suits that hid their shoulder holsters.

Detective Sergeant James Clancy got out from behind the driver's seat, looked over the group and grinned.

"Not regular cruisers for this address, eh, Sir?"

"The super-rich get special treatment, Jim, you know that! And that's why your fabulously superior, heroic Chief Superintendent is here to do the arrest, not some lowly sergeant!"

Clancy suppressed his laugh. "I don't think I've ever even *been* on this street!"

"And never likely too again, Sergeant, except to arrest some murderous bastard like the one who lives here."

"Right sir," agreed Clancy.

"Shall we proceed, Sergeant? I'm looking forward to this."

* * *

The blue and silver police car of the North Rhine-Westphalia State Police drove at a moderate rate along the road out to the hills above Bonn.

Two unmarked black vans followed demurely a few hundred metres behind.

"We were lucky to draw this assignment, Wolfram," said the man in the front passenger seat.

"Indeed, sir and a beautiful day for it," replied the man in the back seat. "So nice to get out of town occasionally. And to have a driver as well!"

The uniformed man behind the wheel grinned, but said nothing. The man beside him smiled cheerfully.

"Quite. Have you ever stayed at the Steigenberger Grandhotel Petersberg?"

"Good grief, Sir! On a sergeant's pay? Not a chance! Have you?"

"Just the once, Wolfram. My wife and I had the first two days of our honeymoon there, but I must admit, her father paid for it! Luckily, he seemed to like me."

"Quite an experience, I imagine, Sir!"

"To be honest, Wolfram, it was a bit rich for my blood. We've never done anything like that since. Karen and I prefer to go camping in the forests like everybody else."

"What about the man we're calling on? I imagine he spends every weekend there."

"Well, he lives almost in its shadow, so he wouldn't need to. I went to his house once, some formal police occasion, it's fairly mind-boggling. Black and white tiles, Greek statues, lines of ferns in the hall, all that sort of stuff. It reminded me of an expensive funeral parlour. I could fit my entire house in the lobby."

"Yes, I imagine so, Sir."

The remaining few minutes of the drive passed in silence before the caravan arrived at massive steel gates on the hill. The famous hotel could be seen just a few kilometres away.

The car stopped by the grille and the Captain pressed the button.

"This is Captain Helmut Oehler and Sergeant Wiederhold of the State Police. Please open the gates."

The silence from the speaker lasted a few seconds before an irate voice came on.

"Do you idiots have any idea who you're fooling with? Get away from my house or I'll have you all arrested in minutes."

The captain looked round at his sergeant with amusement then returned to the grille.

"Baron Krauskopf, you may open these gates now or I'll have my men blow then open. Your choice. I have full authorisation to enter and to take you prisoner."

The other man's rose even more in volume.

"Oehler, I'm about to call the Chancellor. What do think she will say about this insanity? Count on it, you will not have a job by the time you get back to Bonn and not your freedom either."

The connection was broken.

"Well, let's see, shall we?" murmured the Captain and closed his eyes.

They waited just three minutes before the gates swung open under power.

"It seems the Minister's briefing about the honourable Baron to the Chancellor last night had its effect," said the Captain.

"I wish I could have heard the Baron's conversation with her," replied the Sergeant and looked back to make sure the two black vehicles had followed them in.

* * *

"I remember when this dacha was owned by one of the Politbureau," said the Major. "As a kid, I used to walk round the fence, wondering what it was like to live in such a place. And then the guards chased me away."

"Not much has changed," said the Lieutenant seated next to him as the large Mercedes staff car drove up the half-kilometre driveway. "A few still have the power and the wealth, the rest of us stand back and wonder."

The major twisted round and checked that the two black, windowless vans were close behind.

"And now I wonder just what has this man done that earns him our visit," he said. "He's a personal friend of Putin and Medvedev, half the Russian Government is in his hands, but it's the President himself that's ordered this little episode."

The three vehicles stopped before the wooden porch of the enormous country cottage that was still the symbol of prestige, wealth and power in post-Communist Russia. The two army officers climbed out and waited while the black vans stopped and a dozen heavily armed men emerged and fanned out round the building.

"What is this?" asked a voice from the front door. A tall, white-haired man with a lined, authoritative face stood there, arms folded.

"Valissy Petrovich Basargin, we are here on the order of the Minister of Justice at the direction of the Minister of Defence. We need to see you inside."

"You will not see me inside. Now get off my land or I will call Putin immediately. You think you can go against *him?* You will be Privates in the Siberian outposts within a week!" Basargin's voice showed no anger, just the calm of absolute authority.

The Major turned and nodded at one of the armed men behind him. He levelled his rifle and a red spot of light appeared over the heart of the man on the porch. He looked down for a second and resumed his calm stare at the Major.

"This is supposed to frighten me?" he said with a smile.

"It should," replied the Major and made a small gesture with his right hand.

Basargin's chest exploded and blood and flesh splattered against the wooden wall behind him. The remains collapsed onto the ground.

The armed men returned to their transports and the two army officers climbed back into the Army staff car.

"I wonder what he did?" said the Lieutenant.

"It must have been pretty bad," replied the Major.

The ride back into Moscow passed in silence.

Chapter 24 – The Final Whistle

David sat quietly at his desk. The silence and peace was almost therapeutic. After many months, he had nothing to fear, no horrors to fill his dreams with terror, no hunt to follow. And he'd made a major decision.

He rose from his desk to go and see Charlie Simpson. He opened his door and walked into the corridor.

"Hello, David," said Angela.

They stared at each other for an endless moment. He hadn't seen her since she had left in Charlie's protective arms as he led her from the killing room in Kinsella's house. She was wearing a blue suit with a short skirt and a white shirt open at the neck. She was very beautiful, he thought.

"Hello Angela," he finally said.

"Are you all right?" she asked.

He gazed at the flawless skin, deep brown eyes and elfin ears. He wanted to touch her face but restrained himself.

"I'm fine," he replied. "You?"

"It took a while. You know, for a doctor, it took me a ridiculously long time to recover."

"Hardly surprising. We were just seconds from being dead."

"But strange, isn't it? I spend my days cutting up dead bodies of people who have been killed violently. But when it was suddenly me that could be on that slab..."

Tears broke from her eyes and ran down her cheeks. He couldn't help himself and wiped away a pair of drops from her right cheek.

She smiled. "Nowhere near as bad as I was in that room." She took a tissue from her handbag and carefully dried her eyes. She looked at him again. "I'll never forget how we talked in there."

He smiled. "I think it helped us both. I know you didn't mean any of it."

"No, no, of course not. It's just all the horrible things that were going on."

"Of course."

For a few more seconds they looked at each other.

"What are you going to do now, David?"

"I'm just going in to see Charlie."

"Oh." She seemed to understand. She flung her arms round his neck and hugged him. "Take care, David," she said into the side of his neck.

He held her lightly by the waist, knowing he didn't dare do more or he might lose control.

"You too, Angie," he whispered and released her.

She walked on down the corridor and David went in to see her husband, his superior officer and a man for whom he had enormous respect and affection.

"You're leaving?"

Bill Hamilton spoke in resignation. The others of his group in the conference room stayed silent, but the expressions of dismay were obvious.

"I have to," said David. "I've reached the end. That last episode with Kinsella was just too much for me. I'm sorry to sound like a wuss, but I could sense what was happening in me. I've seen too many dead bodies these last few weeks and I came just too damn close to being another one, me and Angie also. And I've seen too many good cops go down with Post Traumatic Stress Syndrome. I didn't want to end my career in a mental institute."

"So what are you going to do?" asked Rachel. She didn't try to hide the tears on her cheeks.

"I've taken my shrink's advice," David replied.

"Your shrink?" Barrie Roche looked puzzled. "I didn't realise you've already been seeing a shrink."

"Me," said Jack Savage. "Remember? I'm the not-wanker shrink!"

The laughter in the room was almost hysterical, a mix of relief, sadness and a need to find something to laugh about.

"I've bought some acreage up the coast, not too far from this old bastard," said David. "Might try my hand at growing a few things, maybe alpaca. They seem pretty nice animals."

"What about grandkids?" asked Hamilton.

"They can wait. Anyway, there's a stage before them and I haven't reached that one yet."

Jack caught his eye and David nodded. Time to end this or he'd get maudlin.

"Behave yourselves, boys and girls," he said. "Don't make me come back here and straighten you out."

He waved, turned and walked out before he broke into tears.

Jack Savage smiled at the group and followed him out.

Chapter 25 – A New Season

The police patrol car came to a gentle stop by the entrance to the underground car park of the office block in Chatswood.

The woman police officer who was driving pointed her flashlight at the entrance.

"Nothing I can see there," she said.

"The kids were pretty clear," replied her partner, a tall, skinny young constable. "They said it was way inside."

"Okay, let's do it," the woman said and they both climbed out, advancing on the entrance with their flashlights.

"Yes, over there," said the woman, directing her light at the middle of the parking area. They walked nearer then stopped, almost overwhelmed by the sight.

A man was hanging by his wrists from a beam. He wore only his underpants. A hideous gash across his stomach had released a dreadful pile of guts, blood and fluids on the floor.

Struggling for self-control, the young woman played the light over the man's body. She saw something unexpected. The man's little toes had been cut off both feet and lay on the ground amid the hellish mess.

"Oh shit," said the constable and reached for her radio.